Praise for the Alberg & Cassidy

"Excellent writing, inventive plots and realistic characters
distinguish Wright's mysteries.... The suspense
becomes tormenting as the author leads readers
through blind alleys and, finally, to an astounding revelation
adroitly concealed until the story's close."
—*Publishers Weekly*

"The author is unrivaled in her talent for casting an ever-so-
light layer of menace over ordinary scenes and situations."
—*The Star-Phoenix*

"Every bit as good as the novels of
P.D. James and Ruth Rendell"
—*People*

"Magical...[Wright is] unexcelled at rooting violence
in the rhythms of everyday life and banal desires"
—*Kirkus*

"Wright has become a master of the psychological
thriller. Her characters are totally recognizable
people whose actions are the result of complex
motivations and who strive to rebuild their lives
on the rubble of too many demolished dreams.
Powerful reading for all readers, not just mystery fans."
—*Booklist*

"Wright's skill and subtlety make [her subplots] equally
interesting and riveting....She has an uncanny ability to make
us pity the malefactor, even as we revile his actions"
—*Edmonton Journal*

Fall from Grace

Fall from
Grace
MURDER IN A SMALL TOWN

L. R. Wright

Felony & Mayhem Press • New York

All the characters and events portrayed in this work are fictitious.

FALL FROM GRACE: MURDER IN A SMALL TOWN

A Felony & Mayhem mystery

PRINTING HISTORY
Fall from Grace
First Canadian edition (Seal Books): 1991
First U.S. edition (Viking): 1991
First Felony & Mayhem edition: 2010
Second Felony & Mayhem edition
(*Fall from Grace: Murder in a Small Town*): 2024

ISBN: 978-1-63194-319-5

Manufactured in the United States of America

Cataloging-in-Publication information for this book
is available from the Library of Congress.

This book is for James Cardwell…
and for his widow, Jewel

Author's Note

There is a Sunshine Coast, and its towns and villages are called by the names used in this book. But all the rest is fiction. The events and the characters are products of the author's imagination, and geographical and other liberties have been taken in the depiction of the town of Sechelt.

Acknowledgments

The author wishes to acknowledge the continuing advice, assistance and support of her family and friends, with particular thanks to John—facilitator; and to Elaine Ferbey, Katey Wright and Brian Appleby for sharing their specialized knowledge; any inaccuracies are her own.

CLASSIC MAYHEM

Devoted to the best traditional mysteries of the 20th century, both Golden Age charmers, written before about 1960, and those from the Silver Age, which shine just as brightly and have much in common with their older cousins. If you love twisty puzzles, witty characterizations, and the art of the civilized crime novel, pull up a chair!

More Classic Mayhem

L.R. WRIGHT
The Suspect
Sleep While I Sing
A Chill Rain in January
Fall from Grace
Prized Possessions
A Touch of Panic
Mother Love
Strangers Among Us
Acts of Murder

PAMELA BRANCH
The Wooden Overcoat
and coming soon...
Murder Every Monday
Lion in the Cellar
Murder's Little Sister

JUANITA SHERIDAN
The Chinese Chop
and coming soon...
The Kahuna Killer
The Mamo Murders
The Waikiki Widow

EVELYN E. SMITH
Miss Melville Regrets
and coming soon...
Miss Melville Returns
Miss Melville's Revenge
Miss Melville Rides a Tiger

Fall from Grace

Prologue

Spring 1980

The evening rain fell into the thick rhododendron hedge behind the high school, making a crackling noise, like the sound of fire.

People hurried from the parking lot toward the building, their greetings muffled by the rain, identities obscured by umbrellas.

"Stop for a minute, Warren," said Annabelle to her brother. They had come to see their friend, Bobby Ransome, graduate. "Smell. Spring's in the air."

"Come on, Annabelle," said Warren, hunching his shoulders against the rain.

"What a sourpuss you can be," Annabelle chided. "You act like an old man sometimes, you really do."

She swept past him, up the steps and into the school, and Warren, squinting upward, saw a billion raindrops falling like silver tracers through the light that flooded from the wide-open doors.

Inside, he hung his jacket on one of the big hooks attached to the corridor wall and ran his hands over his hair, shaking rainwater onto the floor. He looked around him, trying to summon nostalgia; he'd graduated from this school himself only a year ago.

"Yo, Warren." A former classmate rushed past, hand in hand with a girl Warren didn't recognize.

"Yo, Ken," Warren called after him heartily.

He saw Old Man McMurtry approaching and felt immediately guilty, as if he were still a student. The principal stuck out his hand. "Good to see you, Warren," he said as they shook hands. "I hear you're doing well." He clapped Warren on the shoulder and moved on.

How would he know if I'm doing well? thought Warren resentfully. Then he remembered that it was McMurtry's wife's Ford Escort he'd been working on all week. And that made him feel damn pleased.

Meanwhile, the rain pattered steadily upon the forest that blanketed the steep hillside behind the rhododendrons.

Warren saw Annabelle chattering away to her friend Erna, so he sauntered into the auditorium—well it was a gym, really, but it had been set up like an auditorium, with a groundsheet on the floor and a couple of hundred metal chairs, and the red curtains drawn across the front of the stage—and looked around for Bobby. But he couldn't see him.

The rest of the graduating class was there, though, all sitting together, boys with boys, girls with girls; there was a lot of laughing and fooling around going on and Warren could tell every one of them was feeling damn important. Cock-of-the-walk, that's how they all felt. He looked at them affectionately, remembering.

Near the back of the auditorium, Harry and Velma Grayson watched their son as he documented the evening's events with his camera. Determined, concentrated, he flew from group to group, crouching, standing on chairs, apparently oblivious to protests, plaintive or exasperated. Velma was always relieved when somebody smiled into Steven's camera. Since he obviously wasn't going to be in any of his own pictures, Velma had brought her little Instamatic with its built-in flash, and she raised it to her eye now, and snapped.

A tall young man with dark hair and a bony face, wearing a dark suit and a tie that's too long; a camera is slung around his neck—he's holding it in his right hand; he's caught in mid-stride, heading for the side of the auditorium, looking back over his shoulder at the people spilling in from the back.

Outside, the rain continued. It rattled among the rhododendrons, was absorbed by the forest, and inveigled its way into the small clearing between hedge and forest that was a favorite haunt of students craving a smoke, or a beer, or drugs, or sex, between or after classes.

Bobby Ransome's Aunt Hetty sat in the first row, close to the wall. In her big black purse was a card in which she'd written heartfelt words of commendation. She wished Bobby's parents could have been there, but she didn't mind standing in for them. Widowed years earlier by an automobile accident, she had no children of her own. And her pride in her nephew was particularly welcome now. It was a distraction. Her older sister, Lucy, had just left Sechelt to live in Barbados, and Hetty was by herself in that great big old house. That great big empty old house.

Mr. McMurtry finally dimmed the lights, and the audience hushed.

The red curtains were drawn back, revealing the school choir. Annabelle, sitting next to Erna, smiled to herself at the sight of Bobby Ransome up there. He was not a person you'd expect to find singing in a choir. He'd been a bad boy once, Bobby had. He was a lot older than the rest of the graduating class, because by rights he should have finished four years earlier, at the same time as Annabelle. But he'd gotten into trouble, and dropped out, and Annabelle considered it nothing short of miraculous that he'd eventually gone back.

His fair hair hung long and thick over the collar of his shirt and Annabelle, watching him as the choir began to sing, was filled with tender, private feelings. Oh he'd been trouble, all right. But she had loved his muscular thighs.

She couldn't hear his voice among all the rest. But then there was a song that he sang alone, and Annabelle, watching, listening, was at first surprised, and then enraptured.

"Amid the dark shades," Bobby sang, "of the lonely ash grove." He leaned into the music, and Annabelle felt invisible, in the near-darkness, as if she were watching him dream.

"I first met my dear one," Bobby sang, "the joy of my heart." Annabelle's eyes were on his face, on the flat planes of his cheeks, the green glinting of his eyes, on the chunk of hair that had fallen across his forehead—and on his mouth, which moved, as he sang, in a manner somehow foreign. And yet it seemed familiar.

"With sorrow, deep sorrow," she heard Bobby sing, "in search of my love." The piano accompaniment wandered in glorious dissonance and Annabelle watched Bobby's mouth and thought: maybe his lips moved like that when they touched my breasts, my body; as if they were singing. She turned to look across the aisle at Wanda, but saw only the flood of Wanda's dark, unruly hair, and the slightness of her body. Then Wanda lifted her hand to smooth her hair away from her cheek and Annabelle saw that her face was flushed. Annabelle nodded, satisfied.

His aunt, hearing him sing, recognized the voice of Bobby's father when he was young.

Warren, hearing him sing, grinned and shook his head admiringly, and thought, people sure do keep a lot of secrets.

And outside the spring rain spattered soft and gray into the clearing, which was for the moment empty.

Later, Annabelle shrugged into her coat, which she had draped over the back of her chair, and told Warren, "I'll get a ride home with Erna."

Bobby swung down from the stage and went first to his aunt and then to Wanda, who blushed crimson at the sight of him. "Not here, Bobby," she said, as he leaned toward her.

A broad-shouldered, fair-haired man in his early twenties wearing gray pants and a light tweed sport coat, bending to a young woman with a mass of dark, curly hair, his lips pressed against the curve of her neck; the young woman's face is lifted, her eyes luminous, lips slightly apart.

"Goddamn it," said Wanda furiously to Steven Grayson and his camera.

Bobby turned so fast that Annabelle blinked.

"Beat it," said Bobby, and Steven shrugged and laughed and backed away, but not before he'd snapped another photograph.

A face with a wide forehead, high cheekbones, a strong chin; the eyes are narrowed; the man's right fist is raised, and his face is suffused with anger.

"Fuck," said Bobby, taking a step forward, but Steven had melted into the crowd.

Annabelle said quickly, "I heard you guys are getting married." She smiled at them. "Congratulations."

Warren, hearing this, was embarrassed. He felt it wasn't proper for a recently divorced person to be congratulating other people on getting engaged.

"Thanks, Annabelle." Bobby pulled Wanda close to him and rested his chin on top of her head; his hands held her firmly, almost—but not quite—cupping her breasts. Wanda tried to push his hands away.

"I may be getting married again myself," said Annabelle, "before too long."

Warren looked at her in amazement; this was the first he'd heard of it. Bobby looked surprised, too. And Wanda looked relieved, which Warren could certainly understand.

Annabelle reached up to pat Bobby's cheek, and then she leaned down and gave Wanda a kiss on the cheek. "Be happy," she said, and sashayed off toward the door, where Erna was waiting.

"That's quite a woman, your sister," said Bobby to Warren, watching her.

At the door Annabelle put her arm around Erna's shoulder. "Ready?"

"Sure. Let's go," said Erna.

On the way out to the parking lot Annabelle said, "Guess what, Erna. I'm pregnant."

A woman laughing in the rain, her head flung back; thick, tawny hair spills across her shoulders, her hands are jammed into the pockets of her raincoat; she's illuminated by the light from a lamppost on the edge of the parking lot.

Warren left the school with Bobby and Wanda and Bobby's aunt, and he and Wanda waited awkwardly in the rain while Bobby saw his aunt to her car. They watched, at a distance, as she fumbled in her big black purse and handed something to him. A card, it looked like. Bobby read it, and gave her a hug.

A small, lanky woman with gray hair pinned on top of her head peers around a young man's broad back; her expression is cautious—curious. The shot is taken from behind some shrubbery. She is looking directly into the camera.

The rain was still falling. Warren heard it in the rhododendron hedge, and he glanced in that direction and saw the extravagant blossoms glowing fitfully, stroked by somebody's headlights.

Bobby slapped the roof of his aunt's car and waved as she drove slowly away. Then he joined Warren and Wanda. He grabbed Wanda and kissed her.

Fair-haired man, dark-haired woman in an embrace; next to them, a man of medium build with short, dark hair, wearing a poplin jacket; his left hand is pressed against the back of his neck and he's looking toward the school, his face scrunched up in embarrassment.

Bobby released Wanda. He turned to Warren, his face aglow. "I am looking into my future, Warren," he said, "and I am seeing it shine, I am seeing it shine."

Warren was uncomfortable with this kind of talk. But he saw the truth of it in Bobby's eyes. He punched Bobby's shoulder, and they grabbed each other in a mock wrestling match, and their laughter and Wanda's shrieks drifted through the evening with the rain.

Summer 1990

i

"Happy birthday, Mom," said Steven, and Velma's eyes filled instantly with tears.

"I knew you wouldn't forget," she said into the phone. She turned and looked out the front window of her small house, into the branches of the willow tree; their green tendrils hung low enough to brush the lawn.

"I never forget," said Steven. "Have I ever forgotten your birthday?"

"No," said Velma, smiling at the willow tree.

"Or Mother's Day?"

"No," said Velma, "no, you haven't."

"Or Christmas? I've never forgotten Christmas, either, have I?"

Velma laughed aloud at this.

"I thought about sending flowers," he said, "but that would have been coals to Newcastle, right?"

"Right," said Velma, smiling. It was the middle of June, and her garden was ablaze with roses. And she had red geraniums in the windowboxes, and pink ones in pots on the patio. And in hanging baskets she'd planted fuchsia and petunias and verbena and trailing lobelia. Yes, if there was anything she didn't need more of, it was flowers.

"It's particularly lovely out there today," she said, "with the sun shining so bright. I wish you could see it." She said this deliberately, knowing that it might upset him, because she resented the fact that she hardly ever got to see him. After all, it wasn't as if he was half a continent away, like Lettie Charles's boy.

"Yeah, me too," he said, which she didn't believe for a moment. He was a real Vancouverite now, Steven was. "Now I've got you on the phone," he went on, "what's the news?" He used the exact same phrase, every time he called.

Velma, smiling, reached into the kitchen for the stool that sat next to the refrigerator. "Well," she said, looking out at the willow tree, marshaling her recollections, "let's see." She made herself comfortable on the stool and offered him, one by one, all the fragments of information that had come her way, since the last time they'd talked.

Velma was extremely surprised when at the close of her narrative Steven said, "I've got an idea, Mom. How would you feel about putting me up in my old room for a while?"

She didn't understand him, at first. She turned around on the stool and focused her gaze on the telephone, which was attached to the wall. She pressed the receiver more tightly against her ear. "What did you say, dear?"

Steven laughed. "I've got an urge to come home for a while, Mom."

"But Steven," she said. Her heart was soaring; amazement had done it. "Steven. Oh, Steven."

"I'd have to tie up some loose ends first," he said. "Take me ten days or so. I could be over there—say by the end of the month. In time for the July First weekend. How about it?"

"I'm absolutely delighted, Steven. I'm so happy I feel like crying," said Velma, blinking rapidly.

When she'd hung up, Velma went outside and got her clippers. She picked an enormous bouquet of roses, pricking her hands in the process, but it was worth it to bring such gorgeous blooms inside.

She stood in the middle of the yard, holding the clippers, the basket of roses over her arm, and looked for a moment at the house. It stared back at her, squinting through narrow windows. She thought for some reason of the first house they'd lived in, the one Harry had built with his own hands, on three acres out in the bush. Steven had had a room upstairs whose windows looked out into the branches of a big tree. He'd gone in and out of that window as often as he'd used the door.

The house was blurry because of her tears.

At long last, Steven was coming home. After ten years of self-imposed exile, Steven was coming home to Sechelt.

Summer days stretched before her warm and fragrant and she saw Steven sunning himself in her backyard and Steven lounging in front of the television and Steven laughing at one of her jokes and Steven smacking his lips over homemade hamburgers cooked on the barbecue and Steven taking pictures, of course, always taking pictures. And some of these images were true and some were shot through with lies.

Velma peered into the hot summery future and a small black presentiment lodged itself inside her. She placed her hand flat upon her chest, pretending her hand was a magnet: she would pull that bad feeling right out of there and fling it into her compost heap.

And then it retreated, and Velma was relieved. She looked again with eagerness toward the future, and did not know that the murder of her son awaited her there.

ii

The highway was clogged with traffic; the two o'clock ferry had arrived, having crossed Howe Sound from Horseshoe Bay, just northwest of Vancouver. The ferry had docked at Langdale, a village at the southern end of the forty-five-mile-long strip of British Columbia that is known as the Sunshine Coast.

Among the vehicles heading away from Langdale that bright day in June lurched an elongated pickup truck, the back of it loaded, the load covered with a tarpaulin.

After Langdale and Gibsons Landing, the road wound inland through countryside occupied by people on acreages. There were horses in some of the pastures, and chicken coops near some of the houses. On some of these properties old car bodies and chunks of unidentifiable machinery lay about. There were swing sets in some of the yards, and tires hung from tree branches, and from behind the wobbly fence fronting one piece of property an ancient dog, irritable with toothache or stomach distress, barked at the slowly passing traffic.

The highway wended northwest from Gibsons, carrying its burden of traffic toward Sechelt, and about halfway between the two villages it made an abrupt ninety-degree turn and headed directly for the sea. But a gravel road continued northward. To the right a long, narrow strip of cleared land bordered the gravel road, backing up against a forest that spilled quickly upward to cover the flanks of a low-flung mountain. In the middle of the clearing, a building stood behind two old gas pumps, long since disconnected.

It was a small, rectangular, wooden building with a sharply peaked roof. There were little windows in the gables, and underneath the one facing north another piece of roof stuck out, like an eyeshade. In the long roof that looked toward the gravel road was a dormer with two tiny side-by-side windows, and in the bottom part of the roof, where it angled and the pitch became less steep, there were three skylights, one in the middle, one at each end.

A glass wall wrapped around the building on two sides; from the road, it looked like a greenhouse with a second story.

On this sunny afternoon the traffic, vehicle by vehicle, lurched up to the turn in the highway, lumbered dutifully around it, and aimed itself west, at the Pacific Ocean.

All but the pickup truck.

When it reached the corner, the pickup continued forward onto the gravel road, crunched along until it got to the building, swerved off toward the old gas pumps and came to a halt between the pumps and the glass-walled house.

For a while it just sat there. Then the driver's door flew open, and Herman Ferguson got out.

"Annabelle!" he hollered. He wore a white T-shirt through which a mat of dark chest hair could be seen. He wasn't very tall. He was wiry, unshaven, and had a lot of thick black hair.

Two of his teeth were missing. Sometimes, when he got excited, he made a whistling sound when he spoke.

"Come on here, you guys," he yelled to the children who had appeared around the corner of the building. "Where's your ma? We've gotta get this thing unloaded."

Bowlegged and cocky, he strode to the end of the truck, where he hoisted himself up and started undoing the ropes that connected the tarp to the sides of the vehicle.

The oldest child, a girl, was nine. She had blond hair tied in a dispirited ponytail. Pieces of it had come loose and were hanging around her face. She was wearing baggy jeans that wouldn't have stayed up on her skinny frame except for a cord drawn through the belt loops and tied firmly around her waist. On top, she wore a short-sleeved pink T-shirt.

The boy was eight. He was called Arnold, and he had his father's hair, thick and black, so black that in the bright sunlight sometimes it looked dark red.

The smallest child was a girl, also blond, who was six, almost seven. Her hair was cut so short that it was hard for some people to tell she was a girl. She could run very fast and she climbed trees very nimbly and her name was Camellia.

Her sister was called Rose-Iris.

Annabelle hurried around the corner, breathless, pushing a strand of hair away from her face. "I was in the garden," she said. She smiled at her children as she approached them, gathered at the rear of the truck. "What on earth have you got there?" she said to Herman.

From his position on the truck bed Herman whipped off the tarpaulin, revealing a collection of wire cages. "Take a look at that," he said triumphantly.

"What is it?" said Camellia, standing on tiptoe, straining to see.

"Animals," said Rose-Iris disbelievingly, peering into the truck. "It's animals. In cages."

"Let me see, let me see," said Camellia, all excited. Rose-Iris lifted her up, staggering a little.

"I got 'em from Tyrone," said Herman.

"I thought you went over there to get money," said Annabelle, her hands on her hips. "I thought Tyrone owed you some money."

"He did owe me, and now he's paying me. He's sending more next week, too." Herman gestured impatiently to his wife. "Come on over here. When the monkeys and the skunks get here there's gonna be enough critters for a zoo, and that's what I'm bound to have, a zoo, a mini-zoo, two dollars for adults and a buck each for kids." He threw back his head and laughed. "How's that for a summer project?" he said to Arnold, with a wink.

Rose-Iris put Camellia down again. "Can we play with them?" said Camellia.

"Don't be silly," said Rose-Iris sharply. "They're wild animals. You don't play with wild animals."

Annabelle had ventured nearer, and now she stared into the interior of the cages. She saw raccoons, and squirrels, and foxes. All of the animals were panting. Some of them were quivering. Their eyes were huge and dark; fathomless, thought Annabelle. Urine and excrement had fouled the bottoms of the cages, which were lined with newspapers.

"Well come on, don't just stand around," said Herman. "These critters need a drink. Climb on up here, Arnold, help me get these things off here. We'll set 'em up out back, where there's some shade."

Annabelle stood back and watched as the cages were unloaded. Her heart was hammering in her chest. It's the heat, she thought. Really, it was uncommonly warm, for June.

She smoothed her dress with her hands, tilted her head, and managed to clear herself a passageway through the threat of turmoil.

"I'm having nothing to do with this," she said, her tone flat and implacable. "I'm going back to my garden."

The rest of the family watched, silent, as she walked quickly toward the house.

"I think she's scared of those animals," said Camellia finally.

Rose-Iris gave her a push. "Ma's not scared of anything," she said, glancing up at her father.

"She'll get used to them," said Herman, staring at the corner around which Annabelle had disappeared. "She'll damn quick get used to them."

iii

"Wanda, it's five to four."

"I know it's five to four."

"Well come on."

"It's five to four, Warren. Not four. We're leaving at four o'clock, that's what you said."

"Yeah, well, it's that now."

"It's not four, it's five to four. I'll be ready at four. I told you I'd be ready at four, and I'll be ready at four."

Warren Kettleman let the screen door bang shut behind him and went down the walk to the street, where his van was parked in front of the house. He unlocked it and opened the windows, and left the passenger door open, too. It was like an oven in there.

The clock on the dashboard said 3:57. He knew it would read exactly four o'clock when the screen door slapped open and Wanda came out.

And it did, too. Warren shook his head wearily. She was so damn stubborn. She'd never give him the satisfaction of coming out early, even when she was all ready to go early, even though she knew how much he hated being late.

But he didn't say anything. He just started the motor and waited patiently while Wanda flounced down the walk, hipped herself into her seat and slammed the door. He continued to wait, gazing out through the windshield, and finally Wanda made a sound of exasperation and put on her seat belt.

And Warren felt inexplicably lighthearted, all of a sudden. He didn't know why, but he felt very good. He leaned swiftly toward Wanda and planted a kiss on her ear. She gave a little screech, then grabbed his head and kissed him hard on the mouth. Warren growled in his throat, which he knew she loved, and Wanda's eyes got darker, and she said, "Let's go back inside," and Warren damn near said, "Yeah."

As soon as they arrived, Wanda smacked a kiss onto her mother's cheek. Wanda's dad tossed Warren a can of beer and her mom poured Wanda a big glass of iced tea made from a mix.

"What are we having?" said Wanda, peering into a pot on the stove.

Her mom gave Wanda's hand a little slap. "Get outta there. 'Portuguese Fish Soup.'"

"Geez, Ma," said Wanda, dismayed.

Warren felt dismayed, too. In five years he'd never had the same thing twice, at the Prestons' house. He'd given up telling Mrs. Preston when he especially liked something because he knew he'd never get it again anyway. But maybe he ought to start letting her know when he didn't like something. For instance, he didn't like fish. He couldn't stand fish. He was pretty sure he was almost allergic to fish. Maybe if Wanda's mom had known that, she wouldn't have made Portuguese Fish Soup.

"What else?" said Wanda, which Warren wanted to know, too.

"Buns and a salad," said Mrs. Preston, pouring herself some iced tea. "And blueberry crumble for dessert, made with blueberries outta my freezer."

He could fill up on buns and salad, thought Warren. And although he didn't know what the crumble part would turn out to be, he liked blueberries.

"Come on outside," said Wanda's dad. "I want you to take a look at my exhaust."

Warren took a big swig of beer. Yeah, he thought, buns, salad, blueberries, that'd be okay. He threw Wanda a wink and followed Mr. Preston outside.

He was lying on a creeper under Mr. Preston's Ford when gleeful shrieks started coming from the house, female shrieks interspersed with male laughter. He froze, under there, because as soon as he heard the guy laugh he knew who it was.

"Warren! Warren!"

Wanda was outside before she called his name for the third time. He could see her feet dancing up and down on the concrete of the driveway.

"Guess who's here!"

He scooted out from under the Ford and stood up, dusting off his hands, but there was grease all over them and just as he realized he was glad of that, at least he wouldn't have to shake hands, Bobby came outside, a grin on his face, with Mrs. Preston right behind him.

"Hiya," said Bobby. He looked just like he'd looked in high school, even though that had been ten years ago. Except his hair was a lot shorter, of course. Big, tough, and easy moving, Bobby was, and his hands were shoved into the back pockets of his jeans.

"Hi," said Warren. "Long time no see."

"You got that right," said Bobby, nodding. A hunk of hair fell down over his forehead and Warren watched him toss it back with a shake of his head, just like in high school. He wondered what Bobby had been up to in the last year and a half, since he'd gotten out of the slammer.

"Came back to Sechelt to see your stepdad, did you, Bobby?" said Mr. Preston sympathetically, resting his foot on the front bumper of the Ford. "I heard he was pretty sick."

Warren couldn't believe this, how friendly they were all being.

"Yeah," said Bobby to Mr. Preston. "My mom called me. So I'm gonna stay a while, I guess. Maybe take a few days, go camping."

Warren had known he was back in town, of course. Wanda had heard, and Wanda had told Warren. But he hadn't expected to see him. Except maybe on the street, by accident.

"So," said Bobby, "you're still into cars, are you, War?"

"Yeah," said Warren. "Still into cars."

Everybody had felt real bad when Bobby got sent to jail. And Warren could understand that. But the fact of the matter was, when all was said and done, Bobby was guilty. He never even tried to pretend he wasn't. And so he'd deserved to go to jail, hadn't he? Warren couldn't understand why Wanda got so mad whenever he pointed this out.

"You got some grease on your new shirt," said Wanda reproachfully, and he looked down and saw that she was right. But she came over to him and took his arm and hugged it to her breast, and Warren felt good about that.

"You make a cute couple," said Bobby, with another grin.

Into Warren's head came a picture from high school, of Bobby and Wanda necking in the hallway. He'd felt disgusted to see this, because he didn't like public displays of affection, but it had made him hard, too. Everything made him hard then, he reminded himself, staring at Bobby. He wondered what it was like to be in jail.

"You want to stay for supper, Bobby?" said Mrs. Preston.

Warren couldn't believe his ears.

Bobby looked at Wanda. "Does my ex have any objection?"

Wanda shrugged, and let go of Warren's arm. "I don't care one way or the other," she said.

"What are you having?" said Bobby to Mrs. Preston.

"'Portuguese Fish Soup,'" Warren blurted.

"Can't pass that up," said Bobby. "Whatever the hell it is." He grinned again, but his eyes were funny, and Warren saw with a little shock that he really didn't look at all like he'd looked in high school. There was this layer of watchfulness over him; and he kind of glowed empty, even with the sun shining right on him.

"Good," said Mrs. Preston, beaming at her former son-in-law.

Nothing good, thought Warren, staring down at Wanda's shiny brown hair, can possibly come from this.

He looked at Bobby, who was leaning against the side of the garage with his arms crossed, looking back at him, and he had a bad feeling, a very bad feeling, right in the middle of his gut. He gazed searchingly at Bobby, trying to see him clear, becoming more and more apprehensive without having any idea why; wanting to protect himself, and Wanda—and Bobby, too, for that matter—from whatever stupid mess Bobby might be heading into.

Warren was always having bad feelings. It was in his nature. But even at his gloomiest, his most pessimistic, the thought of Bobby killing somebody would never have entered Warren's worried mind.

Chapter One

On the Sunshine Coast that year, summertime was long and hot and dusty, and the world smelled of raspberries and roses.

For weeks the sky remained utterly clear, and the air was hot and still.

The waters that lapped at the western shoreline were such a deep blue they looked as if they might stain the skin. The nearer islands in the Strait of Georgia were etched fine and clear, every tree and every rock sharp-edged; the islands somewhat farther away were soft dark shapes against the sky; the most distant islands were purple shadows in the far-reaching sea.

Old-timers said they'd never seen a summer like it. The trees by the roadside were heavy with dust thrown up from the gravel shoulders. Garden-watering was limited to every second day, and people weren't wasting it on their lawns, which were rapidly becoming brown.

Roses thrived in the heat. So did marigolds. All sorts of flowers thrived in it. Some people did, too.

That summer was an aberration. Impatiens, fuchsia, begonias both fibrous and tuberous—all were wilted, weakened, disabled by the relentless heat of the astonishingly tropical sun.

Some people were, too.

On a Monday in early July, Staff Sergeant Karl Alberg pulled his white Oldsmobile into the fenced lot behind the Sechelt Royal Canadian Mounted Police detachment. He left the windows open when he climbed out of the car. He moved slowly and cautiously, but the heat pounced on him anyway, and swept over his body in a suffocating wave. As he plodded across the gravel and around to the front of the building he felt like he was wearing entirely too many clothes. A pair of pants, a shirt, underwear, socks and shoes: it didn't sound like much. The pants were made of cotton. The saleswoman had told him they'd be cool because cotton was a fabric that breathed. Alberg had never conceived of clothes as breathing.

The pants might be cool but they wrinkled awfully fast. The shirt was cotton, too; everything he had on today was breathing. If he listened carefully he could probably hear it. The shirt he wore had long sleeves. Alberg hated short-sleeved shirts, except for T-shirts. There was something unseemly about the way the sleeves flapped around. He didn't mind T-shirts because their sleeves gripped his biceps firmly. But T-shirts weren't appropriate for work, he felt. So he wore long-sleeved shirts to work, and rolled up the cuffs a couple of times, casually.

Isabella had found a fan somewhere, the kind that rotates, and Alberg got a whoosh of cool air in his face as he opened the door. The fan sat on the counter in front of Isabella's desk.

"Good morning to you," she sang.

Isabella Harbud, the detachment's middle-aged receptionist and secretary, was the only person Alberg knew who was actually relishing the weather. For once she was coming to work wearing only one layer of clothing. Her mane of graying auburn hair was pulled back into a ponytail and her face glowed with goodwill.

"Lookee here," she said, pointing to a bunch of flowers on the end of the counter.

"Very nice," said Alberg. "Are they from your garden?" He hoped it wasn't her intention to try to put them in his office. Isabella frequently thought of things to do for him that he didn't want done.

"They're from Mavis Furley," said Isabella.

Alberg looked at the flowers for edification.

"She got her car stolen," said Isabella. "Remember? We found it for her. Corporal Sanducci found it. Abandoned on a logging road. None the worse for wear. Remember?"

"I remember," said Alberg.

"This bouquet," said Isabella, "is an expression of her gratitude." She waited. "My lord," she cried, exasperated, "hasn't anybody ever given you flowers before?"

Alberg stared at the flowers. He noticed a card, and took his reading glasses out of his shirt pocket. He put on the glasses and read the message on the card. Nodding to himself, he put the card back. "Very nice," he said, and leaned close to the flowers so he could sniff their fragrance. "Very nice." He put his glasses away, gave the counter a brisk slap, and ambled down the hall, smiling at nothing.

The smile faded when he opened the door to his office. It was stifling in there, and upon his desk sat a pile of personnel forms that he'd managed to put out of his mind overnight.

He pulled up the venetian blinds and shoved the window open as wide as it would go. He left his office door open and sat behind his desk, staring gloomily at the paperwork that awaited him.

After a while he called Cassandra Mitchell and they arranged to meet later that day. When he hung up Alberg thought about Cassandra, about him and Cassandra, and wondered what that was, anyway—him-and-Cassandra.

His ex-wife was getting married, on the long weekend in August. In Calgary. To an accountant.

Alberg pulled out a desk drawer, rested his feet on it, put his hands behind his head and studied the photograph of his daughters that hung on the wall. It was time to take a new one. This one had to be at least six, seven years old. Diana was staying with him for the summer and in a couple of weeks her older sister, Janey, would be joining them for a few days. He could take their picture on a boat, maybe. But he didn't have a boat. He could rent one. Except they didn't like boats. They'd grown up in inland places and were distrustful of the ocean.

Alberg smoothed his hair, pulled in his gut, and tried not to let himself get depressed. It was so damned hot, though.

He ran his hands over his cheeks and jaw and considered quitting the Force and growing a beard. His hair was getting thin on top, he was pretty sure. It had some gray in it, too. But that wasn't noticeable, because his hair was blond. If he grew a beard, though, what color would it be? Blond? Gray? Or something else entirely? He kind of liked the idea that it would grow in a different color entirely.

Yeah, he thought; he'd buy a boat, grow a red beard and retire. He'd spend his days sailing up and down the coast; wearing his new beard, a seaman's hat and cutoffs. He'd be a character. People would write books about him.

"Knock knock," said Sid Sokolowski, peering around Alberg's open door.

With an effort, Alberg managed not to drop his hands, put his feet on the floor and try to look busy. "Come in," he said.

"How're you doing with the evaluations?" said the sergeant, maneuvering his considerable bulk into the office.

"Fine, fine," said Alberg briskly. He pulled his glasses case out of his shirt pocket. "What're you up to today, Sid?" he asked, peering at the pile of forms on his desk.

"Couple of B and E's," said the sergeant. "Otherwise it's pretty quiet."

"It's the heat." Alberg stood up, putting the glasses case back in his pocket. "I'm going into town, have a coffee, touch a few bases here and there."

"Staff," said Sid Sokolowski, but Alberg was already out the door, heading for the reception area.

"Staff," said the sergeant, lumbering close at Alberg's heels.

"I'm going into town," Alberg told Isabella, who was just hanging up the phone.

"You want to look after this?" she said, handing him a piece of paper on which she'd scribbled a message.

Alberg took it from her, held it at arm's length. "A 'death threat'?"

"That's what the man said."

"Here, Staff, I'll do it," said Sokolowski, his hand outstretched. "You better get at those evaluations, eh?"

Alberg looked at him with dignity. "Of course, Sid. Of course I'll get at them. Just as soon as I've dealt with"—he peered again at the piece of paper—"with Mr. Ferguson's complaint." He gave Sokolowski a beatific smile, and left.

A few minutes later, Alberg drove off a gravel road, parked next to a pair of nonfunctioning gas pumps and climbed out of his car. He slammed the door, fanning at the cloud of dust created by his arrival. His skin was sore. It felt thin and insufficient, as if the sun were weakening it.

Alberg thought about the RCMP volunteers who'd gone to Namibia. That kind of adventure, despite the heat of the African sun, would be good for a man, he thought. Therapeutic. He stood next to his car and looked around him. He felt the heat and listened to the grasshoppers, and he smelled the fragrance of dry grass—he might as well be in Africa, he thought, and wished passionately that he were. Adventure, that's what I need, he thought; I need an adventure.

There and then he decided to buy himself a sailboat. Right away. Right now. To hell with waiting until he retired.

He walked toward the house, thinking about his boat. He might get a Grampian 26. Or possibly a San Juan 24. There was a nice-looking CS 27 for sale at the Secret Cove marina. Or maybe he should have an Alberg 30, he thought, smiling to himself; he lifted his head and found himself staring through glass at a woman, who was holding a watering can and staring back at him. He stopped, confused, his mind for a moment not registering the fact that he was looking through an entire wall made of glass. Then he saw that the woman was standing among a vast array of plants. The place was a greenhouse, then.

A door slammed, and a man appeared from behind the building. He saw Alberg and shouted, "Get the hell off my property."

Alberg pulled out his notebook and flipped it open. "Are you Herman Ferguson?" he said.

"I'm the owner of this property, that's who I am," said the man, waving his arms. "And I want you the hell off it." He was about five eight and a hundred and seventy-five pounds, and he wore jeans, a sleeveless white undershirt, somewhat grimy, and suspenders. His feet were clad in hiking boots.

"I'm Staff Sergeant Alberg, Mr. Ferguson. From the RCMP."

The man stopped waving his arms. "Well how the hell's a person supposed to know that when you got no uniform on?" He added grumpily, "It's about damn time you got here. Yeah, Ferguson, that's me. Come around back here and see for yourself."

Alberg glanced again at the greenhouse. The woman was bent over, watering a small tree. He saw that all the plants were in pots, although the floor of the building seemed to be dirt. Behind the woman, a child entered from a doorway, through which Alberg could see that the building wasn't a greenhouse after all. "Interesting house," he said, but Ferguson had vanished. Just then he appeared again, around the corner, gesturing impatiently at Alberg.

The back of the house looked normal. There were a few windows, and two doors. The place stood in a clearing that was covered with brown grass. About fifty feet away the trees began, sweeping up the incline, foresting the mountain.

In the shade of the trees, near the house, was a small, windowless shed. Farther away but still in shade was a collection of wire pens, each about five feet square. In each pen was a pair of animals. Alberg didn't know much about animals. But a couple of them were foxes. And there were some raccoons, everybody knew what raccoons looked like. And in one of the pens, double-wired, so the chinks were smaller, there were a few squirrels. And Jesus, he thought, monkeys, too, little monkeys.

"Lookit this, just lookit this," said Ferguson excitedly, and some spittle flew from his mouth. He gestured at the last pen, which was empty. Alberg looked. The wire had been cut, and the side of the pen pulled back. "I had two skunks in there," said Ferguson.

Alberg nodded. He saw that the guy was missing a couple of teeth.

"Well what the hell are you gonna do about it?" said Ferguson.

"I'm confused," said the staff sergeant. "I thought somebody here had gotten a death threat."

"Me," said Ferguson, banging his chest. "I got it. I got a death threat. Somebody did this here damage, and stole my skunks, and left me a note that threatens to kill me."

"Have you got permits for these animals?" said Alberg, watching the monkeys.

"I gotta permit for every flamin' one of them," said Ferguson.

Alberg sighed and wiped his forehead. He was being punished, he thought, for trying to avoid those evaluations.

"Where's the note?" he said.

"Inside," said Ferguson, heading for the house. "I'm layin' a charge. Out of my way," he said to the boy who pushed open the screen door just as Ferguson got to it. "This is the cops. I'm layin' a charge. Out of my way, boy." The boy backed away into the house.

Alberg followed Ferguson through the door, across a hallway that stretched the length of the house, and into the kitchen, where the woman he'd seen through the glass wall stood with three children, looking at him curiously. "Hello," he said, smiling at them. "My name's Karl Alberg."

"I'm Annabelle," said the woman. "This is Rose-Iris. And Camellia." She glanced at the boy. "And Arnold," she said, reaching out to rumple his hair.

"Get out there, boy," said Herman to his son, "and give those critters some water."

Arnold left, reluctantly.

Annabelle leaned against one of the kitchen counters and crossed her arms. Her face was shiny with sweat—it was no cooler in here than it was outside. Her light brown hair was pulled back into a thick braid. She was wearing a sundress, and no shoes. Her daughters moved close to her; she put an arm around each of them.

"Sit down," she said to Alberg. "Would you like some iced tea?"

"This ain't no social call, Annabelle," said her husband. "The man's here on police business."

"I'd love some iced tea," said Alberg gratefully, pulling out a kitchen chair. He and Ferguson sat down. "Okay. Tell me about it." He glanced at Annabelle, who had put ice in a tall glass and was pouring tea from a glass pitcher she'd taken from the refrigerator.

"Okay, right," said Herman. "I went out to water them. Started with the far cage, saw it right away. The cage was broke, and the death threat was stuck in the wire, like," he said, jabbing at the air. He reached behind him and snatched something from the top of an old buffet that stood against the wall. "Here. Take a look at that."

The envelope had Herman Ferguson's name on the front. It had been torn open. Alberg pulled out the sheet of paper inside. The message, like the name on the envelope, had been put together from words cut out of magazines and newspapers. It read: "A RIGHTEOUS MAN REGARDETH THE LIFE OF HIS BEAST; BUT THE TENDER MERCIES OF THE WICKED ARE CRUEL." Alberg looked dubiously at Ferguson. "You think this is a threat on your life?"

"You're damn right I do," said Ferguson, with fervor. "And I know who left it there, too. You take this off and fingerprint it," he said. "Then you take that old hag's prints, and they're gonna match up. You betcha."

"Herman," said Annabelle. She set a glass down in front of Alberg. "You can't go around slandering people like that," she said. She went back to the counter, held out her arms, looking at Alberg, and drew her daughters near.

"You shut up, there," said Herman, his face turning red. He was straddling one of the kitchen chairs, clutching its back; the heel of his boot tapped the linoleum rapidly, in a nervous tic. "It's her, all right. It's that bloody woman that did it," he said to Alberg.

Alberg asked Annabelle for a plastic bag, into which he carefully slid the note and its envelope. Herman watched him, mollified. "Who are you talking about?" said Alberg.

"That crazy old hag with all the cats," said Herman. "She's the one. She'll do more, too, if she's not locked up."

"Herman," said Annabelle. She laughed.

"Shut up," Herman yelled. "I told you. Just shut up."

"Hey, hey," said Alberg mildly. "Take it easy." He lifted his glass and took a long drink. "It's good," he said, with a nod to Annabelle. Then he turned to Herman, who was muttering to himself, his heel still tapping the floor. "What's this woman's name?"

"I don't know what the hell her name is," said Herman. "People like that, what the hell difference is it what their name is? She's crazy. A crazy person. Pedals around town on that damn bike, talkin' to herself. It's a disgrace, to the whole damn town."

Annabelle rolled her eyes heavenward. She gave her daughters a gentle push. "Go on, you two. You've got things to do. Go attend to your chores."

They left the kitchen and Alberg heard them whispering in the hallway.

"What makes you think she's got anything to do with this?" he said to Ferguson.

"I seen her lurkin' around here," said Herman. "Drivin' her damn bike on that road out there."

"Once," said Annabelle. "You only saw her once, Herman. She was going up to Erna's, to buy a chicken."

"Besides," said Ferguson, ignoring his wife, "she's an animal freak, and we don't got another one of those around here, as far as I know. Last winter I seen her attack some poor woman wearing a fur coat."

"What do you mean, 'attack'?" said Alberg.

"Screeched and yelled at her, hollered, jumped up and down." Ferguson shook his head, disgusted. "Crazy. She's a crazy person. And she's after me, and I want her arrested."

Annabelle yawned and stretched her hands high above her head, arching her back. Then she padded across the room and sat down at the table with them. "She probably doesn't even know about your animals," she said to Herman.

He stared at her, momentarily speechless. Then he said, "What the hell are you talking about? The whole damn town knows about my animals." He turned to Alberg. "They're the talk of the whole town, my animals are. Why, the paper's gonna send somebody out here to do an article on my mini-zoo." Suddenly, almost casually, he cuffed Annabelle on the side of the head. "Shut up, you don't know anything."

"Hey," said Alberg, grabbing Herman's arm.

Annabelle had grown very pale. "It's all right, Mr. Alberg. I make him mad sometimes." She pushed back her chair. "I'm going to water my garden." She left the room, and Alberg heard the screen door creak as she pushed it open.

He let go of Herman Ferguson's arm.

"She makes me mad," said Ferguson sullenly. "She knows it, but she goes ahead and does it anyway."

Alberg stood up.

"Can we get back to business, here?" Ferguson looked up at him plaintively.

"We don't have a hell of a lot of business to get back to," said Alberg, and Ferguson got up, too, sputtering protests. Alberg looked down on him for a moment, liking it that he was taller and bigger than the other man. "That's not a threat you got," he said, heading for the door.

"The hell it isn't," said Ferguson indignantly, trailing after him.

Alberg pushed open the screen door. "Have those animals been inspected?"

"Certainly they've damn been inspected!" said Ferguson. "The damn wildlife guy's been here two, three times."

Alberg went down the steps, looking around for Ferguson's wife, but he couldn't see her. "I'll check it out," he said.

Ferguson came through the doorway, the screen thwacking shut behind him. "Well what the hell are you gonna check out," he said bitterly, "if I ain't been threatened?"

Alberg stopped and turned around. "Vandalism. Theft. Intimidation. That sound okay to you?"

Ferguson frowned, uncertain, and rubbed vigorously at his thick black hair.

"I'll be in touch," said Alberg. He rounded the corner. "Let me know," he called out, "if it happens again." He was pretty sure that it would.

Chapter Two

Warren Kettleman saw his life as a horizon, and his worries as clouds upon it, and his aim, the thing toward which he struggled, that which he would have called nirvana, was to be able to gaze at that horizon and see it clean, clear and pale, uncluttered by so much as a wisp of cloud. If he had ever accomplished this he might well have felt that it was a consummate achievement; he might well have promptly, quietly, and with intense satisfaction shut down all systems and, utterly fulfilled, died.

Which would have been a big shock to Wanda, because Warren was a husky, healthy guy who, having just turned twenty-nine, had a lot of years ahead of him.

He awoke this Monday morning fifteen minutes before his alarm was set to go off, which is to say, at five-fifteen.

Warren turned onto his back. The fan purred from the top of the dresser, and daylight edged the window blind. Warren and Wanda were covered only by a sheet. Warren, staring at the window blind, thought about his wife's thin brown body. The blind moved slightly, fingered by a breeze. It was going to be another very hot day.

Warren started to go through his worries; nervously, skillfully, ritualistically—like a cardsharp shuffling a deck. This was something he did every morning and again at night, just before he went to sleep. He believed in naming his enemies, and looking them straight in the eye.

There was always money to worry about, of course. Warren knew he'd never have enough money. He and Wanda both earned a decent salary. Compared with lots of people, they lived a comfortable life. But Warren wanted them to have a lot of money. He craved RSP's, and CSB's, and GIC's—anything that smacked of savings. Wanda got impatient with him about this. She was frugal, too, most of the time, but every so often she wanted to do something extravagant. This caused Warren to break out in a cold sweat. What if one day he couldn't dissuade her, and she used up all her recklessness in one fell swoop, and spent all the money they had on a Mercedes? Or, worse—on something that couldn't be sold? He didn't know what. He just had visions of all their money disappearing.

He turned onto his side and looked at Wanda's shoulder. He touched it with his tongue and tasted salt. He glanced at the clock, then moved closer to Wanda, and pressed his erection against her buttocks. Wanda gave a little moan but it turned out to be a moan of protest. She pulled away from him and in her sleep flung off the sheet. Warren propped himself up on an elbow and looked down at her, small and brown and shiny, except for the parts covered by her swimsuit when she sunbathed, which was every chance she got. These parts weren't big enough, as far as Warren was concerned. He lay down again.

Money. Annabelle. Annabelle was a worry, too, but that worry was something that was never going to change and never going to go away, either. It was something he'd learned to live with, he told himself. Although every once in a while he felt a great surge of bitterness toward his sister. He envied her, even though her life was such a total mess, and it was his envy that made him bitter.

Money. Annabelle. And now, Bobby Ransome. Bobby loomed large among Warren's worries, these days. But then he'd always loomed large in Warren's life—and Warren had always been surprised about this, because theirs was a sideways relationship that had never felt important until later.

He sat up and swung his legs over the side of the bed. He sat there looking down at the rag rug and bewilderment flooded him.

He switched off the alarm, stood up, quietly got clothes from the closet and his dresser drawer, and went to the bathroom to shower.

When he got home from work he took cheese and a can of beer from the fridge and crackers from the cupboard and sat at the kitchen table, sipping, munching, listening to a soft-rock music station on the radio. Then he put his dishes in the sink and started in on his current project. These days he was applying aluminum siding, white, to the garage. He'd never done this kind of work before so he was proceeding slowly and methodically, learning as he went. When he'd finished the garage, he planned to start in on the house.

After a while he was pretty hot, so he went inside and got himself a can of pop, and drank half of it in the kitchen, staring out the window above the sink. He took the rest back out to the garage, and resumed work on the siding. And as he worked, his mind wandered again to Bobby Ransome.

When Warren was twelve and Annabelle was fifteen they'd lived next door to Bobby. Warren's granddad had an old '59 Chevy he wanted to get rid of and Warren, who'd loved cars even then, bought the car from his granddad for a hundred bucks, which he earned doing a paper route and collecting bottles and beer cans.

Warren's folks owned an acre out near Halfmoon Bay, and there was a shed on the property that Warren's dad let him use as a garage. So Warren bought the Chevy—which was a gut-ugly Biscayne with huge fins, but Warren loved it because it was his first car. And the clutch was slipping, so he bought used parts from Joe Fourquin the auto wrecker guy and set to work to fix it. Which meant he had to first remove the drive shaft and take out the transmission. And Bobby Ransome started wandering over from next door to see what was going on.

Bobby didn't know a whole lot about cars. Except he knew how to drive, of course. Which Warren did, too, even though he was only twelve. So Bobby watched him working on the Chevy, and he asked him stuff, and at first this made Warren nervous but then he decided he liked it. This big kid squatting on his heels, arms resting on his thighs, hands linked, seriously watching, asking Warren serious questions. It felt good.

But when Warren got the Chevy put back together again, it wouldn't work. He was some embarrassed. Had to take the damn thing apart all over again. Drive shaft. Transmission. The whole works.

And then finally he figured it out. He'd put the clutch fork in backwards.

Warren, smiling at the wall of his garage, recalled a summer evening. He'd been working on the Chevy all day. And this time, he got it right.

Warren remembered that he gave a great whoop and banged his palm down on the steering wheel, and honked the horn excitedly, which brought Annabelle running outside and Bobby running over from next door. Both of them jumped into the front seat with him and Warren proudly drove the Chevy out of the shed and across the yard behind the house, and they were all three laughing fit to bust a gut and Warren figured he'd never been so happy, before or since.

"Yoo-hoo," Wanda called from the back porch. "I'm home."

He put away his tools and went indoors.

"I'll set the table if you like," he said as he washed his hands.

"It's far too early, Warren, honestly," said Wanda, pouring diet ginger ale into a tall glass. "I need to put my feet up." She added ice to her drink, then took it into the living room, and Warren followed.

He sat on the sofa and listened to Wanda chatter away about the bank, its employees and customers, and he attempted some aimless conversation of his own but his heart wasn't in it.

Finally, "I've been thinking," he said.

"Uh-oh," said Wanda cheerfully. "A dangerous sign."

"Wanda, I really would like us to have a baby."

She rolled her eyes and groaned. "We've been through this, Warren. I told you. When I'm thirty."

"But that's three more years."

"It's not three more years. It's two years and three months."

"Still—," said Warren.

"I want two more years to enjoy life, thank you very much, before I tie myself down with kids. I told you when we got married, Warren," she reproved him, "that I wasn't keen on having kids right away. I don't think it's very fair of you to keep bringing it up all the time." She picked up her glass and drank some ginger ale.

"Wanda, the thing is—"

"Oh for goodness' sake," said Wanda. She was curled up in a big easy chair. She banged the arm of the chair with a small fist. "No more, Warren. Please."

"But I read something," said Warren earnestly, leaning forward on the sofa. "Just listen. Okay?"

She heaved a great sigh, which Warren took as permission to continue.

"See, I read that the best time to have your first baby is when you're eighteen, something like that."

"Well I messed up that opportunity good and proper, didn't I," she said.

"Yeah, but anytime from eighteen to about—" He stopped, floundering. "Oh, thirty or so," he went on, "early thirties, somewhere in there, that's good. And then once the body's done it once, why it knows how, in a manner of speaking." Wanda, he noticed, was looking at him incredulously. "And then you could wait a couple of years before having another one, and you could go on having them right through your thirties, and every time gets easier."

Wanda now had a grim expression on her face.

Warren went on: "But if you wait until your body starts to—to—to, stiffen, see, stiffen up, before you have your first one, why then you're gonna have trouble, and then probably you wouldn't want to have another one, so you'd end up with only one kid."

Wanda gazed at him stonily.

"And that's what worries me," said Warren.

Wanda didn't say anything.

"Having only one kid isn't good," said Warren lamely. "A kid should have company, growing up."

"I've got the perfect solution," said Wanda.

"What?" said Warren cautiously.

"No kids at all. Ever." She stood up.

"But you'd've had them with Bobby, wouldn't you?" Warren said quickly, bitterly.

Wanda became very still; she looked like a statue, standing there, facing the hallway.

Warren heard the words repeat themselves over and over again in the stillness, like they were echoing in the air between him and Wanda. Maybe he shouldn't have said them. But no; they had to be said, he figured.

Wanda turned to face him.

"And don't try to deny it," Warren said. "Because we both know better."

Wanda snapped her mouth closed. She swept past him and he heard her march down the hall into the bedroom, and the door slammed.

Warren imagined rows and rows of his unborn children, retreating from him, reproachful and sorrowing.

Chapter Three

Annabelle hadn't been expecting him. Not exactly.

When he came she was very glad there was nobody else at home.

He knocked on the wooden frame of the screen door, because the inside door was open; the day was already hot, although it was still young. Annabelle moved through the kitchen into the hall and saw him, blurry through the screen, sunlight behind him, and she smiled in spite of herself. But she put a frown on, while she unlatched the door. She pushed it open just a bit, and pretended surprise and exasperation. "For heaven's sake," she said. "Bobby Ransome. Whatever are you doing at my door?"

He smiled at her, of course, but she ignored that and told him calmly and politely to go away.

"Give me a cup of coffee at least," he protested. "And get me caught up on stuff. I hear you're married, for instance."

"Yes I'm married," said Annabelle primly, "and I have several children, too."

"Several?" said Bobby. "What's that, 'several'? Whaddya mean, 'several'? How many've you got?"

"Three."

"Three's not 'several,'" said Bobby, and he stretched out his arm and pressed his hand against the side of the house, leaning there. "Three's three."

"All right then, three," said Annabelle. "Now I'm very busy, Bobby, and you have to leave right away." He was wearing jeans and a T-shirt and he was tanned very brown. She wondered where he'd been since he got out of jail. She thought he must have had an outdoor job of some kind, to have gotten so brown.

Finally he shrugged. "Okay," he said, and she watched him amble across the yard toward the road, where a small blue car was parked. She was still watching when he reached it, and somehow he knew this because just before he got there, while still sauntering away from her, he lifted his arm and gave a wave; and then quickly turned to look at her over his shoulder. He shook his head, laughing, to see Annabelle still standing there.

She was flustered by her encounter with Bobby Ransome, and went into her garden to calm herself.

It was a very private place, virtually surrounded by trees and brush, about thirty feet behind the house. It was small, about twenty feet long by fifteen feet wide, including the small lawn she had built there, with strips of grass purchased from the garden shop. At the east side of the garden, where it shouldered into the hillside, was a stand of alder trees. On the other three sides there was brush, which Annabelle kept cut back, and down, so that it gave privacy to her garden without keeping out the sunlight.

She looped the handle of her pail over her left hand, took a pair of pruning shears in her right, and began a slow inspection. Carefully she removed several dead blooms from one of her rosebushes, cutting them off at the first five-leaflet leaf that faced away from the center of the plant. The flowers were oyster-colored. They fascinated Annabelle, who had never seen roses that color before. She also had a bright yellow rose, a dark red one, two pink ones, and one that was the color of an apricot.

She was wearing a blue-and-white-striped sundress, and her feet were bare. Her back was sweating, and under her arms. Annabelle lifted her face and closed her eyes and stood quietly, feeling the heat of the sun, listening to the bees nosing at her flower beds and the birds murmuring in the alder trees. Her feet seemed to be gripping the earth like roots. She let her body sway slightly; the smell of roses and crisp dry grass was thick and sweet. She heard leaves rustle and opened her eyes, slowly, and with a sleepy smile turned to greet her child, whichever one it might be who was coming through the brush.

But it wasn't a child.

The smile stayed on her face, forgotten, as she looked at him. He was holding branches apart with both hands. He stepped toward her and let go of them and they sprang together again, closing the gap. Now they were together, she and Bobby, in her garden.

Annabelle didn't think to say anything to him. He was looking at her intently, and he seemed much nearer to her than he actually was. She wondered why they weren't speaking, either of them. She wondered what he'd heard about her, since he got back. She felt the smile tremble on her face and thought it was going to disappear, but instead it changed.

Oh, well, thought Annabelle, only vaguely aware of having made a decision.

She looked up into his green eyes, and there grew inside her joy and mischief and exhilaration. She allowed her smile to bloom. She saw that Bobby was holding his breath, but Annabelle breathed deep and slow, giving him her blazing smile.

"I didn't say goodbye," he said, after a long time. He stepped close to her. "Annabelle—"

"Shhhh," said Annabelle, laying her index finger across his lips.

"Mama!" cried Camellia, crashing through the bushes. She stopped in confusion to see a strange man in the garden with her mother.

Annabelle stepped away from Bobby Ransome, toward Camellia.

Bobby looked at the child, and then at Annabelle. She imagined that she could hear his heartbeat, fast and hard. Finally he nodded, and backed through the brush, and was gone.

Chapter Four

Cassandra Mitchell leaned back in the swing, letting her long dark hair hang down behind it. "Maybe she *is* crazy," she mused. "She could be crazy. She talks to herself, after all." She closed her eyes, and the day was still so bright that light filtered through her eyelids, creating a field of pink.

"Me, too," said Alberg. "I talk to myself, too."

Alberg's daughter Diana, who had a summer job with the local newspaper, was working that evening. So Alberg and Cassandra had gone to Earl's Café for hamburgers. Now they were sitting on a garden swing in Cassandra's backyard, drinking lemonade and talking about Hetty Willis.

"Probably you're both just eccentric," said Cassandra tolerantly.

Hetty Willis pedaled about the town on an elderly bicycle, a brown-paper shopping bag riding in the wire carrier. She wore a black shawl all the time, whatever the weather; it was draped around her shoulders and tied in a knot in front. She was never seen wearing a jacket or a coat; she never carried an umbrella.

"She lives in that big house all by herself," Cassandra went on. "Except for her cats."

And she did talk to herself—often, and unintelligibly. Sometimes she came into the library, to peer at the spines of books, and her incoherent mutterings could empty the place in minutes.

Cassandra lifted her head. "So, tell me. Why're you asking about her?"

"I have to talk to her," said Alberg.

"What about?" said Cassandra. She didn't really expect him to tell her. "See, look at that, now," she said in disgust, pointing at him.

"What? What?" said Alberg.

"Your face gets all closed off. It smooths itself out and closes itself off. That makes me so mad, I cannot tell you how angry that makes me." She pushed herself off the swing. Sometimes she thought she didn't know him any better now than the day they'd first met, in the Harrisons' restaurant for lunch, after he'd replied to her "Companions" ad in the *Vancouver Sun*.

Alberg, smiling, stood up and put his arms around her. "I like the way you smell," he said. "I like the way you look, too."

"I'm overweight," said Cassandra into his shirt. "I'm getting old."

"You don't know nothin' about old," said Alberg with a sigh, "until you're staring fifty in the face."

She gazed at him, thoroughly exasperated. Was it a good thing, she wondered, or a bad thing, that he'd forgotten she was only three years younger than he.

He touched the side of her neck with his tongue and moved his lips to her ear. "I love you," he said to her ear; he didn't even know for sure that he'd said it out loud. But then she turned her head and drew back to look at him, and there was such solemnity on her face that he knew he must have actually said the words. And he was dismayed. And this must have shown in his eyes, because she shook her head and laughed at him.

The blue house stood on the east side of the road, high on the hill that dropped down to Davis Bay. He pulled off the highway onto a chunk of concrete that was cracked and crumbling, with weeds growing from every seam and fissure, weeds now brown and dead, killed prematurely by the brutal summer.

Alberg cut the motor and rolled up the windows. He got out of the car and locked it, then looked up. The house stood at the top of a very long flight of cement steps. He couldn't imagine an old woman lugging bags of groceries up those steps. There had to be a back entrance.

From this angle the house looked like the house in *Psycho*. Except that it was bright blue. And painted not so long ago, either. It was a particularly noxious shade of blue, he thought, to use on a house.

The steps went up, and up, and up. There was a railing beside them. Alberg put a hand on it and gave it a quick shake and watched as the resulting wobble scurried upward; the whole damn railing all the way up the hillside shuddered. He squinted upward at the blue house, a bright blue shriek against the fading evening light, and started climbing.

He labored up the crumbling steps thinking about his upcoming birthday—it made his heart grow cold to acknowledge that he would be fifty in less than three weeks. But my God my wind's better since I quit smoking, he thought, beginning to pant.

Halfway up the stairs there was a landing, a concrete pad about three feet square upon which sat a deck chair. Alberg stopped and looked at it approvingly. It was the old-fashioned kind made of wood and canvas, like a hammock with a frame, faded and torn but still usable. For some reason it made him think of his mother's piano, an upright with a stool that you twirled around to make it higher or lower.

He looked up at the bright blue house. He saw no lights, no sign of life at all—except for two cats peering at him from the veranda, beneath a window framed in lace curtains. He grasped the railing and propelled himself up the last six feet of steps and stood in front of the veranda, breathing heavily, eyeing a big sofa that he figured used to be maroon. Three more cats lay upon it. The sofa had been torn almost to shreds.

Alberg walked up the steps onto the veranda and looked for a doorbell. There was no bell and no knocker, either. But there was a little brass crank, which he turned, and he heard it squawk inside the house. Almost immediately the door opened, and an old woman looked out from behind it.

"Mrs. Willis?"

"MizMiz," she said, unblinking.

Alberg thought for a moment. "I beg your pardon?"

"MizMiz. NoMissus."

"I'm sorry," said Alberg. "Ms. Willis."

She wasn't much over five feet tall. She seemed a collection of sticks and knobs, with very little hair; it was long and gray, what there was of it, and he could see her scalp through it.

"My name is Alberg. I'm with the RCMP. Can I talk to you?"

"Ohohoh," said Hetty Willis. She stared at him for a few more seconds. Then she pulled the door open wider, and scurried inside.

Alberg stepped through into the house. He realized that he had been aware for several minutes of an unpleasant odor, which now surged out of the house and smacked him in the face. It was the smell of cat urine. He tried to breathe through his mouth.

Hetty Willis had hurried on stick legs through the vestibule and was now crossing a large entrance hall from which a wide stairway led to the second story. There were three doors, all closed. She scuttled toward the door on the left, and as she neared it she started to make high-pitched crooning noises around quick repetitions of the word "Hurry." Her hand reached

for the glass doorknob; a roar of animal clamor rose from behind
the closed door, surely too big and too loud to be coming from
a few domesticated cats—Christ, thought Alberg, images of
rough-coated cheetahs and cold-eyed lions springing to his
mind. The old woman turned the handle and pushed open the
door, releasing a tide of normal-sized cats that streamed across
the threshold and into the hall. It undulated speedily across the
worn hardwood floor toward Alberg.

There were dark cats and light ones, sleek cats and fat ones,
large cats and small ones. Alberg, who had acquired two cats of
his own, had begun thinking of himself as someone who
respected and appreciated cats. At this moment, though, it was
difficult not to at least flinch as the swarm of feline bodies swept
around him; what he really wanted to do was get the hell out of
there.

"How many have you got?" he said to Hetty Willis, who
had squatted to stroke several of her cats, her voice thrumming
wordlessly. "Miss Willis? How many cats have you got?" She
stood up and hustled across the hall to the doorway opposite.
Oh my God, thought Alberg, but this time when she opened
the door nothing emerged. She motioned to him. The cats
swirled around her feet but when she went through the doorway
they didn't follow. Some sat, some wandered back to the room
from which they'd come, some disappeared into the shadowy
reaches of the hallway, some climbed the stairs. Alberg followed
Hetty Willis into what seemed to be a parlor.

"Sixtytwo," she blurted, perching on a straight-backed
chair.

The room was dark and cool. Heavy curtains hung at the
windows; they were dark green, and might have been velvet,
Alberg thought. There was a large fireplace at one end of the
room, with two loveseats in front of it, facing one another over a
long, low table. Opposite the fireplace was a wall of bookcases.
A rolltop desk stood nearby, and a couple of easy chairs, each
with a standing lamp behind it. There were two large rugs on
the floor.

"Sixty-two cats," said Alberg, stunned. He looked around. "You don't let them in here?"

She shook her head. Her gray hair hung to her shoulders. She looked at him steadily, with brown eyes that were hooded and wary.

Alberg tried to imagine sharing a house with sixty-two cats. He wondered how much it cost to feed them. "Do they all have names?"

Hetty Willis moved to the desk. She put into the drawer what looked like an unfinished letter, and began stroking the back of the chair with nervous, restless fingers. She wore a shapeless tweed skirt and a long-sleeved gray blouse that buttoned up the front. On her feet were socks and sneakers. She touched her throat. "Insidemyhead."

"Pardon?" said Alberg.

"Insidemyhead."

"Inside your head," said Alberg, slowly and carefully.

She nodded. "Catnames. Catfaces."

"The—your cats' names are inside your head?"

She nodded again. She stared at him fixedly. "Onaroll ofpaper. Insidemyhead."

Alberg gave a helpless shrug. "I'm sorry," he said. "I don't understand."

"Can't seethemall," she said, and he saw how hard she was working. "Playerpiano," she said finally. "Like a playerpiano."

Words yearned to fall from her lips with the profuseness and rapidity of raindrops; she fought to subdue them, in order to control their disposition.

"Catnames. Catfaces."

But there was a momentum created by every word she spoke that wanted instantly to pull forth more and more; those she allowed to escape slid bumpily from her lips, colliding in midair.

"On thepaper." She swallowed repeatedly, editing in her mouth. "Rollspast. Can't seethemall."

Alberg didn't know whether her disability was physical or mental. He was fascinated.

"Justsome." She was holding tight to the back of the chair. "Then it rollspast."

Alberg listened for a code; and found it, finally, in rhythm.

"Somemore." She made a circle in the air, again and again. "See morenames. Morefaces."

Alberg grinned. "Gotcha," he said. "Like a player piano."

She sat down, and pointed at one of the easy chairs.

"Thank you," said Alberg. He pulled his notebook and pen from his jacket pocket. "Do you know about that place off the highway, with the animals in cages?"

"Didn'thave," said Hetty Willis, fingers once more against her throat. "Didn'thaveit. Twodollars."

Alberg was confused for a moment. Then, "Ah," he said. "You mean, the admission?"

She nodded.

He frowned at her, thoughtful. "Anybody who's got sixty-two cats must care a great deal about animals."

"Cats," she said. "Aboutcats."

He looked at her sharply, wondering if she'd smiled, just for a second. "So it's only cats that you love?"

"Don'tbesilly," she said sharply, then clapped a hand over her mouth.

"What's silly?" said Alberg, feigning hurt. "How am I silly?"

She shook her head. "Lovelovelove. Nolove. Nolove."

"What, you mean you don't love your cats?"

She regarded him with infinite weariness.

Alberg looked down at his notebook. "The guy calls the place a mini-zoo. Somebody stole a couple of his animals. A couple of skunks, I think it was." He glanced at Hetty Willis, who was impassive. "Maybe let them loose, I don't know."

Hetty looked back at him and said nothing.

"And there was damage done, too."

Hetty sat quietly and said nothing.

"And whoever did this left a note behind for the man who owns the place." Alberg put his notebook back in his pocket.

"We're having it checked for prints," he said casually, but Hetty
was apparently indifferent. "The guy took it as a threat." He
clicked his ballpoint pen closed and put that in his pocket, too.
"I figure it was more of a warning," he said, standing up.

Hetty stood up, too, and led him back into the hall, where
cats were waiting to rub against her ankles and meow for
her attention.

She watched from the window as he climbed down the
steps and disappeared, and she waited until she saw headlights
come on, and a car drive away. Then she returned to the sitting
room and sat down at her desk. She got the letter from the
drawer, put on her reading glasses, uncapped her pen, and
resumed writing to her lawyer.

"Out on the Redrooffs Road," she wrote, "some new people
have moved into the McNeil place. They've got several cats, a
big black dog, and a horse. Their children run about with virtually no clothes on and I cannot believe that they treat their
animals any better." She peered through her half glasses,
rereading what she'd written. "Not that I think animals should
be clothed," she added, and put down her pen for a moment, to
stretch her fingers.

That policeman is full of curiosity, she thought. It bubbles
out of his skin.

"Nothing has been done about that so-called zoo, yet," she
complained to the lawyer. Her penmanship was as exquisite as
ever; but it was an art more and more difficult to practice.
"There's no place for such a thing in this community. I know
you say the man isn't breaking any laws. But there are laws,"
Hetty wrote, "and there are laws." Again she put down her pen,
and flexed her hand.

It doesn't bother him to feel inquisitive, she thought. He
can ask, or not ask, and get an answer, or not get one, and it
doesn't bother him.

"Now to the other side of the ledger," she wrote, "where I
fear the pickings are scarce, as usual. There have been eleven
adoptions from the SPCA. Mr. Thomas took three kittens; Mrs.

McMillan, Mr. George, Mr. Samuelson and the little Gazetas girl each took a cat. Three young dogs were taken by Mrs. Adamson (of Halfmoon Bay), Miss Jacobs and Mr. Pupetz. And Miss Wachowich, bless her heart, took a grown dog with asthma, a wall eye and a limp.

"And that's all I have to report." Her hand was aching badly now, but she persevered, because she knew that if she put down her pen again she wouldn't finish the letter today.

At the door the policeman had scrutinized her face, and she had felt his curiosity, detached, powerful, not necessarily benign. He'd been going to say something—and then he'd changed his mind.

"When you come to see me next," Hetty wrote, laboriously, painfully, "I have a personal matter to discuss."

He'd smiled at her instead. And she'd been surprised at the sweetness of his smile, and wondered if it was genuine.

"I want to change my will," Hetty told her lawyer. "Because my nephew Bobby has come back."

Chapter Five

They'd lived out of town when Steven was growing up. On three acres out by Porpoise Bay. He was an only child, so he spent a lot of time by himself.

Velma, walking home from work—slowly, because of the heat—smiled to think about those days. They constituted the part of her life she had labeled "Happy"; a parcel of days, a piece of time that she had put away on a shelf, tied up with red ribbon, wearing a big red bow. And Steven's reappearance in Sechelt seemed to have returned those days to her.

She wondered how long he would be able to stay. She was full of plans for the two of them.

Velma waved through the window of the drugstore at Peggy Allan, who worked there, and turned the corner to walk up the hill toward her street.

She remembered the summer Steven had made a sword out of two pieces of wood: he must have been about five, she thought. He'd gone howling through the woods slashing at the underbrush with his makeshift weapon, and it was always breaking, or coming apart, so that he'd have to make himself a new one. He used to come home with his legs and arms all scratched, and pieces of the forest in his hair.

Velma walked up the hill, swinging her handbag, squinting a little against the bright sunlight. She and Steven had gone to Percy and Edna's for dinner last night—it had been so good to feel like a family again!

There'd been a stream running through their acreage, she remembered, with a little field of grass next to the water, and Steven had found wild strawberries there. And salmonberries, in the woods. And blackberries.

She was slightly winded when she got to her corner. Not much, though. She was in pretty good shape, for a woman her age.

He hadn't had many friends, when he was a child. Harry was always trying to get him to join the Cubs, or a hockey team, but Steven wouldn't. He'd had *some* friends, though, thought Velma, plodding along the side of the road. She remembered one little boy he brought home to play—he had an odd talent, she recalled vaguely; birdcalls, or something.

She glanced across a tumbled-down fence into the front yard of an empty house with a FOR SALE sign tacked to one of the posts that held up the porch. She wished she could afford to live on a nicer street.

Less than five minutes later she was trudging up the walk to her front door, feeling tired, now, and looking forward to putting her feet up.

As she climbed the steps she saw through the screen that Steven was on the phone. He was facing the wall, holding the receiver to his ear with his right hand, and his left hand was splayed out and pressed against the wall above his head. Velma opened the door silently and slipped inside, not wanting to startle her son.

"Do you know who this is?" she heard him say, in a voice curiously thin and dry.

Then, "It's—it's me."

Velma put her purse on the floor by the closet and clasped her hands together.

"Steven." He paused. "Steven Grayson."

Velma stood quietly; courteous.

"Listen," he said. "I've got to talk to you. I've—it's important. It's very important."

She watched as he pulled his hand away from the wall and took a quick step forward, toward the kitchen.

"Please don't hang up, don't—"

He replaced the receiver. Velma saw that the back of his shirt was soaked with sweat.

"Steven?"

Slowly, he turned around.

"What's wrong? Who were you talking to?"

She saw in his eyes that he had no intention of telling her.

Chapter Six

That night, Herman wanted to make love. Afterward he fell asleep and started snoring, but Annabelle still wasn't tired. She lay on her back with her hands under her buttocks and didn't feel sleepy at all.

After a while she got up and went into the kitchen. She poured herself a glass of milk and sat down at the table, in moonlight that spilled through the window. The glass had a blue-white glow even after she'd emptied it, created by the shadow of the milk still inside it, and the moonlight touching it.

Annabelle lifted her hands and spread them wide and looked at them in the light from the moon; rough, short-fingered hands. There was a thin gold ring on the left one. Annabelle took it off and set it down on top of the table. She spread her hand again: she could see a faint mark encircling her finger, now, a circle of skin paler than the rest of her hand.

The refrigerator began whirring. It was a sound that Annabelle liked. She enjoyed knowing that the refrigerator held so much good food; milk and eggs and butter and vegetables and fruits. She wanted a freezer, too. She'd put lots of chickens in it, bought from Erna Remple's place up at the top of the road, and maybe they could buy a quarter of beef—lots of pot roasts and stew meat and ground beef and chuck steak, and a few good steaks and roasts for special occasions. She'd get strawberries in June, and raspberries in July, and blueberries in August, and she'd freeze them, too. And she might set one day a week aside for baking; at the end of that day she'd have bread and coffee cakes and muffins and all kinds of things to put away in the freezer. She'd get a copy of the *Buy-and-Sell* and find out how much they cost, secondhand.

Annabelle got up from the table and wandered quietly through the house, peeking in at the children, keeping an ear open for sounds from the cages out back.

She wished Herman would get rid of those animals. She didn't like them in her life. They gave her inexplicable feelings of foreboding.

She went into the glass-walled room and sat down in a lawn chair. The moon was large and bright in the sky and it flooded the place with light; the potted plants shone, wide awake in the moonlight.

Annabelle stretched her legs out in front of her. Her bare feet, bare legs, the white nightgown with pink polka dots that came to her knees—everything looked glossy and silver in the moonlight. She thought she could even feel it on her skin, deep and soft like satin.

She thought about the first time she'd seen this place. Herman had trundled them out here in the pickup and she'd gazed in horror upon an abandoned building, and two old rickety gas pumps, and a wooden sign, the paint faded and peeling, that once had said "CAFÉ." Somebody had painted "CLOSED" across the sign in big black letters that were almost as faded as the word beneath. She'd gotten out of the truck very reluctantly. This was going to be their new home, this falling-down dilapidated dejected-looking place, and Annabelle hadn't liked the idea one little bit.

She'd climbed out of the truck, though, and while Herman was lecturing the kids about something or other she'd wandered closer to the building. The panes were encrusted with grime but light still managed to poke through, and the dirt-floored area between the glass wall and the wall of the house was crowded with weeds, some as tall as small trees, a thick, urgent forest of weeds that pressed against the glass walls as if against the walls of a prison.

What on earth would Warren think of this place? As if things weren't bad enough on that front, she'd thought.

At least it was close to Erna, though. That was in its favor.

One of the skylights in the roof was broken, and one of the dormer windows, too, but the window walls were in surprisingly good condition; several panes were missing, glass glinted dully from the dust, and one pane was cracked, that was all. But there was steady, relentless pressure upon the glass from the greenery behind it, and it was clear that the weeds were eventually going to bring the whole thing crashing down.

Annabelle went over to the window wall, where she cupped her hands around her eyes and leaned close, to squint through the grimy glass.

"What do you think, Ma?" said Rose-Iris tentatively. She'd come up next to Annabelle and was trying to see inside.

Annabelle smelled the thick, rich smell of weeds triumphant, and saw in her imagination the weeds ripped out and replaced with exotic flowering plants, in pots.

"There's surely a job to be done in there, all right," she'd muttered crossly to Rose-Iris, but excitement stirred in her chest. Then she'd turned and said loudly to Herman, who was leaning against the truck, watching her, "There's a job to be done in there, I can tell you."

"You can handle it," Herman had said.

Annabelle, looking around now at her indoor garden, thought that he'd been right.She went back to bed. She climbed in beside Herman and turned so that her back was to his back, and she shut her eyes and prepared to go to sleep.

Vancouver came into her mind. She imagined herself walking along a street there, downtown it would be, maybe she'd be on Hastings Street, in front of Woodward's, near the restaurant where she used to work. There she is, walking along, thinking about her shopping list; she's taking her time, looking around her, enjoying herself, minding her own business...and all of a sudden there's a touch on her arm. She turns and sees that it's Bobby. "Why Bobby," she says, cool as a cucumber, "what on earth are you doing here?" (She tried to imagine what he'd be wearing, strolling along the street in Vancouver, but she couldn't. So she went on.) He tells her why he's come to town, and then he looks at his watch and says, "Why it's almost lunchtime. Would you care to join me?" And Annabelle frowns a little and then says, "Well I guess that would be all right, as long as I don't miss my—my dental appointment," she tells him, "which is at one o'clock." (No, thought Annabelle, in bed with her eyes closed. She did a revision.) "As long as I don't miss my dental appointment," she says to Bobby. "And what time is your dental appointment?" Bobby asks. "It's at two o'clock," says Annabelle. He takes her by the arm. "I'll make sure you don't miss it," he says in her ear, and propels her down the street.

Annabelle turned onto her back. She couldn't remember the last time she'd been to Vancouver on her own. Not since she lived there, before she got married to her first husband, could she remember walking down a street in Vancouver on her own.

"Hey," said Herman the next morning, and Annabelle turned from the stove to see him holding up her wedding ring. "What's this doing here?"

"My finger started to itch," said Annabelle smoothly. "I think I'm allergic."

Chapter Seven

"Yeah," said Bobby into the phone. It was a week later.

"It's me again."

"Jesus Christ. I don't believe this."

"All I want is to talk, I just want to talk to you," said Steven. "Listen—don't hang up—you don't understand. Please. Don't hang up."

They could hear each other breathing.

"I—you see," said Steven, "I've been working on this for a long time. It's been on my mind for a long time. I've got something for you."

"Like hell you have."

"Yeah, I have, really."

"You got nothin' I want, Grayson."

"No, but listen—"

"Lay off. Stay away from me. Or I'll have your ass."

Chapter Eight

Hetty Willis woke at six o'clock the next morning, as usual, when her clock radio came on. She lay in bed for fifteen minutes, getting caught up on the news. There was certainly a great deal of friction in the world. Things could—and did—so quickly, so easily, get out of hand.

She got up, and did some slow, cautious stretching exercises before getting dressed and opening the curtains and making her bed.

It was almost seven when Hetty went out into the hall, where several cats awaited her; her bedroom was one of the few rooms in the house in which cats were not allowed. They roamed freely through most of the house, and in and out of it freely, too, through the pet door in the kitchen.

Hetty made her way downstairs and into the cats' room. Here she refilled the fifteen food and water dishes, which in another life had served as containers for yogurt, cottage cheese, or margarine. Then she went into the kitchen and had breakfast, watched by several cats arranged on the tops of cupboards, on the seats of chairs, on windowsills. After she had washed the dishes, she set about doing the cat chores.

She took a plastic bag into the cats' room and scooped into it the droppings from all fifteen litter boxes. Then she selected three of them for a thorough cleaning, dumping the litter into a plastic garbage bag, scouring the boxes, sprinkling them with baking soda, and adding clean litter. Each day she did three boxes in this way.

She took a wicker basket from the cat cupboard and checked its contents: brush, flea comb, a dozen new white flea collars, felt pen, ointment. Then she climbed the stairs and proceeded to search the house, room by room. Each cat she came across along the way got checked for fleas, and for scratches or other minor injuries. When she found a cat whose flea collar was dated more than three months earlier, she replaced it. Every day she flea-combed all the cats of the same or similar coloring; today it was the black ones. She didn't bother to try to keep track of the cats as she inspected the house, looking for them; she had decided long ago that the odds were she'd encounter all of them frequently enough to keep everything under control—health, cleanliness, fleas. But she had to look for them diligently—under furniture, on top of bookcases, behind curtains—because cats liked to hide, and they especially liked to hide if they weren't feeling well. Today Hetty found nobody injured, nobody sick, and the flea situation wasn't bad, either: it must be the heat, she thought.

She made preparations for lunch, and then sat down on the couch in the cats' room with a cat on her lap—a Siamese—and four more arranged around her. She stroked the Siamese and did a bit of planning for the end of her life, which she judged to be about eighteen months in the future. In twelve months she would be seventy-five and it was at seventy-five that each of her parents had died; and her sister, Lucy, too, in Barbados just last year. Hetty spent a small portion of each day considering this matter. Careful planning was essential to the success of any endeavor, including death.

These preparations had become more urgent, lately, with her nephew's reappearance in her life. It's an ill wind, she thought...It was his stepfather's recent heart attack that had brought Bobby out of exile and although God knew she meant the man no harm, she was happy that Bobby had come home.

Oh what a bad time he'd had, she thought. He deserved to have some happiness come dancing into his life.

Hetty took the cat's face in her hands and looked into his eyes. She often did this; searching for cat-souls, she called it. But she never found any, had never spotted a cat-soul: they kept them well hidden.

First, he'd gotten married. Right out of high school. To a girl so young she was practically still a child. Hetty had suspected that the girl was pregnant, and that had turned out to be true. Bobby's mother, Rachel, had been furious.

And then his father, Wallace, dying like that. Hetty's brother. Hetty had tried to blame everything that happened next on Wallace dying, on the pain and confusion his death created, but she couldn't. People had to be held accountable for their actions no matter how much pain they were in, or else there would be chaos.

The Siamese sat up and rubbed the top of his head against Hetty's chin, and the sound of his purring comforted her.

She got up from the couch and went into the kitchen, where she brushed her skirt almost clean of cat hair and washed her hands. Then she prepared lunch and put the coffee on to perk.

A few minutes later Bobby arrived. He gave her a big hug and lifted her into the air, laughing.

She hustled him into the sitting room and poured coffee into two mugs. She sat on the edge of her straight-backed chair nodding, smiling, pleased by the sight of him. He was a strong, healthy-looking man with wide shoulders, slim hips and clear skin. There was a scar, a little one, on his forehead that hadn't been there before he went away.

He didn't have much to say, but that was all right.

"How long?" she said, after a while.

"Dunno. Depends," he said. "I'm going away for a couple of days," he told her, scooping more sugar into his coffee. "But I'll be back. At least for a while."

He stirred his coffee absently. Then he stood up, and walked over to the window. He stood staring out at her side garden, his hands in the pockets of his jeans. Hetty watched him for a few minutes. He didn't move, just stood there, staring outside. He looked different, of course. Ten years was a long time.

She had written to him while he was in jail. Sometimes he wrote back, and she taped his letters carefully into the scrapbook. He had phoned her when he got out, from Vancouver, to tell her that he wasn't coming home right away. She hadn't heard from him again until three weeks ago, when she'd opened her front door to see him standing on the porch, smiling down at her.

She got up and went to him, and lifted her hand and put it on his shoulder. She didn't know what exact thoughts were in his mind, but she knew that they were sad ones, maybe angry ones. She knew he was in turmoil. She wanted him to start his life all over again, and she thought he wanted that, too. But it's not possible, thought Hetty, her hand on his shoulder, gazing outside at the small patch of brown grass between her house and the neighbor's rickety fence. You can't start your life again. You can only resume it. Continue. Proceed.

"This guy wants to see me," he said absently. "I dunno why." He gave her a grin meant to be reassuring. "You got anything to eat around here?"

She had made ham sandwiches, and bought some cinnamon buns.

She would have liked to be closer to him than she was. But she thought she was probably as close to him as anybody would ever get. A couple of outcasts, Hetty thought. That's what we are.

He seemed to shake off his sadness, if that's what it was, while they ate, and drank their coffee. He talked, and even made some jokes, and when he stood up to leave, he seemed almost lighthearted.

"Wait," she said, a bony finger tapping at his chest. Then she pointed to herself. "Speak."

Bobby folded his arms. "Shoot."

Hetty was excited about what she had to tell him—too excited for her crippled speech. Frustrated, she hurried to her desk and scrawled a message on a piece of her stationery.

She thrust it at him and waited, impatient.

"'You're in my will,'" he read. He glanced at her, and she nodded vigorously. "'The house,'" he read. "'And money.'"

Bobby folded the paper, slowly, in half, then folded it again. He held it loosely in his right hand, head down. Hetty patted his arm, making soothing sounds. He put both arms around her and held her for a while.

Hetty walked with him to the door and watched through the window as he made his way down the long, crumbling flight of steps that led to the highway. So many wasted years, she thought.

And he'd deserved that, too; she admitted it.

Bobby had done wrong.

Chapter Nine

"**I**'m going into town, Ma," said Rose-Iris the following day. "To the library."

"Okay," said Annabelle, stirring a pot of homemade chicken noodle soup.

"Can I come? Can I?" said Camellia.

"No," said Rose-Iris, hurrying out the door.

Camellia pelted after her, and Annabelle went to the door to watch, through the screen, as Camellia danced around Rose-Iris and then ran, backward, in front of her, pleading and pleading, until finally, as Annabelle had known she would, Rose-Iris, with a furious, jerky motion of her arm, granted Camellia permission to accompany her.

Annabelle went back to the stove.

Pretty soon Herman and Arnold came home, and Annabelle dished up the chicken noodle soup, along with some cheese sandwiches and bowls of raspberries for dessert.

After lunch Arnold was allowed to go and play with his friend who lived down the highway; work was over for the day, because the paper was finally sending a reporter over to inter-view Herman about the mini-zoo.

"I'm at loose ends," said Herman, watching Annabelle do up the dishes. He was straddling his chair, and his chin was resting on his arms, which were folded along the back of the chair.

"I can think of a few things for you to do," said Annabelle.

"Like what?" said Herman, dismayed.

But Annabelle knew he wasn't dismayed at the prospect of being asked to do a chore or two; it was the idea that there were any left that he hadn't already taken care of that bothered him.

She laughed. "Nothing. I'm teasing you. Why don't you relax? Watch some TV, or something."

She let the water out of the sink, wiped the countertops, and wrung out the dishcloth.

"Annabelle," said Herman.

His voice was so quiet that Annabelle turned around swiftly, thinking something was wrong. She could tell from the look on his face that nothing was wrong—but she didn't know what it did mean, either, that look.

"What?" she said.

He shook his head. "Nothing. I just felt like saying your name."

She felt a great tenderness for him, sometimes. And always, always, there was the gratitude. She went to him and kissed him on the forehead. "I'm going to work in my garden," she said.

Annabelle set to work weeding the perennial bed; the dirt felt silky under her bare feet. She looked into the thick breathing forest as she worked, smelling the greenness of it. The dirt of her flower bed, the forest, the heat—it brought to her mind a book she'd read as a child, called *Girl of the Limberlost*. She remem-bered it as being about summer, and the healing power of the sea, and sun-hot tomatoes eaten right off the vine.

Eventually she heard a car, and she knew the reporter had arrived. She weeded for another few minutes, and then curiosity got the better of her, and she went through the brush onto the path that led to the house.

And there was Herman, his arms going around like a pair of windmills, gabbing at a young woman holding a notebook. She looked so thoroughly out of her element that she reminded Annabelle of the reporter in that movie about Nashville; the one who wandered around in a parking lot full of school buses making things up for her tape recorder. Annabelle realized, as she got closer, that the difference between them was that this young woman knew she was out of her element, and it was making her furious.

"Here's the lady from the paper," said Herman. "This is my wife," he said proudly to the reporter.

Annabelle smiled. "Would you like some iced tea?"

The girl shook her head. Her face was flushed. "No, thank you," she said. She was an attractive person, thought Annabelle. She had long, wavy hair and a heart-shaped face and a figure that was both curvaceous and sturdy.

"How come you didn't bring a camera?" said Herman.

"I'm a reporter," said the girl stiffly. "Not a photographer."

Annabelle sat down in a lawn chair near the house. She didn't move it into the shade of the trees because she didn't want to be that close to the animals.

"You can't have a story like this and not have pictures," Herman was protesting.

"If my editor wants pictures he'll send a photographer later."

"Okay, fine," said Herman. "Now here's your raccoons," he said, leading the way. "You saw your squirrels, you saw your foxes, you saw your monkeys, now here's your raccoons."

He'd changed his clothes, Annabelle noticed. He'd put on a white shirt over his undershirt, and a belt was holding up his jeans, instead of suspenders.

"Have you had a lot of people stop by?" said the reporter, clutching her notebook to her chest.

Herman hesitated. "Not yet. Not enough people know about it yet. I gotta get more signs put up. Your piece in the paper'll help a lot."

"What'll happen to them in the fall?" said the girl, staring at the raccoons.

"Whaddya mean, what'll happen to them? I put more stuff in their cages," said Herman, "so they can make nests, like, keep themselves warm."

"How much do you know about animals, anyway?" said the reporter, and Annabelle heard the dismay in her voice, even if Herman didn't.

"Not much," he said stoutly. "I'm learning from the wild-life guy. He tells me what I gotta do, and I do it."

"I don't understand," said the reporter, shaking her head. "I mean, you can't possibly be earning your living doing this."

"Never said I was," said Herman. "Carpentry's my livelihood."

"Then why?" said the young woman.

My goodness, thought Annabelle, suddenly pensive. She's practically in tears.

"Why what?" said Herman, exasperated.

"Why cage up these animals?" the girl shouted.

"Well how the hell," Herman shouted back, "how the hell can I have a goddamn zoo without goddamn cages?"

They stared at each other.

The girl snapped her notebook closed. "I've got all I need, thank you," she said, and marched off toward her car.

Herman glanced at Annabelle, who quickly wiped from her face the pity she'd felt there.

Chapter Ten

Cassandra helped the Ferguson girls load their books into two plastic grocery bags and watched as they went off up the street, the younger one skipping. Then she went to the staff room, which she shared with several part-time volunteers.

It was reached through a doorway behind the library's U-shaped counter, next to the shelves of books being kept on reserve. It contained a couch, an armchair, a round kitchen table with three straight-backed chairs, two coffee tables and a stand-up lamp. The floor was covered with strong but ugly carpeting that was the color of cement.

Cassandra looked around glumly, and made a half-hearted attempt to gather up armloads of *Publishers Weekly*, *Quill and Quire* and *B.C. Book World*. But there were newspapers everywhere, too, and the sink was cluttered with dirty glasses and coffee mugs, and the small refrigerator probably needed cleaning, and certainly the drip coffeepot sitting on the counter did.

There were no windows in the staff room, only skylights, and on summer days like this one the heat was merciless.

Cassandra slumped into the green plastic armchair; there was a tear in the seat, and the back of it was coming off. The Sally Ann wouldn't take this chair, she thought, fingering its bilious arms, as a gift. If she wanted to get rid of it she'd have to pay somebody to cart it away. Which was probably exactly what had gone through the mind of Betty Trimble before she had graciously donated the damn thing—on condition, of course, that Cassandra arrange for its transportation to the library.

Cassandra no longer uttered automatic bleats of gratitude when people offered her things. Now she spoke a cautious thank-you and said she'd be by to look it over, whatever it was. She resisted telling potential donors to take a hike, or call the junk man, because after all, the library had come by its coffeepot and its fridge, as well as the hideous green chair, through people like Betty Trimble.

I really must get this place cleaned up, she thought, surveying the room. She pulled a tissue from the pocket of her dress and dabbed at the sweat on her face. But not today.

One of the volunteers appeared in the doorway. "There's somebody out there wants to see you."

It was Diana Alberg. "Do you have information here about animal rights?" she said.

Fifteen minutes later Diana was seated at a table in the reading area, surrounded by books and pamphlets and magazines. Cassandra, cataloging books behind the counter, glanced up once in a while. She was thinking about the framed photograph that she'd seen on the mantelpiece in Karl's living room. It was a picture of his two daughters with their arms around his smiling ex-wife. Maura was tall and slim. She couldn't be called beautiful, exactly—but she was striking; dramatic-looking. Janey, the older daughter, resembled her. Cassandra had felt awkward, looking at the picture, and then depressed, and then royally pissed off. She hadn't said anything, but the next time she'd found herself in Karl's living room the photograph had been gone.

Diana was taking notes, absorbed in the material Cassandra had helped her find. Cassandra thought she looked very young, even though she'd graduated from university several months earlier.

They didn't know each other well, yet. Cassandra had found Diana to be intelligent; opinionated; impatient. She had a sense of humor. And a healthy curiosity about the world.

And what, I wonder, thought Cassandra, gazing at Karl Alberg's younger daughter, does Diana think of me?

After a while Diana closed the books, piled the magazines and pamphlets on top of them, picked them up, and went back into the stacks.

Cassandra followed her. "You don't have to do that," she said. "Here, give them to me, I'll put them away."

"Thank you very much," said Diana politely. "You've been a great help."

Cassandra took the material from her. "Are you doing research for an article?"

"Sort of," said Diana. She glanced quickly at Cassandra. "Have you any opinion," she said, "about animal rights?"

Cassandra looked thoughtfully at the three *Ficus benjamina*, each seven or eight feet tall, that stood near the floor-to-ceiling windows. "I believe that they have some," she said carefully.

"Do you wear fur?" said Diana.

Cassandra shook her head. "I eat meat, though," she admitted.

"Yeah," said Diana.

Cassandra thought for a while. "I wear leather, too, I'm afraid."

"Yeah," said Diana. "How depressing. So do I."

Cassandra thought some more. "I only buy cosmetics from The Body Shop," she said. "You know. No experiments on animals."

"That's good," said Diana, nodding. "Me, too." She looked at Cassandra and said, "I think people should take action, when they believe in something."

"I think so, too."

Diana glanced toward the door. "Well, I'd better go. Thanks again," she said, turning away.

"You're welcome."

Diana hesitated, then faced her again. "You and my dad," she said.

Cassandra's heartbeat became faster, lighter. She lifted her chin slightly, and straightened her shoulders.

"What—uh—," said Diana, flushing. She stopped and lifted her hands in a gesture of helplessness. "My mom's getting married."

"I know."

"Do you think Dad will go to the wedding?"

"Do you want him to go?"

"I just want—I wish it were possible for everybody to be friends."

Cassandra nodded. "That would be good, wouldn't it," she said gently.

Chapter Eleven

"**J**esus Christ." There was more weariness than anger in his voice this time.

"I just want to talk to you," Steven said quickly. "That's all."

"Yeah, but I don't want to talk to you. What are you, asshole, some kind of moron? Don't you understand English, or what?"

"It's not so much to ask, is it?"

"It's a helluva lot to ask, you creep. I never want to lay eyes on you again."

"Look," Steven pleaded. "Just once. Just for ten minutes. Maybe only five. Let me say my piece, and give you this—this package I've got for you, and then I'll never bother you again. I promise."

Bobby didn't hang up. Finally, "Shit," he said.

"Okay?"

"Damn you."

"Okay?"

"You'll have to come to where I'll be."

Steven rested his forehead against the wall and closed his eyes. His relief was so great he thought he might weep. "Anywhere," he said. "I'll go anywhere."

Chapter Twelve

Warren got home from work at the usual time on Friday but he didn't go to work on the siding, he changed his clothes and then he just sat in a chair in the living room for two solid hours and worried, and fretted, and agonized. By the time he heard Wanda coming up the steps he was damn near frantic. He knew it would probably be a good idea to pour her a ginger ale and let her sit down first, but he just couldn't wait.

He rushed to the door. "Wanda," he said, blurting it out, "I saw you today."

"Oh?" she said, putting down her purse on the little table in the hall.

"Yeah," said Warren miserably. "I saw you with Bobby."

He didn't know what would happen now. He was relieved to have it out in the open, but he was terrified, too.

"At the coffee shop, you mean?" said Wanda, taking off her high-heeled shoes one at a time, putting them side by side in the hall closet.

"Yeah," said Warren, who ached all over.

"Well why didn't you say something? Why didn't you sit down with us?"

He'd gone in there with Norman, from work, and Norman had spotted them right away. "Don't look now," he'd said out of the side of his mouth to Warren, "but there's your lady all cozy with her ex." And it had cut Warren to the quick to hear this, and then to see it.

"Oh Wanda," he cried, "don't lie to me; you're seeing him, aren't you—you're seeing Bobby."

There was such astonishment on Wanda's face that he knew instantly how wrong he'd been. And first he felt relief, a torrential amount of relief, and then he felt so stupid he could have died from it.

And of course Wanda got mad. She put her hands on her hips and glared up at him. "You are such a jerk, Warren Kettleman. I don't know how I ever let myself get mixed up with such a total jerk." She stomped off down the hall, her bare feet banging on the hardwood floor.

He sat down in the living room again, and waited. Patiently, for once.

And finally she emerged from the bedroom, wearing a red dress with her hair all soft and curly, looking like some kind of a flower. This was a big relief to Warren. It meant they were still going out for dinner.

He wished he hadn't said anything to her. But he knew that if he hadn't, it would have eaten away at him.

"You look real good," he said, in apology, and took hold of her hands. He'd planned to kiss her, but she turned her head away.

"Come on," she said. "I'm hungry." She swished past him and out the door and he followed, locking the door after him, hurrying to catch up with her.

When they were in the van, driving, Wanda said, "It's your sister you ought to be keeping an eye on." She gave her hair a shake. "Not me."

Warren damn near drove off the road.

"I don't know anything," Wanda said quickly. "Not for sure."

Warren was shaking his head disbelievingly.

"But I heard he went out to her place the other day."

"He wouldn't," Warren protested. "He wouldn't get mixed up with Annabelle. She's a married woman, for Pete's sake."

"Oh don't be stupid, Warren. He doesn't care if she's married or not." She looked out the side window. "Bobby'll do whatever he wants."

"Yeah, but Annabelle…"

He felt Wanda's gaze on his cheek, and felt himself flushing.

Chapter Thirteen

Late Saturday morning Annabelle went to the Super-Valu store for groceries, and she saw Bobby in the lineup next to hers.

She ignored him. But her body didn't. She felt fluid, as though she'd been turned into a mountain stream, clear and savory. As she moved groceries from her basket onto the countertop she knew that this was how dancers moved their arms, leading with the elbows and the wrists, making intricate, alluring patterns in the air.

He hadn't seen her yet.

When he did see her he was reaching to put a can of soup on the counter and because he was looking at Annabelle he missed, and the soup fell and hit his foot. He leapt backward and exclaimed in pain, and Annabelle laughed.

They went out of the store and into the parking lot together, she trundling her shopping cart in front of her, he carrying a paper bag of groceries he said were for a camping trip.

"This is my truck," she said when they reached it, and turned to face him. The sun was very bright. She started lifting bags out of the shopping cart. Bobby put a hand on her arm.

"Wait," he said. "I'll do it."

She looked at his hand, very brown against her bare arm. Her whole body was extremely warm, because it was, again, such a hot day. Where his hand rested, her skin was at first cool, then even warmer than the rest of her. He was wearing denim cut-offs and a dark blue tank top.

"Okay," she said. She stepped back, easing her arm out from under the touch of his hand, and gestured at the shopping cart. "Go ahead," she said.

When he'd loaded her bags into the back of the truck she said, "Well, thank you," but he stood between her and the driver's door.

"How about a coffee, Annabelle?"

She shaded her eyes with her hand, looking up at him.

"Christ, Annabelle," he said after a minute. "We're old friends, remember?" He leaned close to her. "I thought you might write to me," he said sadly. "But you never did."

"Oh don't you give me any of that tripe, Bobby Ransome," said Annabelle. "You were a married man. At least at first. Old friend or no old friend, I don't correspond with other people's husbands."

"So how about it?" said Bobby, leaning against the back of the truck. "A coffee at Earl's can't do you any harm."

Annabelle sighed, and frowned. "Oh, well," she said. "All right."

From a table next to the window Diana watched them enter the café, and she gave Annabelle a tentative smile when their eyes met. Then she turned to Alberg. "Your garden's wilting, you know."

"What garden?" said Alberg, studying the menu. "I don't have a garden."

"You've got rosebushes in your backyard," said Diana, fanning herself with her hand, "and hydrangeas in your front yard. They're all wilting. Because you haven't been watering them."

"You don't water things around here, Diana," he explained patiently. "This isn't Calgary. Nature takes care of itself out here. The rain will come, and then things will stop wilting."

"I've been here for weeks now and it hasn't rained. There isn't a cloud in the sky. Face it, Pop; it isn't going to rain."

Earl, the Chinese proprietor, came over to take their order. When he'd left, Diana said, "I've got something bothering me, Pop."

Alberg looked at her hopefully. He always welcomed an opportunity to provide his daughters with sage advice. "What is it?"

"There's a place near the highway that's got animals," she said, leaning closer to Alberg, keeping her voice down. "Mr. Moran sent me out there to write a story about it."

"Uh-huh," said Alberg, noncommittal.

"It's supposed to be a tourist attraction, I guess. Or at least that's what Mr. Moran thought. But it's an awful place, Pop."

"Uh-huh," said Alberg again. He felt trouble looming.

"Just awful. The animals are in these little cages." Diana shrugged. "I don't know what I expected. There's this game farm near Edmonton; maybe that's what I expected. Big fields for them to run in. I don't know."

When Diana was a child, she had often brought home stray dogs and cats. Her mother, exasperated but tolerant, had always allowed her to feed them until their owners could be located. But Maura had brought this practice to a halt the day Diana appeared with a black Afghan, female, whose owner banged on the Albergs' door only minutes later complaining loudly of theft.

"I mean it's ridiculous," Diana went on. "Squirrels. Raccoons. Foxes. You can't call that a zoo. He should let them all go, that's what he should do. It's really very upsetting, Pop." She sat back and took a sip from a tall glass of diet ginger ale.

Alberg wanted to be sympathetic and useful. But he was worried about the time; he was supposed to pick up Cassandra at one o'clock, and it was already past noon.

He wondered if Diana knew about the missing skunks.

Diana leaned closer again. "You paid for me to go to school. So you ought to know that I actually learned a few things there."

"Good," said Alberg warily.

"A couple of times something happened to make me see the world differently. Do you know what I mean?"

He nodded.

"Once was in a third-year philosophy course. Ethics."

She was looking at him intently, so he nodded again.

"We had a unit about animal rights."

Alberg sighed, without having meant to. He looked longingly out the window.

"Oh Pop just listen, will you?"

"I'm listening," Alberg protested.

"And keep your damn mind open."

"My damn mind is always open."

She threw him such a filthy look that he flinched.

"Ajar, then," he said, and although she didn't smile, he thought she softened. "Go on, honey. Please."

"The prof asked us to make lists," said Diana. "First we made a list of the things that animals can do better than us. Then we made another list, of the things we can do better than animals."

Alberg looked around for Earl, but Earl was busy at the cash register.

"And once we'd done that," said Diana, "and they were up on the board where we could all see them, we started talking about what things were more important. You know, thinking, for instance, as opposed to running fast."

Diana had hair like Cassandra's, Alberg realized. It got all frizzy in this heat. Diana's hair was very long, and she was wearing it in some kind of knot that was pinned on top of her head, but bits of it were coming loose and curling around her face in little spirals. Like Alberg, she didn't tan; but unlike

Alberg, who burned easily, Diana's skin when touched by the sun glowed like the skin of a peach.

"Are you listening?" she demanded.

"Yes, of course I'm listening."

"And up until then I'd always just assumed that it was better to be able to think, and create things, and have a sense of right and wrong, and a complicated memory—" She looked around the café, as if seeking explanations there. "I'd just *assumed* that those things were the most important things, and therefore humans were more important than animals. I just *assumed* it, Pop. Without even thinking about it."

Alberg, who had heard this stuff before, was nevertheless respectful. He enjoyed Diana's passions, and was proud of her because she was stern and uncompromising. He also found her slightly intimidating. He was glad she was his daughter, and young. He was sure he would have sometimes quailed before Diana, if she'd been his contemporary.

"Here," said Earl, setting down a hamburger platter for Alberg, and a shrimp salad for Diana. "Enjoy."

"We're so arrogant, Pop," said Diana when he'd left. "You know?"

Alberg nodded dutifully. He wondered if it would be okay to start eating.

"And right then a whole bunch of things looked entirely different to me," said Diana. "It was like I was considering—the world, and life—from an entirely new point of reference."

What would his life be like right now, Alberg asked himself, if both his daughters had come to Sechelt for the whole summer, as they had originally intended? Maybe they would have been too much for him, both of them together.

"I figure that's why people go to school, really," said Diana, as Alberg picked up his fork and speared a French fry. "That's the bottom line of it. To see things differently, and then to think about life differently. Act differently, too."

Alberg nodded again, munching, feeling slightly stupefied.

Diana studied him for a moment. "Pop," she said.

"Yes?" said Alberg. He took another surreptitious glance at his watch.

"Animals have the right not to live in cages."

Alberg thought about this. "If you're speaking philosophically," he said, "I guess I'd have to agree."

"The day is coming," said Diana, looking into her shrimp salad, "when I'm going to have to become a vegetarian."

Alberg wondered if Hetty Willis was a vegetarian. He picked up his hamburger.

"I've been doing some research," said Diana.

"Oh yeah?" said Alberg politely. He took a bite.

"I'm going to try to get that place closed down, Pop," said his daughter, looking across the café at Annabelle Ferguson.

Alberg stared at her. He felt a fierce pride, which astonished him. And even as he registered this fact: "Shit," he said, with a sinking heart.

Bobby had offered her lunch, but Annabelle declined. She was bored and impatient all of a sudden, and wanted to get home before the milk she'd bought with her groceries turned sour in the heat. She looked fretfully around the café listening with one ear to Bobby talking about his stepdad's heart attack. She crossed her legs, bare beneath her blue-and-white sundress, tapped her sandaled foot in the air, uncrossed her legs, crossed them again. She nodded, and sipped coffee, and nodded some more. She watched lunch orders being delivered to the surrounding tables. She heard very little of what Bobby was saying. Why on earth had she agreed to come here? She felt odd. Awkward and resentful. She wanted to be in her garden.

"Excuse me," she said finally. "I have to go now." She stood up.

He stood, also, and left money on the table.

Annabelle walked toward the door. He was right behind her. When they reached the door he placed his left hand flat against the small of her back. Annabelle shivered.

Out on the street, half a block away from the café, he put his hands on her shoulders and turned her around so that he could look into her face. She looked back at him, at his green eyes. I wonder if anybody I know is seeing this, thought Annabelle, but she didn't try to move away from him, and her pulse felt like the thrumming of a bird's wings.

"I'll walk you back to your truck," he said, and she nodded. Halfway there he said, "My mom'll be at the hospital. Do you want to come to the house for a minute?" His voice sounded perfectly normal. Annabelle nodded again. He took her by the elbow and led her around a corner, up a hill, and through a gate.

They went into a small house with a sun porch. Inside there was a little hall, a stairway on the left, a living room on the right, and at the end of the hall Annabelle could see part of a kitchen. It was cool and quiet. There were venetian blinds in the living room and they were mostly closed, letting in little slivers of sunlight. Annabelle stood in the hallway looking at the floor, which was made of wood, probably oak.

"Annabelle," said Bobby, and she looked up.

His brown legs had a fuzz of hair upon them. He wore sneakers but no socks. She looked at the muscles in his calves, and thighs.

He put his grocery bag on the hall table.

Annabelle looked down again. She let the strap of her handbag fall from her shoulder. She leaned over to put it on the floor. It was going to be all dusty, when she picked it up again.

She felt him moving toward her. He took her chin in his hand and tipped it up. She saw that he was looking at her mouth. He reached out to kiss her, and Annabelle opened her mouth to him. They kissed each other for a long time, and then he took her upstairs.

The mole was still there, next to his left hipbone, and once more his body was long and strong against hers, and her hands and her mouth remembered him well.

Chapter Fourteen

That morning Warren got the eight-thirty ferry from Langdale. He spent the thirty-five-minute trip on the deck, which turned out to be the only half hour in a month that he'd felt cool.

He watched a tug chugging along, pulling a log boom; he'd considered that line of work himself, once. Might have done it, too, if it hadn't been for Wanda, who hadn't liked the idea of his being away from home that much.

There were a lot of things that Warren knew how to do. It was a good feeling, knowing you could earn your living in more ways than just one. It gave you security. He'd learned this from his first employer, Bobby Ransome's dad, a busy, jolly person who'd had all kinds of irons in the fire.

A couple of kids were fooling around by the railing, brothers, Warren figured, about eight and ten years old. Warren was just about to warn them about falling overboard when their parents came up and did it for him. Then the father tried to get the kids to go with them to the cafeteria for a cold drink, but there was no way those kids wanted to go inside. So their folks sat on one of the benches on deck and watched the boys run up and down.

Warren soon saw Horseshoe Bay in the distance, and he returned to the van.

By noon Warren had done his Vancouver errands and was waiting for a table in the White Spot at Twelfth and Cambie. He had a burger, fries, and a chocolate milk shake and used the washroom, then climbed back in the van and headed east on Twelfth, which eventually led him onto the freeway. Half an hour later he turned off at the Fort Langley exit and made his way toward his parents' house.

They'd moved to the Valley ten years ago, to a house on two acres. Warren had always thought it was far too much property for them. But his folks—especially his mom—liked to garden. There were great huge pieces of lawn, and a whole bunch of rhododendrons, but there was also a place his mom called her cutting garden, where she planted flowers to bring inside. And there was a vegetable patch, too. Also raspberries, gooseberries, strawberries and rhubarb. Warren didn't have the faintest idea what happened to all this produce.

Warren was glad of his folks. It was one thing he had over Bobby Ransome, he thought. Bobby's real dad was dead, now. And he'd died in a peculiar way, too.

Warren turned off the country road onto a driveway bordered by ornamental plum trees that were covered in pink blossoms every spring. Now their leaves were a rich shade of maroon.

It had happened more than ten years ago, just before Bobby got arrested. Mr. Ransome was looking for bottles and beer cans by the side of the road and up came this big buck. It charged, and Mr. Ransome got gored and trampled to death. Apparently it was mating season.

Warren pulled into the parking area near the front door and tooted his horn. His mother came out onto the porch and shaded her eyes with one hand, waving at him with the other. She was kind of dumpy, his mom was, but she had a sweet face and her gray hair was thick and curly.

The worst part of it all, to Warren's mind, was the fact that the damn deer was still standing over Mr. Ransome's body hours later, when a cop car stopped to see what was going on.

The unnaturalness of it is what had troubled everybody. Deer didn't go around killing people, for Pete's sake. And if once in a blue moon something weird happened and they did, why they sure as hell wouldn't stand around and gloat over it. You wouldn't think.

Warren's dad appeared from around the house. He was wearing a pair of old jeans and an undershirt with no sleeves. He said it was the thing he enjoyed most about being retired; he didn't have to get dressed up every day. But Warren thought there was a big difference between not getting dressed up and going around looking disreputable.

He got out of the van and went up to his mom and gave her a big hug and a kiss on the cheek.

"Wanda's not with you?" she said, peering back at the van, shading her eyes again.

She knew Wanda wasn't with him. When Warren was being brutally honest about his life he admitted to himself that his mother wasn't all that fond of Wanda. And so she tended to forget important details like the fact that Wanda had a job.

"No, she's not with me, Mom," he said.

"Come on around back," said his dad, putting his arm around Warren's shoulders. "I'll take a break. We'll have a beer."

"Maybe you want to go in the pool, Warren," said his mom. "I'm sure I can find you a suit."

"No thanks, Mom," said Warren. "Not today."

He followed his dad around the house and they sat at a patio table in the shade of a big yellow umbrella. After a while his dad remembered the beer, and got up to get it. Warren noticed the big lawn mower parked under a tree beyond the pool. He frowned.

"You're not mowing the lawn, are you? In the middle of the day? In this heat?" It was even hotter out here in the Fraser Valley than it was in town.

"Nah," said his dad. "Just checking the carburetor."

Warren looked at him fondly. His dad had made his money selling real estate, but he was every bit as good with machinery as Warren was.

His dad, knowing what Warren was thinking, winked at Warren and said, "It's in the genes, boy."

After a while his mother came out with a plate of sandwiches. Warren gazed at them hungrily. "Why'd I have that burger?" he said, and reached for a sandwich anyway.

They ate the sandwiches, and Warren and his dad had another beer, and then his dad got up and wandered back to the lawn mower. His mother watched him until he was far enough away to be out of earshot.

"So how is she?" she said quietly.

Warren shook his head. "This is downright ridiculous," he said. Then he sighed. "She's okay."

"How are the kids?"

"They're okay, too." He pulled his wallet from his back pocket, opened it, took out a photograph. "Here. This is for you." His mother looked at it like it might bite her. He poked it at her, impatiently. "Here. Take it."

Slowly his mom reached for the photograph, turned it right side up, and looked at it. She looked at it very hard, so hard that her shoulders hunched over and her forehead creased. Then she put it down on the table and fumbled in the pocket of her slacks for a Kleenex. She dabbed at her eyes, blinked at Warren, and pushed the photograph at him.

"Really, Mom. This is so stupid."

"It isn't my doing. Not anymore."

When Annabelle was fifteen she'd gotten pregnant. Warren did not like to think about this because it was Bobby Ransome that did it. (What the hell *was* it about Bobby Ransome, anyway?)

"Talk to her again," he said to his mom. "I wish you would."

His mom had made Annabelle get an abortion. Which seemed like the best thing at the time. But it ended up being a very bad thing. It ended up being something Annabelle never got over.

"She won't listen to me. She'd hang up on me, if I tried."

And then later, Annabelle got married. And then she got divorced. Warren and Annabelle's folks did not approve of people getting divorced.

"When was the last time you tried?" he said to his mom. "Huh? When did you call her up last? Or write her a letter, to that post office box she's got?"

And then she got married again. To Herman. Which turned out to be the last straw for the folks, because they thought Herman was definitely not right for Annabelle. So they refused to speak to her anymore. They said they were disowning her.

(Warren remembered telling Annabelle this. All she said was, "As if they'd ever owned me in the first place.")

His mom stood and picked up the sandwich plate. "I send her a card every Christmas."

And then, later, when they changed their minds, why it was too late, for Annabelle had turned against them.

"When did you phone her last? Talk to her? Tell her you love her?"

His mom gave him a look that made him hurt down to the bottoms of his feet. "What good would that do?" she said bitterly. "Annabelle doesn't care if we love her or not." She went into the house.

Warren put the photograph back in his wallet.

He leaned forward, his elbows on his knees, and stared at the pool. It was funny how the water was really colorless; it was the pool that was bright blue, not the water at all.

Everybody figures that family problems get themselves sorted out, after a while, thought Warren. Everybody always thinks, this'll pass, this'll mend itself. But sometimes, Warren knew, things didn't pass, they didn't get mended. Sometimes they just got worse and worse, without anybody meaning for that to happen.

His father returned to the table and sat down. He pulled out his handkerchief and mopped his face. "Where's Mother?"

"Gone inside," said Warren.

His dad glanced through the open patio doors into the empty family room. "So," he said quietly to Warren. "How's Annabelle?"

Warren felt very weary. He took out the photograph. "Here," he said, handing it to his dad. "See for yourself."

Chapter Fifteen

Steven felt the late-afternoon sun on his back as a series of hot breaths, as though it were a large animal following him, silently following him up the steep incline. It burned into his back, and then he passed among trees through shade and coolness, and emerged once more into sun, felt it sear his skin through the thin white T-shirt.

There was a path, of sorts, that led steeply upward, curving around the carcasses of fallen trees, brushing against banks of ferns, steering him through a tunnel of greenery that smelled rank and moist despite the heat. He climbed confidently, though he'd never been here before, never been on this side of the cliff before. It was like being backstage in a theater. So this is what holds it up, he thought, as he climbed, his camera hanging around his neck.

He was sweating in the heat but he didn't mind; he could feel the wetness gathering in the middle of his back and under his arms, soaking his T-shirt, and he didn't mind; he liked the feeling that he was working hard, it reflected his hope that perhaps, finally, he could be once more deserving of reward.

On either side of the path grew brush and ferns and tree trunks and stinging nettles. Steven heard nothing, as he climbed, except his own labored breathing, and the scuffling of his sneakers on the hard-packed trail. He climbed on, aware of the money belt hugging his waist, aware of the muscles in his thighs and calves, aware of his sweat.

He had to stay calm, he told himself, and speak reasonably, and if he did that, everything was going to be okay. Staying calm and speaking reasonably, that was the important thing. He would make his declaration, and present his offering, and he would be respectful and repentant.

He'd gone over and over it in his mind, while lying in bed staring at the ceiling; while walking the streets of Sechelt; while mowing his mother's lawn. He'd been going over it for days, and finally he was calm, finally he was ready.

Suddenly he stumbled, and threw out a hand to break his fall, but his feet went out from under him and he had to scuffle on his hands and knees to keep from tumbling down the path. "Shit," he muttered, breathless, his camera swinging wildly from its leather strap, striking him on the chin. He edged cautiously off the path and clung for a while to the slim trunk of a young fir tree. Then he checked his camera, brushed dirt from his legs and hands and started upward again, moving more slowly, taking more care.

The sun watched and waited and from between the trees pitched shafts of fire at his back; they struck at the nape of his neck and started a headache there. He could see it in his mind—a flame of an ache created by the sun striking against the bones of his neck.

The sweat was dripping from his forehead and when it got into his eyes it stung.

He hoped he would arrive first. He was feeling shaken and uncertain, now; rattled by almost falling, and by the heat-ache in his neck. The words he'd had ready had fled. He knew he could get them back again but he needed a little bit of time.

He wiped sweat from his face and floundered upward, assailed by the sun. His mouth was dry and his heart was pounding and his head hurt. This was not an easy climb at all, he thought, and tried not to feel angry about that.

Then the path turned, abruptly, and he was on even ground, standing alone in a clearing. Tall grass, sun-dappled, grew beneath the trees. It was very quiet. His breathing sounded loud in the stillness, and his heart was making a lot of noise, too.

But he would soon be composed again. Then he would repossess his arguments and when it was time he would present them, he would be prodigiously convincing, and all would be well, he would be free, and his life would stretch before him unblemished and beckoning.

He looked around with satisfaction at the level, grassy place. He stood in shade and saw sun-shafts piercing the dry grass, and saw the brush that concealed the cliff edge, and saw the trees soaring skyward.

And saw a figure emerge from the forest.

"Hello, Bobby," said Steven, turning to face him.

Chapter Sixteen

"We're only going out for a couple of hours, right?" said Cassandra. She was staring up at the mast of Alberg's rented sailboat. It seemed disproportionately high; she thought it likely that an error had been made, and that as soon as they tried to hoist the sail the mast would crack and, with a bleating sound, break in two.

Alberg was getting red in the face, hauling sailbags up from below and squinting at whatever was stored within.

"You should be wearing sunblock," said Cassandra. "Maybe they've got some at that place that says 'Groceries.' I'll go see, shall I?"

He fumbled in his shirt pocket and held up a container of lotion.

"Oh," said Cassandra. "Good." She glanced around the boat and rubbed her hands. "What can I do?" she said brightly.

Alberg got up and went over to her, took her by the shoulders and planted a kiss firmly on her mouth. "Sit down and shut up," he said.

They motored out of Secret Cove, past Turnagain Island and into Malaspina Strait, and then Alberg raised the mainsail.

"I hate it," said Cassandra a few minutes later, "when it tilts itself over like that." Her voice sounded thin, and higher than usual.

"You don't say 'tilted,'" said Alberg. "You say 'heeled.' I thought you told me once that you knew how to sail?"

Cassandra hesitated. "I exaggerated."

Alberg, one hand on the tiller, hugged her with the other and laughed. "Look around you," he said. "Go on." He gave her shoulders another squeeze. "Look."

And Cassandra looked.

It was a dazzling day; a perfect day. It would not be possible, she thought, as the twenty-seven-foot sailboat slid through the water, to make it more perfect. They were sailing through a world painted in multiple shades of blue. The sky was pale blue, and glowing. The sea was dark like ink, or grape juice, and the sun shot sparks from it. The sea sometimes rippled, and then small flecks of white appeared upon its blue-black surface. Cassandra felt the deep heat of the sun, yet the surface of her skin was cooled by the sea breeze.

There was land to every side of them, falling back from them in layers. The nearest islands were so close Cassandra could see the dried grass on the hillsides, and almost smell its hot, hay-like fragrance. Then there were more islands, farther away, and she could still see details of their geography but it was less defined; these islands were tinted blue, as though blue forests blanketed them. Still farther away, the land was bold blue shapes, smooth and featureless, like dark glass. The most distant island of all, Vancouver Island, was pale blue and fuzzy, looking like a mirage.

Alberg said, "I'm going to tack now." He pushed the tiller toward her. "Change places with me."

She scrambled in front of him, while the boom and sail swung flapping to the other side; then the sail filled again with wind. The sail was so enormous that the thought of having to manipulate it, assisted only by the capricious wind, caused Cassandra's heart to stutter.

Soon Alberg poked her and said encouragingly, "Go on out to the pointy part."

Cassandra felt herself challenged. And besides, she wanted to feel alone; she wanted to get a sense of being all by herself on the big ocean in only a sailboat.

She made her way forward, clutching at the lifelines and the shrouds, and sat down with her back against the mast.

It was very quiet out on the water. But it was a quietness full of exuberance and motion; it was a quietness made conspicuous by what could be heard: the rippling of the water as the sailboat sliced through it, the motors of far-off powerboats, the lazy shrieks of seagulls.

Suddenly a flock of small birds appeared, swooping and swirling in perfect unison, as though they comprised a single being; their concentration absolute, their wings creating a soft, fervent whir.

Twice a seal popped a gray-brown head above water and watched with large calm eyes as the boat swept by.

Cassandra marveled at herself. Here she sat, right up in the front of the damn boat, hardly nervous at all, exhilarated by the blueness of the ocean and the panorama of sea, sky and islands that stretched before her.

"Hey!" called Alberg, and she turned to see him grinning at her from the cockpit. He gestured, vigorously, and she made her way cautiously back to the stern. "Gotta lower the sail," he said, starting the motor. "See there?" He pointed. "We're going in there."

"What is it?" said Cassandra.

"North and South Thormanby Islands," said Alberg. "Here. Take hold of the tiller."

"Oh God," said Cassandra. "I can't steer this thing."

"You don't have to steer. Just keep it going into the wind."

"What do you mean, 'into the wind'? What's 'into the wind'?"

Alberg changed course slightly and the sail emptied and began to flap.

"Oh God," said Cassandra.

"Find yourself something on land to aim at and just keep it there, right where it is," said Alberg, and he climbed up onto the cabin top to haul down the sail.

"Oh God," said Cassandra, gazing blindly, fixedly shoreward.

"It's hard to believe you've never been here before," said Alberg a few minutes later. They were passing a group of small islands on their left.

"I haven't been here," said Cassandra, "because it isn't a place you get to in a car."

"Anybody who decides to live in this part of the world ought to have a boat," said Alberg.

As they proceeded into the bay, drawing closer to land, Cassandra saw that the gap between North and South Thormanby Islands was spanned by a long, wide isthmus of sand. Several sailboats and powerboats were anchored offshore, and there were people sunbathing on the beach. Beyond the sandy isthmus Cassandra saw the broad, deep waters of the Gulf of Georgia winking in the sun.

Cassandra took the tiller again while Alberg went forward to drop the anchor. When he cut the motor she could hear children laughing on the beach. They had anchored next to a green sailboat; Cassandra saw swimming clothes and towels hung over the lifelines to dry, and she realized again how hot it was.

Children were splashing in tidal pools on the isthmus, and adults were swimming in the bay. South Thormanby, to the left, was much the bigger of the two islands, with rolling, rocky hills; North Thormanby presented to the sandy isthmus, and the children playing there, a steep cliff face with a thick forest crowding the top. The cliff was pale, like the sandy beach at its foot.

Alberg beamed fondly upon the landscape, as if he had created it. "Buccaneer Bay," he said. "Didn't I tell you? Is this the most beautiful beach in the world, or what?"

Cassandra, smiling, gazed at the children playing in the sand, and raised her hand to shield her eyes from the sun's glare—and something caught her eye. She looked quickly to the right; her eye had captured a memory; a sharp streak of movement. "Karl," she said.

He turned quickly, hearing something in her voice.

"The cliff," she said.

And they both watched, and saw sunbathers sit up, uncertain, and somebody wearing brightly patterned shorts clambered to his feet and began to walk, tentatively, toward the base of the cliff. Halfway there he beckoned urgently; something in his hand flashed in the sun; Cassandra thought it was maybe a can of beer. Two more men got up from the sand and started toward him.

Alberg hauled the dinghy up from below and inflated it. He tied it to the stern pulpit and dropped it overboard. They climbed down the ladder into the dinghy, first Alberg, then Cassandra.

It was strange to be suddenly so much closer to the water, thought Cassandra.

It was very hot. She felt trickles of sweat on her temples, and there were beads of it on her forehead, and the small of her back was damp.

She looked apprehensively toward the land, where everyone, it seemed, was being drawn slowly but inexorably to the cliff.

They beached the dinghy and splashed up onto the sand. Alberg strode off toward the small crowd, and Cassandra followed.

When they got there, Cassandra saw a shape covered by an orange tarpaulin. All she could see was the shape's left arm; it was smooth and brown, obviously male, obviously young.

People stood around quietly, some holding children by the shoulders, pressing the children's faces to their thighs. The place was a jumble of bare limbs, brown or reddened or freckled.

Cassandra felt the oiliness of sunscreen and smelled the sweet innocent smell of summer sweat, and she knew that the children huddled against their parents would never forget this sight, and that neither would she.

Alberg identified himself to the crowd and shouldered his way gently through it. He hunkered down next to the body. He lifted the tarp, and felt in vain for a pulse.

"What happened?" said Alberg, studying the body closely. There was a wide, thick, zippered, belt-like thing around the waist of the dead man.

"Nothing. I mean, I don't know. I heard this great jeezly thunk and there he was. He fell, I guess. He must've fallen. Jesus, man—"

"Take it easy," said Alberg. He pulled the zipper. The belt was stuffed with money. Alberg looked quickly around him; nobody but the kid wearing the bright flowered shorts was close enough to see, and he was looking resolutely away. Alberg pulled the zipper closed and replaced the tarp.

"I covered him up as quick as I could," said the young man. "I didn't want anybody else seeing it. Kids. Jesus."

Alberg beckoned to Cassandra. People looked at her curiously as she made her way through them to get to him.

"Go back to the boat," he said. "Get on the radio to the detachment, tell them we need the police boat with a full crew, and the doctor, right away. I've got to stay here. Okay?"

Cassandra couldn't speak. She couldn't remember how to operate the radio. She nodded, feeling sick and helpless.

"You got a dinghy?" said the young man, looking at her.

"Yes," said Cassandra, and cleared her throat.

"I'll row you over." He turned to Alberg. "Okay?"

"Okay," said Alberg. "Thanks." He watched them traipse across the sand together, Cassandra and the young man wearing the flower-patterned shorts.

He turned to the small, shaken crowd. "Better get back to your boats, folks. But don't go anywhere. We'll need to get statements from you."

They drifted off to pick up blankets and picnic baskets, herding their children toward the dinghies scattered along the water's edge.

Alberg sat down on the sand next to the body.

He thought it a very strange thing, this accident. The kid was carrying at least ten or fifteen thousand dollars. Who the hell came to Buccaneer Bay wearing ten or fifteen thousand dollars?

Beneath the orange tarpaulin the young man's blood trickled into the sand.

Alberg listened to the soft lap of the sea, and felt the heat of the summer sun.

It was a dazzling day.

Chapter Seventeen

Fifteen minutes later Alberg was still sitting by the body, waiting for reinforcements.

"The tide's gonna come in, you know," said the young man in the bright shorts, who had hair the color of straw.

"I know."

"How long will it take your guys to get here? Should we move him?"

"They'll be here soon. It'll be okay." He looked at the young man, sizing him up. "What do you do, kid?"

"I'm a student."

"What kind of student?"

"U.B.C. Economics."

They were sitting side by side on the sand. Alberg's sunblock had long since worn off and he was red wherever his skin was exposed—legs, arms, face, neck. He was wearing deck shoes and socks, and brown shorts, and a yellow T-shirt. He sat there in the sand next to the tanned student from the University of British Columbia and felt himself burning, and tried to ignore it. He picked up a handful of sand and let it trickle through his fingers. "What's your name?"

"Joseph Dunn. Joe."

Alberg studied Joseph Dunn. He was a big, sturdy kid. He didn't look like he ought to be so pale and nervous. By now he should be recovering; getting his confidence back.

As casually as possible, Alberg asked, "Was he still alive when you got to him, Joe?"

The young man gave him a swift look. "Yeah."

"How come you didn't mention that?"

Joe held up a hand. He was sitting with his legs crossed. He looked down at the sand and took a deep, ragged breath. "I can't believe what I'm seeing, right? All of a sudden there's this thump, and out of nowhere a guy's lying on the sand—he's bounced down those rocks, he's all battered and bleeding. So I figured—he's gotta be dead. And all I can think of—I want to make sure nobody else has to look at this, the place is crawling with kids." He shuddered, and hunched his shoulders. "So I turn around and wave the other guys back. So they stay back, and they keep other people back, too, and I go over to the guy…"

Alberg said, "Go on."

Joe clasped his hands, which were broad and strong and brown, with big knuckles. "So I'm leaning over him, he's lying sort of on his side and…shit." He shuddered again. "And then, I see his eyes open. And I see he's still breathing. So I get down on my hands and knees next to him." He looked at Alberg again, horrified. "I'm thinking, like—what the hell do I do? I start hollering for first-aid stuff, does anybody on the beach have a first-aid kit, but he reaches out to me and he's trying to say something to me, see?"

"Take it easy," said Alberg.

"So I get down there right next to him," said Joe. "'It's okay,' I tell him. Okay, shit, the guy's dying, I know it, he's a totally broken person. But I tell him it's okay. 'You're gonna be okay,' I say. He doesn't move anymore. But he says, 'Help me.' Oh Jesus."

Alberg reached over and gripped his shoulder.

"'Sure I'll help you,'" said Joe, rushing it now. "And then he says, 'Hold my head. Help me.' And I know what he means, see? That's the thing. He doesn't mean, 'Help me,' he means, 'Help me die.'" Joe swiped at his face, at the tears there. "So I put my hand on the back of his neck and in a minute he was dead."

Alberg gave his shoulder a hard squeeze, and let go. He looked out into the bay, where his rented sloop was anchored, and saw Cassandra leaning on the stern pulpit.

"Is that all he said? Are you sure?" He lifted his hand, and Cassandra waved back.

Joe nodded. "Positive."

There was nobody left on the beach. They were all on their boats, watching Alberg and Joe and the orange tarp. The sun was very hot, and the water had begun to rise.

"You did good," said Alberg to Joe.

Chapter Eighteen

The signs read "warning: Do not climb on these sand banks. The cliffs above are eroding and can fall at any time."

The forest on top leaned over the edge as if to stare down at the body on the sand. North Thormanby Island was swathed in forest, except for this high cliff at its southern end, which bore the striations of sandstone. The beach below it would be swept clean by the tide, made new for morning: no trace of the young man's blood would be found, no trace of his dying would remain there.

Alberg squinted upward, looking for something by which to orient himself. He saw a log he had spotted earlier, a tree trunk bare of branches extending perhaps forty feet straight out from the top of the cliff. He remembered noticing it from the boat. When Cassandra had said, "Karl, the cliff," he had turned and looked at the top of the cliff, and had seen a perfectly horizontal line stretching out into space.

Alberg looked up at the tree trunk, trying to estimate how far it was from the eastern edge of the cliff. Above him a flock of crows was curiously circling, circling.

The sea had reasserted itself between the Thormanby Islands and was slowly, steadily, devouring the beach. Alberg turned and called out to Sid Sokolowski, and the two of them walked eastward, around the corner to Grassy Point. Wild grass grew upon the sand here, among the driftwood, and as the tide encroached upon the island Alberg and Sokolowski found a path that led inland, steeply upward, along the floor of a deep fissure.

Trees had fallen across the path, some completely uprooted, and they had to climb over them, or under them. Alberg's sunburn was throbbing; every tree branch he encountered seemed to scrape against him; the whine of mosquitoes stung his ears; even the whirring of bird wings unsettled him.

"Christ," he said, sweat stinging his face as he vaulted clumsily over a huge, rotting log.

"It'll be easier on the way back," said Sokolowski behind him, panting. The sergeant wore the RCMP summer uniform of navy pants with a yellow stripe down the leg, and a short-sleeved tan shirt.

The greenery was thick on either side of the so-called path, and trees loomed inward from the top of the chasm; Alberg kept expecting one of them to crash down upon them.

Finally the trail leveled out, and its boundaries became less steep, and then very suddenly they were at the top, looking across the gap at South Thormanby Island.

"Christ," said Alberg, grabbing at a tree trunk. "If we'd been doing anything faster than a plod, we'd have gone right over."

Cautiously, he shuffled through the brush. He leaned forward a little, looking through the trees along the edge of the cliff, and spotted the log that extended out over the brink; it was about fifty feet away.

Alberg and the sergeant trudged through the brush, keeping well away from the cliff top, until they reached the log. It was a Douglas fir, at least a hundred feet long and more than six feet in diameter. Two-thirds of it soared out into space; the remainder lay upon the ground, swathed in ferns and climbing plants that Alberg couldn't identify, pressed in upon by the restless, verdant forest.

"No sign of anything on this side," said Sokolowski. "You want to go around? Or over?"

Alberg went to the edge of the woods. The recumbent tree trunk disappeared into greenery so thick that he figured he'd need at least a machete and maybe a bulldozer to find the end of it.

"Over," he said, eyeing the log gloomily. "Hoist me up." Sokolowski leaned against the dead tree and bent to make a stirrup with his hands.

Alberg was propelled firmly upward. He clutched at the decaying bark, got hold of the jagged end of what had once been a branch, and pulled, and found himself spread-eagled on top of the log.

It had lain there for years. The wind had blown at it, and the rain had pelted it, and the wind and the rain hadn't budged it. There wasn't any reason to think that two hundred pounds of Karl Alberg was going to send it flying over the edge—yet he thought it probably would. He pictured it in his head, the damn tree shooting out into the sky with him riding it, riding it, all the way down to the ocean. He wondered how deep the water was out there between the islands; maybe not deep enough, yet, to drown in. And then he saw himself jumping clear of the log in midair. Which would land first, Alberg or the log? He peered down the long, long length of the dead tree and it was like peering down the barrel of a rifle. He was afraid to move. He hung on to the rough dead bark and stared straight ahead of him and saw the tree extending for what seemed miles, and across the sea-flooded gap stretched the shaggy green roof of South Thormanby Island.

"Are you okay, Karl?" said Sokolowski.

Alberg nodded, and coughed. "Yeah. Fine."

Slowly, he relaxed his grip upon the tree. Warily, he wriggled a few feet closer to the root end. Then he pushed himself around and dropped to the ground. He looked down at himself and saw that his thighs and knees were scraped and bleeding.

"See anything?" Sokolowski called out.

"I just got here," Alberg snapped. He looked around and, almost at once, saw where the young man had gone over.

The brush was crushed and broken, here, and a fresh chunk of the cliff top had fallen away. A breeze rippled the gray-gold field of tall grass that lay between the brush at the edge of the cliff and the beginning of the forest. Alberg saw that a pathway had been trampled through the grass. He followed it, creating a parallel trail, and was led to the mouth of a path that went steeply down, probably to the beach on the western side of the island. He made his way slowly back toward the place where the body had fallen, scrutinizing the ground.

"Karl?" said Sokolowski, from the other side of the massive log.

"Yeah," said Alberg. Something glinted in the broken grass. He got down on his knees, thinking that the grass looked like some kind of crop—hay, or wheat, or something. "Just a minute," he said.

Carefully, he separated the dry grass with his hands.

It was a lens cap that lay there, gleaming dully in the sun.

Chapter Nineteen

"**I**t's Velma Grayson's kid," said Gillingham, looking down at the young man lying dead on the sand at his feet. "Jesus, what a shame."

The Thormanby Islands floated, separate, in a placid sea. All that remained of the sandy connector was a small beach at the foot of the cliff, and the tide was still advancing.

"Hurry it up, Alex, will you?" said Alberg.

The flotilla of pleasure boats remained at anchor but it looked as if they'd retreated, because there was so much more water, now, between the boats and the body. Alberg imagined himself back on board his rented boat, where Cassandra continued to wait. He would be standing next to her, looking at what was left of the beach. He saw himself and Gillingham and Sokolowski and Carrington and the body: a lonely huddle of the dead and the dying.

"Hurry up," he said again, more gently.

It was late evening, now, and everything was silver-blue—the sky, the water, the islands that rose from the ocean like a tranquil pod of sleepy whales. Everywhere Alberg looked, the world was serene, slumberous, luxuriating in the comparative coolness of evening. There were no clouds in the sky, only the bright sun low on the horizon, blanching the heat from the sky as it descended; there were no waves in the sea, only small silver ripples created by the incoming tide. Alberg's skin burned but the cooler air of evening eased the pain.

He looked down at the body of what had turned out to be Velma Grayson's son, and at Alex Gillingham kneeling next to it.

"Alex," said Alberg.

Gillingham slowly shook his head. "Yeah, well, he's dead, isn't he," said the doctor heavily.

Alberg told Constable Carrington to row the dinghy out to Alberg's boat and motor back to the marina at Secret Cove, then see that Cassandra got home.

He returned to the mainland on the police boat, with Gillingham and the corpse. Sokolowski remained behind with a corporal to finish taking statements; the boat would return later, to pick them up.

The moon was high in the sky when Alberg left Buccaneer Bay. The water was black and silky, except for a long splash of moonlight. Alberg stood by the rail and watched the sea, and let the wind cool his sunburned skin.

Sechelt didn't have a proper morgue. No discreet window wall separated the dead from the bereaved. It would be a face-to-face confrontation, and Alberg hated those.

Velma Grayson's porch light was on. And she must have been waiting up for her son. The door opened right away, and as she looked up into his face Alberg wished that when he'd gone home to hastily wash and change he'd put on the uniform.

She wasn't expecting anything bad. The sight of Alberg standing on her porch hadn't alerted her, even though she knew perfectly well who he was. Yeah, he wished he'd put on the uniform, for once.

She worked in his bank, as a teller. But he didn't know her well enough to call her Velma.

"Mrs. Grayson," he said. "I'm afraid I have bad news."

They drove to the hospital in silence. Alberg was impressed with her calmness. She had listened to him quietly, asked him to wait, and disappeared into what he took to be her bedroom. She came out wearing fresh lipstick, having combed her hair. She was carrying a handbag. She held it on her lap as they drove.

Alberg parked near the emergency entrance and ushered her into the hospital, through an empty waiting room, down the hall and into an elevator. As the elevator took them into the basement he watched Velma Grayson's face, which remained calm, and hoped Gillingham would know somebody they could call to come and be with her, once she'd seen the body, and begun her grieving. The elevator doors opened and she stepped out into the hall, and waited for Alberg to lead the way.

When they entered the anteroom Gillingham was there, and a ripple of dread disturbed Velma Grayson's composure: Alberg saw it pass across her face, a small gray shudder.

"Velma," said Gillingham. He tried to take her hands, but they were both clasping her purse.

She didn't seem to have any interest in Gillingham. She looked around the room, frowning a little. There was a counter next to the door, and several metal chairs were set against the wall.

"Alex," said Alberg.

Gillingham stared at Velma Grayson with an expression Alberg couldn't decipher.

"Alex," Alberg said more loudly.

Finally Gillingham looked at him, then back at Velma. "You'll have to hold the door open for me," he said to Alberg. "I don't want her going in there." Alberg nodded.

Gillingham went through the door that led to the autopsy room. Alberg held it slightly open, watching Gillingham, and when the doctor approached, wheeling a gurney, Alberg opened the door wide to allow it to pass through. Gillingham deposited the gurney in the middle of the anteroom. He stood back and clasped his hands in front of him and stared at the inert, white-draped form.

Alberg was conscious of the room's thunderous silence. It swept around the three of them and the gurney, filling up every unoccupied crevice, and it was so loud that when Velma Grayson spoke, Alberg almost didn't hear her.

"What happens now?" she said.

"I have to ask you to make a formal identification," said Alberg, moving to the head of the gurney. "I'm sorry, but I'm afraid it's necessary." Gently, he pulled the sheet down. "Is this your son, Mrs. Grayson?"

She moved closer to the gurney. She reached out, as if to touch Steven's face, then drew back. Alberg saw her calmness stiffen, become brittle, and begin to crack. He stepped closer to her and glanced at Gillingham, who was looking, anguished, at the corpse. Then Velma Grayson stood back from the gurney and slowly shook her head. "No," she said firmly. "That is not my son."

Gillingham raised his eyes to her face, then looked quickly back at the body, and again at Velma Grayson. "Velma," he said.

She shook her head again. "I know my son. That's definitely not him. That's definitely not Steven." She glanced at her watch. "Can I go home now?"

Alberg looked at her for a long moment. He put an arm around her shoulders. "Mrs. Grayson. I'm so sorry."

"It's not him."

"It's a terrible, terrible thing." He led her to a chair. "Sit down, Mrs. Grayson." He sat next to her and put his hands over hers; she was still clutching her handbag firmly, as if she was afraid somebody would take it from her.

"It's not him," she said.

"He was a very handsome young man," said Alberg.

"Not him."

"Alex said he was a photographer."

She sat rigid in the chair, her feet together, looking intently at the floor.

"You must have been very proud of him."

She raised her right hand to her mouth, and bit down on the knuckle of the first finger.

"It isn't right, is it, that he should die first," said Alberg quietly.

She sagged. Alberg held her close, rocking her. She let go of her handbag and clung with both hands to the sleeve of his jacket. She was gasping. There were no tears.

Finally, she shivered, and pulled herself upright on the chair. "What happened?" she said to Alberg.

"He fell from the top of the cliff," said Alberg.

Her eyes searched his face. "But what was he doing there?"

"I thought maybe you could tell us that," said Alberg.

She shook her head, still staring at him.

"He had a lot of money with him," said Alberg.

"Karl," said Gillingham. "It's very late."

Tears began spilling from her eyes, down her cheeks.

"Can't this wait?" said Gillingham.

Velma Grayson clutched herself around the waist and began to moan.

"Tomorrow, then," said Alberg. "I'll come to your house tomorrow morning."

Chapter Twenty

Alberg made his way along the corridors and out into the parking lot, relieved to be getting free of the hospital. He had been hospitalized three times in his life and had hated every minute of it. He was determined that when he died, it wasn't going to happen in a hospital.

He got into his car and opened the two front windows and just sat there for a while. There were four other cars in the lot—three that probably belonged to doctors, and a battered Volkswagen Beetle, painted yellow. The VW made him recall the birth of his elder daughter. Against all odds, he had been home when Maura went into labor. They drove to the hospital about midnight, and Janey was born eight hours later, and Alberg was with his wife the whole time. It was, he privately believed, one of the more heroic acts of his life. He'd seen other women in labor, he'd even seen one other woman giving birth, but it wasn't at all the same thing as watching Maura do it.

Eventually, he fired up the Oldsmobile and drove away. He would stop in to see Cassandra for a minute, before going home to Diana.

Such an ordinary-looking guy, he thought. Well-dressed, healthy, young. Apparently happy. Apparently successful. Just an everyday, normal person.

Who climbed to the top of a cliff, carrying a hell of a lot of money, and then fell off, to die on the beach.

Or was pushed off, to die on the beach.

Cassandra lived just up the road from the hospital and there were lights on in her house. When he pulled into her driveway it was after one o'clock in the morning, but she heard his car, and opened the door before he had a chance to knock. She was still wearing her sailing clothes; it had been a long day for Cassandra, too, he thought: she probably hadn't encountered a hell of a lot of dead people in her time.

"You're all burned," she said.

He put a hand to his face, which felt tight and sore. "Yeah."

"Come in and have a drink," said Cassandra.

"Coffee, I think. I've got to drive home." He put his arms around her. At least they were finally going to bed together. Not tonight—but at least there was finally something real between them.

It had started six months ago, when they went to Victoria for the weekend. Alberg hadn't known whether to ask for two rooms or one. He'd felt like an idiot standing at the reservations desk stammering and stuttering. He'd been pretty sure they were going to sleep together, for the first time. It was pretty damn clear, after all, he told himself. But when it came right down to it he found himself unable to assume anything; he didn't want to take anything for granted. She must have been amazed, watching his performance. But she hadn't said anything. Not then, and not since.

He'd gotten two rooms. And he was standing in the middle of his room smoldering, furious with himself, when there was a knock on the door. He opened it and Cassandra came in. Without a word, she reached up and began unbuttoning his shirt. He'd felt immense relief, that was his first reaction.

Now Cassandra moved her hands up and down his back, beneath his jacket, and held him close to her. After a minute she pulled away and studied his face, which was as smooth and enigmatic as always. As soon as they'd realized something was wrong on that beach, Alberg had instantly become a cop: detached, dispassionate, concentrated.

"How about a sandwich?" she said.

"Cassandra, I would love a sandwich."

"Come into the kitchen and talk to me while I make it."

He peeled off his jacket and draped it over the back of the leather sofa, and followed her into the kitchen. "I'm sorry I couldn't go back with you. Did Carrington manage the boat all right?"

"I think so," said Cassandra. "How's the boy's mother?"

Alberg took a drink and shook his head. "Gillingham's taking her to a friend's house for the night."

Cassandra left the sandwich fixings on the counter and went close to him, frowning. She put a finger under his chin and turned his face toward the light. "That's a bad burn." She got a tube of ointment from the bathroom cabinet. "Put this stuff on it," she said, and went back to making his sandwich. "I guess you have to do that a lot, don't you? Give people bad news, I mean."

"Yeah," said Alberg, slathering ointment cautiously on the tenderest parts of his face. "I wish I could spend the night," he said wistfully.

"I do, too." Cassandra slapped a piece of buttered whole-wheat bread on top of ham, cheese, lettuce and plenty of mustard. She sliced the sandwich into halves and put it on a plate. "Here," she said, setting down the plate in front of him.

"Thanks," he said gratefully, and began to eat.

Cassandra poured two mugs of coffee from a pot sitting on a warmer and sat down at the kitchen table with him. "You know, Karl, Diana would probably be okay on her own. She isn't a kid anymore."

"Of course she is," he said, amazed.

"Karl. She's twenty-two years old."

"Right," he said, and took another bite of sandwich. "Twenty-two. A kid."

"And how old is that Constable Carrington?"

"That's beside the point, Cassandra."

Twenty minutes later, at the door, he took her in his arms. "One of the things I like about you," he said, "is that you've never asked me if I've ever killed anyone."

Cassandra pulled away, so that she could look into his face. She really was extremely fond of this man, she thought. "Well," she said, "you've never asked me if I've ever killed anyone, either."

Chapter Twenty-One

Annabelle awoke Sunday morning feeling restless and exalted.

"It's getting near the end of the month, Ma," said Rose-Iris when Annabelle got up. She followed her mother down the hall. "Maybe you should pay the bills today."

Annabelle did the family finances—she was very good at it. But she had a forgetful temperament. It was Rose-Iris who kept track of things, and Rose-Iris who made sure everybody's chores got done, too.

Annabelle wasn't much good at ordinary housework but she worked magic in the garden, and with the potted indoor plants, and with illnesses and injuries. She was an excellent cleaner of glass, of windows and mirrors. She would have been a good silver cleaner, too, if there had been any silver for her to clean.

Annabelle stretched, standing on her toes, her bare feet soft and dusty on the bare boards of the living room floor. She stretched high and slow like a cat, arching her back, yawning a big yawn. She put her hands on her hips and a smile on her face, and from the look of Rose-Iris, there, she knew that Rose-Iris didn't recall seeing that particular smile before. And Annabelle thought to herself in wonder that it seemed a very long time since last she'd smiled it. She considered it with affection, this smile she felt on her lips, and realized that she'd be smiling it a lot, now, and that maybe she'd better try not to do it in public.

She shivered a little, and wrapped her arms around her. "I'm going up the road to Erna's," she told Rose-Iris. "I'll pay the bills later."

"Are you going now?"

"As soon as I've watered my garden."

"When will you be home?"

"Oh," said Annabelle vaguely, "I don't know. Maybe I'll stay there for lunch." She gave Rose-Iris a smile that was reassuringly mother-like and said, "Would you do my hair in a French braid?" She stroked the cheek of her oldest child, who was a dreamy, worried little thing. "Please?" said Annabelle.

She sat on a chair in the kitchen, cuddling Camellia, while Rose-Iris brushed out her hair, long and thick and tawny-colored.

Annabelle's skin where the sun had gotten to it was the color of coffee with lots of milk in it. She had a high, high forehead, and eyes like amber. She liked to stand in front of her mirror, twisting from side to side, frowning at herself and saying she was fat. She didn't mean by this that her plump breasts were too big, and she didn't mean that her ample hips were too broad; she was referring only to the extra flesh around her waist. And when she stood straight and held in her stomach, like a person was supposed to, it pretty well disappeared. There was an abundance of Annabelle; but there was not too much of her. That, at any rate, was Annabelle's opinion.

She cradled Camellia and hummed a tune that neither of her daughters could recognize because Annabelle could not hum or sing or whistle in key. Rose-Iris brushed out her hair, and carefully braided it.

"You should tie a ribbon on the end of your braid," said Camellia. Annabelle's youngest child was staunch and reliable, and although she complained about it a lot, she did her fair share of the housework. When she was released, she would spring out the door and head for the woods with the dog belonging to Erna Remple, Annabelle's friend who raised chickens at the top of the road. The dog was a mangy-looking thing. He vaguely resembled a collie. He was always out there waiting for Camellia, but always at a safe distance from the house, since the day Herman had seen him and yelled and thrown rocks until the dog loped away: Herman didn't want any damn dog near his cages.

"Or I could braid a ribbon right into it," said Rose-Iris, "right down the whole length of it."

"Next time," said Annabelle, giving Camellia a hug. She stood up and hugged Rose-Iris, too. "Thank you, sweetie," she said. "I'm going to make you French toast, now."

Camellia grinned at Rose-Iris. The two girls habitually got up early, and Rose-Iris made breakfast for Herman and Arnold and Camellia and herself, before Herman, who almost never took a day off, left to work on his carpentry jobs, taking Arnold along as a helper; Annabelle, in the summer, was a person who slept in.

"We've already had our breakfast, Ma," said Rose-Iris.

"You can have another, then," said Annabelle, swooping and swirling in the kitchen, snatching eggs and milk from the refrigerator, seizing a frying pan from the cupboard.

Rose-Iris sighed and sat down at the table with her chin in her hands, revising the day's schedule in her head.

Annabelle made two pieces of French toast for each of her daughters and poured them big glasses of milk. She sat at the table and watched them eat, smiling, sipping coffee; a nurturer. And when they'd finished, she even did the dishes.

She left the house an hour later. Rose-Iris was singing to herself as she washed the kitchen floor, and Camellia, energetically scouring the bathtub, considered letting her hair grow, so that she could wear it in a French braid.

Annabelle took a quart bottle of pear cider up to Erna's. Erna didn't think of cider as being alcoholic. She thought of it as fruit juice, which amused Annabelle.

Annabelle invited herself to lunch and picked away at a bowl of Erna's homemade stew—surely an odd choice on such a hot day. But she ate some of it, politely, even though it made sweat pop out on her forehead. And then they opened the bottle of pear cider.

Erna had been Annabelle's friend since they were in elementary school together. She was small and thin and crouched-over looking, and an avid, beady-eyed observer of Annabelle's life. Which she considered reckless, and possibly debauched.

"I saw Lionel the other day," Erna said, after her third glass of cider, "up in Garden Bay. Him and his wife have a little store. And they raise Airedales."

"That's nice," said Annabelle with a faint smile.

Erna took a sip, lifted her right leg and crossed it delicately over the left. "I guess he's gotten over you all right, Annabelle."

"I would certainly hope so," said Annabelle, fingering her braid. "It's been twelve years."

"I never heard tell of anybody else," said Erna, "who divorced a man just because he couldn't have kids."

Annabelle, amazed, said, "I can't think of a better reason."

"Do you remember," said Erna dreamily, "the day you met Herman?"

"I do," said Annabelle. She and Erna had been having lunch at Earl's when he came in. There hadn't been any room at the counter, and all the tables had been occupied, so he'd asked Annabelle if he could sit down with them, since the tables seated four. And Annabelle had permitted this.

"I'm drivin' a truck," he'd said. "But I'm a carpenter by trade, lookin' for a place to settle down." One thing had led to another…and soon she had found herself agreeing to accept his generous offer of marriage; an admittedly improbable event which had, predictably, enraged her parents.

Erna bent over, chortling to herself. Annabelle, watching this, felt suddenly peevish. She didn't want to confide in Erna after all. She swept a fretful hand across her forehead. "I have a yen for some fries," she said.

Erna looked up, astonished.

"Come on," said Annabelle. "Let's go down to the beach and get some fries."

Erna stumbled to her feet, not drunk, just taken by surprise, and Annabelle steered her outside. They got into Erna's car and bounced down the narrow dusty road and past Annabelle's house and turned onto the highway.

"You could have had some more of my stew," said Erna, slightly dazed.

"I want some fries," said Annabelle. "I'm not hungry. I just want some French fries."

Erna pulled into the parking lot next to a takeout place across the highway from the Davis Bay beach. They got out and approached the order window. In front of them in the line was a big man wearing a pair of bright green pants. He had an enormous belly, which he was holding onto protectively, looking, thought Annabelle, as if he were a pregnant woman, or a kid with a beach ball.

"I don't want anything," said Erna.

Annabelle nodded distractedly.

"Only a Coke float," said Erna.

There was a hand-lettered sign next to the order window. It read: "A fast food outlet we are not. Your food is cooked fresh, not just kept hot. So please be patient, we will do our best, to get you fed along with the rest."

Annabelle ordered a large fries and two Coke floats. On her receipt was the number thirty-two. As she and Erna made their way across the highway to the beach, the loudspeaker called out, "Number twenty-one."

"Oh groan," said Erna. "We'll be here all day. I've got to get back and feed my chickens." The pear cider, Annabelle observed, was rapidly wearing off.

Annabelle sat down on a log. To her left, a long wharf extended into the bay, and there were a lot of people fishing from it. To the right, the sand and gravel beach was scattered with bright-colored towels, and teenagers were sunbathing, or splashing in the water. Annabelle could see the Trail Islands, offshore, and in the farthermost distance, the blue-purple shadow that was Vancouver Island. Erna plopped down beside her on the log.

For a minute Annabelle felt as if they were teenagers again themselves. There was something dizzying in the summer heat, something intoxicating in the sound of the water swishing languidly onto the shore. Annabelle seemed to hear the squeals and laughter of her teenage summers, and she remembered how it had felt that hot August day when she was kissed—really, seriously kissed—for the first time; how it had taken her breath right out of her lungs.

After a while Annabelle took off her sandals and waded in the water, which was sleek and warm against her skin. She bunched her skirt up around her thighs, while Erna murmured disapprovingly from the log, and walked out until the water was up to her knees. Annabelle looked down into the water and saw that close up, it was green, and she thought about Bobby's eyes; double-lashed, and green like stones shining in the sea.

She glanced at her watch, slipped into her sandals and sashayed across the highway, ignoring Erna's cries of protest.

She walked to one of the bright blue picnic tables in front of the takeout place, and saw Erna peering at her tensely from the beach. Annabelle sat down with her back to Erna and looked over at the parking lot. After a minute she looked away.

A couple of teenage boys wearing wet swimming trunks and dry T-shirts pulled on their shoes and socks.

Annabelle saw that the man in the bright green pants was still waiting for his food.

"Number thirty-one," said the loudspeaker. "And number thirty-two."

Annabelle got up and went to the window. The man with the bright green pants was collecting his order. She got the two

Coke floats and the cardboard container of French fries. They smelled so good that her mouth started watering. She sprinkled them with malt vinegar, and salt, and got a napkin, and turned to see Erna scurrying across the road toward her.

At the same time a small blue car turned off the highway into the parking lot. Annabelle watched as it darted neatly into the space between a pickup truck and Erna's car. Erna came up beside her and the driver of the blue car got out. He slammed the door and looked around him, and saw Annabelle.

"Oh my goodness," murmured Erna, watching as he approached them, his hands thrust into the back pockets of his jeans.

Annabelle realized that she was shivering; a sexy shudder rippled through her body as she watched Bobby walk toward her. She turned to hold out one of the floats to Erna.

"Mercy me," whispered Erna, and began sucking vigorously at the straw in her float.

He came right up to her. "Hello, Annabelle," he said, not smiling, and leaned down and kissed her.

His lips on her temple weakened her. She would have liked to rest her forehead against his chest, and fit her body close to his.

She felt the heat of the sun, and heard the sizzling of the hot oil behind the takeout counter. It must be hot as Hades in there, thought Annabelle: I wonder if they've got a fan.

She looked up into his face. There were deep lines on either side of his mouth. But his body was still hard and powerful, his fair hair was still thick and shiny, his eyes were still bedroom eyes.

She didn't love him. She'd never loved him. But she loved the things he'd given her.

"Hello, Bobby," she said, smiling up at him.

"I gotta talk to you, Annabelle."

"Annabelle!" hissed Erna.

Annabelle felt the tension in him, and misunderstood. She shook her head slowly, smiling. "Not now, Bobby. Not today."

"Oh my, oh my, Annabelle, we gotta go," said Erna, clinging to Annabelle's arm and pitching furtive looks every which way.

"You're making an error, here," said Bobby to Annabelle, ignoring Erna. He put his arms around her, not caring who saw. Erna stepped away from them and scurried toward her car. "Something's happened," he whispered in Annabelle's ear. "And I don't know what to do."

Annabelle, disquieted, pursed her lips. "Well, Bobby, I can't talk to you right now. Surely you can see that."

"Let me drive you home."

"Annabelle!" cried Erna, from behind the open door of her car.

"No no," said Annabelle quickly. "Let me go now, Bobby, or I'm going to spill this stuff."

"Shit, Annabelle," said Bobby furiously, releasing her.

"Tomorrow," said Annabelle, backing toward Erna's car. "I could see you tomorrow."

"Tomorrow, shit, Annabelle." He crossed his arms and glared at her.

"Phone me, Bobby. Tomorrow."

Chapter Twenty-Two

"**I** can't get warm," said Velma Grayson. "So I thought maybe I was getting sick." This was in explanation of Alex Gillingham's presence in her living room.

"I wish I didn't have to bother you," said Alberg.

"I know. It's all right." She was huddled into a corner of the sofa, with only her head visible above the quilt that was tucked in around her. A mug of tea sat on the end table next to the sofa. The house was suffocating, and Alberg could hear the gas furnace working hard to push the temperature even higher; soon, he thought, the place would spontaneously combust. He moved to the edge of his chair, in an attempt to free his back from the clutches of his wet shirt.

Across the room Alex Gillingham looked worriedly at Velma Grayson, leaning forward in his chair, forearms resting on his knees. Alberg felt a spasm of intense irritation toward the doctor—or maybe it was generalized irritation, produced by the heat.

"I've got all kinds of pictures of him," said Mrs. Grayson. "Though they're pretty old." She pushed the quilt aside and began to get up, and he saw that she was wearing slacks and a sweater, and a pair of heavy socks.

"Maybe you could show them to me later," said Alberg, and he smiled at her. He took his notebook and pen from his shirt pocket. "Can we talk first?"

Slowly she nodded, and covered herself again with the quilt. She was about fifty, Alberg figured—my age, he thought glumly. She wore her blond hair short and curly. "I simply can't believe this thing, Mr. Alberg," she said, haggard and desolate. "Falling off a cliff. It's ridiculous. Ridiculous."

"We're going to try to find out exactly what happened, Mrs. Grayson," said Alberg. Sweat was trickling down his temples, and under his arms. "Can you tell me why your son was carrying twenty-three thousand dollars?"

"That's—it's—I haven't the faintest idea." She leaned forward, and the quilt dropped from her shoulders. "Maybe the person he was meeting owed it to him. Do you think that might be it?"

Alberg studied her for a moment. "He was going to meet someone?" he said finally.

She nodded. "That's right."

"Who was he going to meet, Mrs. Grayson?"

"I don't know. He didn't say."

"Well what *did* he say, Mrs. Grayson?"

She looked at him intently. "I knew it was him in the hospital. But dead faces don't look familiar. Even when you know who they are, they don't look familiar." She rubbed wearily at her forehead. "I did know that it was him, though."

"Drink your tea, Velma," said Alex Gillingham.

"Mrs. Grayson," said Alberg, trying to sound relaxed and reasonable. "This is probably pretty important."

"I'm sorry. I don't know who he was meeting, or where he was meeting them, or why. I'm sorry." She began to cry again.

"Karl," murmured Gillingham reproachfully.

"Try to guess, Mrs. Grayson," said Alberg. "Was it some-body from Sechelt? Somebody coming over from Vancouver? A friend? Or was it business? What do you think?"

"I—we hadn't seen much of each other, Mr. Alberg, for the last ten years. I really didn't know anything about his life, I'm afraid."

Alberg sat back with a sigh, and closed his notebook. He was trying to ignore the waves of heat that washed over him, the sodden shirt that clung to him. But he couldn't ignore the sweat that dripped from his forehead. "I wonder," he said, "if I could have a towel."

Alex Gillingham said, "I'll get it, Velma." He stood up and disappeared down the hall.

"I think it must have been somebody here," said Velma Grayson.

"Go on," said Alberg encouragingly.

"Well—" She shook her head, defeated. "I don't know. It's just a feeling. Maybe I'm wrong."

Gillingham returned, carrying, Alberg noticed, not one hand towel, but two. He gave Alberg one and patted his own face with the other before sitting down again, this time in a chair next to the sofa.

"Thank you, Alex," said Alberg, mopping his forehead. He thought longingly of the veranda at the front of the house, and the big weeping willow tree under which his car was parked.

"I don't know when to go back to work," said Mrs. Grayson to the doctor.

"Don't think about that yet," said the doctor. Alberg watched, his irritation rekindled, as Gillingham reached over to pat her hand, which had emerged from behind the quilt to lie limply in her lap. "Take it one day at a time. One thing at a time."

"Mrs. Grayson," said Alberg. "Tell me exactly what he said, when he told you he had to meet somebody."

"Well," she said, frowning at the quilt, "it was Friday night, I guess. I asked him if he'd like to go to Percy and Hilda's for supper on Saturday. That's his aunt and uncle. And Steven said, sure" —her eyes filled with tears—"he had to meet somebody, but it wouldn't take long, he'd be back in lots of time."

Alberg waited while Velma Grayson sobbed, and Alex Gillingham comforted her.

He wondered if all this sweating might end up reducing his weight by a couple of pounds.

"Did he mention the ferry?" said Alberg.

"What?" she said, wiping her face with a tissue. Then she stopped, thinking. "Yes. You're right," she said, nodding to herself. "That's why I figured it was someone from here. Because he didn't say anything about the ferry."

"So he told you he was meeting someone, but he didn't say where, or why, or who."

"That's right."

"And he didn't mention having a lot of money, or being owed money, or owing money himself."

"No."

Alberg glanced at his notebook, trying to hide his exasperation. "Do you know if he'd been in touch with anyone since he arrived?"

She thought for a moment. "Well, once when I came home from work, he was on the phone. But I don't know who he was talking to."

"An old friend, maybe?"

"Maybe. Except—he didn't have many friends, really. I mean, maybe he does now, but not when he was living at home."

"Did he go out? See people? Drive around? Anything?"

She shook her head quickly. "No. I'm sorry, Mr. Alberg, not to be able to help you more— Oh. Wait. He did go back to Vancouver once."

"Tell me about that."

She drank the rest of her tea, and cradled the mug in her hands. "Well, he called me at work. Last Thursday it was. Said he had to go into town. He'd be back on the six-thirty ferry. But I wasn't supposed to hold supper for him. So I didn't."

"What was he going to do in town?"

"I don't know."

"Do you want more tea, Velma?" said Gillingham, and she nodded.

She and Alberg sat there in silence. Alberg thought the room had begun to shimmer, like a highway mirage.

Gillingham came back and set the refilled mug on the end table.

Alberg was convinced that he'd never be cool again. "What c   a   n y   o   u tell me about his life in Vancouver? His friends—hobbies…"

"Nothing," she said dully. "I saw him maybe three times a year. In Vancouver. And he'd call me now and then. But I have no idea how he spent his time, what he liked to do, who he liked to do it with." Once more, she wept. "And now I'm never going to find out."

"When did he leave home?" said Alberg quickly, before her sobs could take firm hold.

"After high school. He went to Vancouver."

"And then what?" said Alberg, after a pause.

She picked up her mug and drank some tea. "Well, first he got a job in retail. I forget exactly what. And then Harry died— my husband Harry was a logger, and he died in an accident that summer, so Steven came home for the funeral and so on. And then he went traveling for a while."

"Uh-huh," said Alberg. He moved a little in his chair, cautiously, and found that his shirt was wetter than ever.

"For—oh, more than a year, it was. But he kept in touch with me. And eventually he ended up back in Vancouver. That was the spring of nineteen eighty-two. And he took photography, and got a job, and—" She looked at Alberg blankly. "And that's all I know."

"Who did he work for?"

"He's been on his own for a couple of years now. Freelancing."

"Mrs. Grayson," said Alberg, struggling to control his frustration, "if I've understood you correctly, your son had been gone for ten years without a single visit home. What brought him home this summer?"

She shook her head. "I don't know."

"You must have been very happy about it."

"Very," Velma Grayson said somberly.

"But surprised, too."

She nodded. "Yes."

"Well?" said Alberg, desperate. "What did he say, when he told you?"

She found a tissue somewhere beneath the quilt and wiped her eyes. "I wish I could help you, Mr. Alberg, oh I do wish I could help you. But he wasn't—forthcoming. You know? He just said he'd like to come home for a while. And I was so glad to have him here, I didn't really care what the reason for it was."

Alberg looked around the living room. It was too damn hot to think straight. Velma Grayson looked ridiculous huddling underneath that damn quilt when the temperature had to be at least a hundred degrees in here. He swiped at his face with the towel.

Mrs. Grayson reached from the cocoon of her quilt to touch Alberg on the arm. She gazed at him searchingly, but didn't speak.

Alberg found he had nothing to offer her; no speculation, no comfort, no judgment. Finally he patted her hand. "May I look at his room now, please?"

Chapter Twenty-Three

"**D**id you hear about Steven Grayson?" said Warren, late that afternoon. "He fell off a cliff."

Annabelle laughed. "Oh sure he did."

"He did," Warren protested. He was in Annabelle's kitchen, pouring himself some coffee. "Don't laugh about it, Annabelle. He died, for Pete's sake."

Annabelle set down her iron. "Died? But—what happened?" she said, sitting down at the table with him.

"I told you, Annabelle," said Warren patiently. "He fell off a cliff. Yesterday, it happened."

"But he—I heard he'd come home."

"He did come home. It happened here. Over on Thormanby Island. You know that bluff at Buccaneer Bay? Well that's where it happened." He shook his head. "It's funny how things work out, isn't it?"

"Now, Warren," she chastised him. "We don't know anything for sure. We just guessed, and we could've been wrong."

"It's water under the bridge now, anyway," said Warren. "Listen, Annabelle." He helped himself to cream and sugar. "I've got to talk to you."

Everybody in the world wants to talk to me, thought Annabelle, exasperated. But she glanced at her brother and thought, you practically can't see the man's face for the worry on it.

"I saw the folks yesterday," he said, and drank some coffee.

Annabelle's eyes narrowed. She got up and returned to the yellow dress she'd been ironing. She'd known that was why he'd come; it was almost always why he came. And she admired his steadfastness, though in this case there was no point to it.

"And how are they?" she said politely.

"Fine, just fine," said Warren. He seemed distracted, though, and nervous. "I gave them a picture of you and the kids," he said.

"You what?" said Annabelle, astounded.

"Remember when I took one that day, a couple of months ago it was, out in your garden?"

"I remember. But you certainly didn't tell me you were taking it for them."

"I wasn't," said Warren quickly. "But it turned out so good. And they hunger for a look at you, you know that, Annabelle."

"Now don't start, Warren."

"You've gotta do something about this," he said doggedly. "It's just so stupid. Those kids, they need grandparents. They could be out there right now, swimming in the pool, eating the vegetables."

"They get vegetables right here," said Annabelle, furious. "And they don't need a swimming pool. Why they've got the ocean to swim in, for goodness' sake."

Warren stood up and went to the door. He looked outside, his hands in his pockets, and for a while neither of them spoke.

Annabelle hung up the dress. It was a yellow one that hugged her breasts and revealed her throat and her arms and had a full skirt that swished around her legs. She would wear it tomorrow, when she saw Bobby, she decided, plucking a blouse from the ironing basket. A small, pink blouse—Camellia's.

Annabelle thought about Steven. It was very hard to believe that someone so young—someone she'd actually known—was suddenly dead. She had to be more stern with Camellia about climbing trees. She spread the blouse on the board and smoothed the fabric with her hand, then picked up the iron.

"Annabelle," said Warren. "Nothing's going right." His voice sounded so bleak that Annabelle lifted her head. "There's stuff going wrong every time I turn around."

"Warren," said Annabelle. "You worry too much. You've always worried too much."

"No," he said miserably. "This is different."

Annabelle unplugged the iron. She went to Warren and led him by the hand to the kitchen table. "Sit down. Tell me."

"Wanda doesn't want to have kids."

Annabelle nodded. "That doesn't surprise me. Not after having an abortion. I know I didn't want to have them, after mine."

"But then you did, Annabelle."

"Yes. I changed my mind. Wanda will change her mind, too. I'm sure of it."

"But it's been ten years, Annabelle."

"Only five since you got married, though."

"She says when she's thirty," said Warren, after a pause.

"Well for goodness' sake, Warren," said Annabelle irritably. "I'm sure I don't know what you've got to be upset about, then."

"But she's only twenty-seven." Then he added, "Twenty-eight in September."

Annabelle said, "That's no time at all. And you'll have plenty to keep you busy, too. Why, you're going to have to fix up a room, and make a sandbox; heavens, you might even want to buy another house."

"That could be," said Warren after a moment. "I hadn't considered that. The preparations."

"Now," she said briskly. "What else?"

Warren hesitated. "I saw you with Bobby Ransome today," he said flatly. "That's a big mistake, Annabelle."

Annabelle started rummaging in the ironing basket. "I was with Erna today, Warren. We ran into Bobby. He just happened by."

Warren was shaking his head sorrowfully. "Annabelle, quit it. There's nobody knows you better than me."

She slapped the ironing board. "Bobby Ransome's an old friend of mine. I guess I can pass the time of day with an old friend if I want to." Her face was hot with anger.

Warren held up his hands. "Listen, Annabelle, there's no criticizing going on here. I'm afraid for you. That's all."

"Well don't be," Annabelle snapped.

Warren sat in silence, his head down.

Annabelle stared at the clothes waiting to be ironed. "You have seriously injured my good mood, Warren."

"I saw him having a coffee with Wanda the other day, too," Warren said miserably.

Annabelle's heart did a little skip but she didn't say anything, she didn't even blink.

"I tell you," he said heavily, "the man's an infestation."

Annabelle couldn't help smiling. He looked so dejected, she got up and gave him a hug. "Warren," she said, "if there's one thing I'm sure of, it's that you don't have to be jealous of Bobby." She sat down opposite him. "Warren—Warren. Look at me." She waited until he did so. "Wanda loves you, and she doesn't love Bobby Ransome. Maybe she used to, when they were married. Or maybe she only lusted after him, like I did." Warren looked quickly away. "But whatever. The only person she loves now is you."

"Maybe," said Warren reluctantly. "Maybe you're right."

Annabelle pushed her chair away from the table. "I'm definitely right," she said, and plugged in the iron again.

Annabelle pressed her children's clothes, dresses and shorts and T-shirts and jeans, and she chatted comfortably to her brother, and she permitted Bobby to move restlessly along the edges of her mind, seductive and dangerous.

Chapter Twenty-Four

Alberg closed the door to Steven's room. He looked around for the heat vent, and closed that, too. Then he hurried to the window, undid the latch and pushed it open as far as it would go. He leaned out, taking great gulps of hot summer air, which by contrast felt cool and refreshing. He thought he might stop at the beach when he left here, and wade into the cold Pacific right up to his neck. And probably have a heart attack.

After a while he turned back to the room. It contained a single bed with a tartan coverlet, a bedside table and a bureau, and in the corner near the window, a desk and chair. On the table sat a lamp and an alarm clock. There was another lamp on the desk.

Alberg opened the drawer in the bedside table and gazed interestedly upon a plastic bag containing what looked like marijuana, an ashtray and a book of matches. He also noticed a roll of butterscotch LifeSavers.

He shut the drawer and went over to the bureau, which held underwear, socks, a pair of pajamas, two pairs of jeans, some gray sweatpants.

There was a closet with a beaded curtain instead of a door. Inside he found two dress shirts, a pair of slacks, a bathrobe, several short-sleeved T-shirts. On the floor were two pairs of sneakers, some slippers, and a pair of good leather shoes. Two sweaters, folded, sat on the closet shelf, along with a shoebox containing shoe polish and brushes. Also two suitcases, both empty.

A gym bag, a shaving case and a camera bag sat on top of the bureau. The gym bag contained several unopened boxes of color film, with a receipt from a local camera store; a checkbook; and a bankbook. The checkbook indicated a balance of $535.23. There was $2,500 in the savings account. In the shaving case were an electric razor, deodorant, a bottle of aftershave lotion, a pair of nail scissors, tweezers, a tube of hand cream, a small container of Tylenol and a nasal spray. The partitioned camera bag contained accessories, but no camera. Alberg compared the lens cap in his pocket to the one on the lens in the camera bag: they were the same.

A photograph was tucked into a corner of the mirror that hung above the bureau. It was a photograph of Steven Grayson and a young woman. They were leaning against the fender of a car—an old, dilapidated import, maybe a Toyota; it must have come from Central Canada, thought Alberg, to be so badly rusted. Steven had his arm around the girl, one foot braced against the car. She was leaning into his shoulder, laughing; a pretty girl, with short dark hair. The sun was shining but they were wearing jackets, and the trees in the background were bare.

Alberg turned from the photo and looked through the room more thoroughly, inspecting under the mattress, and poking behind drawers, and examining walls and floor, and searching the pockets of Steven Grayson's clothing. Then he closed and locked the window, removed the photograph from the mirror, and picked up the gym bag.

Back in the living room, he said, "I'm going to have to take these things with me. We'll return them to you when we're done."

Steven's mother nodded.

"He had some film," said Alberg. The heat was creating thunder behind his eyes. "But I didn't see a camera."

She looked confused. "He had one, all right. It was an expensive one, too."

He showed her the photograph. "Do you know this girl?"

She turned the picture over. "'Natalie,'" she read. She shook her head. "No. I don't know her." She looked at Alberg wearily. "I haven't been much help, have I?"

Alberg took back the photograph. "Maybe Natalie can help us," he said.

Chapter Twenty-Five

It was early Monday morning. The men were crowded into Alberg's office. There were only three of them but they were all big men—especially Sid Sokolowski—and it was another hot day, so it felt stiflingly cramped to Alberg. Someone had suggested that they meet in the interview room. But there was no window in there.

Sokolowski occupied the black leather chair. Carrington had dragged in a straight-backed chair from somewhere. And Alberg sat behind his desk. Each of them had a cold drink that was no longer cold.

"That Ferguson guy," said Sokolowski, "he's complained again. He says somebody's poking around his damn zoo at night. Wanted to know what's going on with the investigation. I told him the lab report's come back and the only prints on the note were his own. He didn't take kindly to this."

"Put Sanducci on it, if anything more happens," said Alberg.

"Right," said Sokolowski.

"Okay," said Alberg. "Buccaneer Bay." He turned to Carrington. "You first."

Charlie Carrington cleared his throat nervously. He was a thin, anxious young man who had arrived three months earlier from a posting in Saskatchewan. "Uh, I ran down the boat, Staff, like you said."

Sokolowski shifted in the black leather chair, causing it to make a faint bleating sound.

"It's a fifteen-foot runabout," said Carrington, fingering his notebook, "belonging to one Keith Nugent, acquaintance of the deceased. We found it beached on the west side of the island, near the bottom of the path that goes up to the top. Nugent says the deceased asked him last Thursday if he could rent it from him for the day, on Saturday. Nugent agreed, and the deceased—"

"Constable," said Alberg. "Don't keep saying 'the deceased.'"

"Okay, Staff. Sorry."

"Go on."

"Uh, yeah, right, so anyway, he, uh, stopped by where Nugent was working on Saturday morning and got the key. Nugent works at that Dairy Queen place over by Davis Bay—"

"It's not a Dairy Queen, Charlie," said Sokolowski.

"Okay. Well, that drive-in place."

"It's not a drive-in place, either," said Sokolowski.

"Sid, for Christ's sake," said Alberg. "We know the place he means, right?"

"Right. But he's got a notebook there. He's making notes and they're not accurate," said the sergeant. "That notebook's got to be right on the money, Charlie," he said to the constable. "And if the staff sergeant here wasn't so irritable with the heat he'd be the one telling you this."

Alberg stared at the ceiling. Sweat crept down along his temples. "You're right, Sid," he said finally. "It's a takeout place, Charlie. Called The Bluebird."

"Okay, Staff," said Carrington. "Thanks." He made a correction in his notebook.

"Go on, Constable." Alberg plucked a handful of tissues from the box on his desk, and wiped his face. Charlie Carrington's arms looked exceedingly skinny, he thought, sticking out from the short sleeves of his uniform shirt.

"This was about noon, he says. When the guy picked up the key. He got to Pender Harbor about twelve-thirty. That's where Nugent keeps his boat. Left his car, a Honda Civic, in the parking lot there. Got in the boat and took off." He looked up. "That's it, Staff."

"Anything in the car?"

Carrington referred again to his notebook. "Just the usual stuff. Registration, maps, an empty fruit juice bottle."

"Wastebasket?"

Carrington nodded. "I went through it. Gum wrappers, mostly. Kleenex. Nothing else."

"Were Nugent and Grayson friends, or what?"

"It doesn't look like it. The deceased—sorry, uh, Steven Grayson, he ran into Nugent in the bank on Thursday. Nugent said he hadn't seen the guy for years. But they'd been to school together, and they got to talking, and Grayson asked if Nugent knew anybody who had a boat. Said he needed one for Saturday. So Nugent said he could use his."

"Didn't he ask what the guy wanted it for?" said Alberg.

"Yeah," said Carrington. "Grayson said he just wanted to cruise around. Said he'd be going back to town soon and he wanted a day on the water."

"And Nugent was at The Bluebird, at work, all day Saturday? You checked it out?"

"Yeah."

"Okay." Alberg sat up and turned to the sergeant. "What did you find out, Sid, talking to the locals?"

"We didn't get anything," said the sergeant. "Which didn't surprise me, seeing as how we didn't know what we were looking for."

"It's always harder," said Alberg agreeably, "when we don't know what we're looking for."

Sokolowski leaned forward, his beefy forearms on his thighs. "See, there's always boats coming and going—and this is on both sides, I mean. The Buccaneer Bay side, and the other side. People beach their boats, or else they drop anchor, and then they wander all over the place, having picnics, hiking, not knowing they're on private land. Or they don't care. They come looking for blackberries. Whatever. So nobody's gonna notice a kid hiking off into the woods, you know? At least, nobody did."

"It's worth going back, doing more interviews," said Alberg. "Somebody must have seen something." He pulled his notebook toward him and flipped it open. "I talked to the bank manager. Grayson tried to make a twenty-three-thousand-dollar withdrawal last Thursday. The local guy told him he'd have to get it from his own branch, in Vancouver. His mother says he went to town that day; that's probably what he was up to."

"Okay," said Sokolowski, "that establishes that if we're talking about blackmail here, he wasn't the blackmailer, he was the blackmailee." He smiled. "Blackmailee," he repeated.

"But it's a very funny business," said Alberg. "The blackmailer apparently sets up a meet—but on top of a cliff? And then what—does the kid get dizzy and fall off? Does the blackmailer shove him off? Without collecting the dough?"

They sat in silence for a couple of minutes. Then Sokolowski said, "We got nothing from the campers, too. And the boaters. Couple of people saw the fall. But that's it." He consulted his notebook. "There's quite a few cabins. Houses, too. People living there year-round." He looked at Alberg. "Some places nobody was home. Or maybe the wife was there but not the husband. You're right. It'd be worth while, going back."

Alberg nodded. "Good. Do it." He took his feet off the desk and sat up. He finished his drink and tossed the can in the wastebasket. "Get me a list of the property owners, Charlie, will you? Both islands."

"Right, Staff," said the constable. He hesitated. "If somebody killed him—"

"Yeah? Go on," said Alberg.

"Well, it surely wasn't premeditated, right?"

"I'd say that's right, yeah."

"Because he wouldn't have wanted him falling onto the beach, making a big commotion down there like he did."

"He also wouldn't have wanted him to take all that money down with him."

"So is that better for us? Or worse?" said Carrington.

"Usually it's worse," said Alberg. "If a guy plans it out, he leaves a trail. But on the other hand, when it's spontaneous—"

"A crime of passion, like," said Sokolowski, helpfully.

"—maybe he panics, does something stupid trying to cover it up." Alberg shrugged. "Could go either way."

Isabella stuck her head around the door. "Dr. Gillingham's here."

"In a minute," said Alberg.

"He flies off the edge of a cliff," Sokolowski muttered, "lands in the middle of a bunch of women and children—" He shook his head in disgust, as if Steven Grayson had plummeted from the cliff top by choice.

The boy had said, "Help me," thought Alberg. Help me die. That's what was in Steven Grayson's mind in the last seconds of his life. Not how he had died, or why. Just the act of dying, and fear of it, and needing help. Alberg was glad Joseph Dunn had been there for him.

He stood up and shuffled through the papers on his desk, searching. "I'll do the victim," he said. "Sid, you and Charlie do the islands again. And keep checking the marinas, in case the perp rented a boat." He looked up at them. "That's it."

Carrington left the office, taking his chair with him, but Sokolowski stayed behind.

"Staff," said the sergeant, "we can handle it all, you know. You got a lot to do here," he said, looking pointedly at the stack of forms on Alberg's desk.

"Yeah, yeah, I know," said Alberg. "It's okay. I appreciate it, but—" He found the lens cap and held it up. "See this? I think the kid had a camera with him."

Sokolowski sighed. "You're kinda behind with this shit, Karl," he said, staring at Alberg's desk. "Vancouver's gonna be on your tail about it soon."

"They're already on my tail," said Alberg. "I'll get it done. Don't worry about it." He slapped Sokolowski on the shoulder and steered him to the door. "Send Gillingham in, will you, Sid?"

"His dad was killed," said Alex Gillingham, "right after the kid graduated from high school. I remember because it happened about the same time Marjorie and I split up." He gave Alberg a rueful look. "Marjorie's moved away, Karl, did I tell you?"

"Yeah, you told me, Alex."

"To Kelowna. She moved to Kelowna."

"Go on. Talk to me about Steven."

Gillingham lifted his right leg and rested the ankle on his left knee. He did this with some effort, since he had recently strained his back while helping a pregnant patient off the examining table. "I was their doctor. I mean the family's, the three of them. Didn't see much of Harry. A Workers' Compensation Board injury once; I sent him to a physiotherapist. With Velma"—he waved his hand vaguely—"nothing serious, just the usual stuff. Steven—" He plucked at the crease in his trouser leg. "He was a healthy kid. A nice kid. I liked him." He looked at Alberg, to make sure he was listening. Alberg nodded. "That summer," Gillingham went on, "after Harry was killed, Velma came to me for sleeping pills. She was hurting real bad. And she was scared, too. She'd never been on her own before."

"Were there financial problems?"

Gillingham shook his head. "Plenty of insurance. No financial problems. But Velma wanted to go back to work anyway. Steven would be gone, she had nobody to look after, and she wanted to keep busy. She hadn't worked for twenty years. But I asked around, and eventually she got on at the bank." He put his foot back on the floor, and Alberg saw him wince. The doctor looked exhausted.

"There's something going on between you and Velma Grayson, isn't there, Alex."

Gillingham shifted in his chair, probably to ease the discomfort in his back. "Not any more."

Alberg tossed his notebook and pen down on his desk and stood up. He went over to the window and looked out at the parking lot, where a couple of patrol cars sat blinking in the sun. Beyond it, the road wandered off toward the village. "I've got a blank space in my head where that kid wants to be," he said. He turned back to the doctor. "Help me out, Alex."

Gillingham hesitated, then looked up at Alberg. "I think he was gay."

Alberg turned this over in his mind.

"I think he was," said Gillingham. "I don't know for sure."

"What about the girl in the photograph? Natalie?"

Gillingham shrugged.

Alberg sat down at his desk and opened his notebook.

"I could be wrong," said the doctor.

"Did he ever talk to you about it?"

"No no," said Gillingham, shaking his head. "It was just—I don't know. It was just a feeling." He rubbed vigorously at his hair.

"What else can you tell me about him?"

Gillingham looked uneasily at Alberg's notebook. "You've got to understand, I wasn't close to the kid. He was always polite, respectful; always had a job, once he got past childhood. But he didn't volunteer much about his private life."

"Was there anybody he might have confided in? How about his uncle?"

"I don't think so. He wasn't close to Percy, either." He lifted his hands. "Karl, I just don't know any more to tell you."

"Okay." Alberg closed his notebook. "Thanks, Alex."

"Karl." The doctor leaned forward. "Velma and I—there hasn't been anything between us for a couple of years now."

Alberg nodded.

"I—she would have married me. But at first I didn't want that. You remember; I was into sports."

Alberg remembered, all right. He'd feared for Gillingham's life, during that period.

"And then, a little bit later, why, I wanted it, but she didn't. So now we're just good friends, Velma and I."

Alberg thought about his ex-wife, Maura, and her upcoming wedding. She'd sent him an invitation. Because they were good friends, too, she and Alberg. The thought of this was suddenly unbearably depressing.

Gillingham gave his thighs a light slap and stood up. At the doorway he stopped and turned back to Alberg. "I can't figure it out, Karl."

"Me neither, Alex," said Alberg.

When the doctor had left, Alberg placed a call to Natalie Walenchuk, whose phone numbers were in Steven Grayson's address book. He reached her at work, and told her about Steven's death.

"I'd like to come over and talk to you," he said.

"Oh God. I can't believe this."

"Is this afternoon okay?"

"I can't believe this. Steven? Oh my God."

Chapter Twenty-Six

That afternoon Annabelle filled the bathtub with tepid water, undressed, and pinned her hair on top of her head. She climbed into the bath and lay there with her eyes closed, languidly scooping water across her breasts. She'd make a salmon loaf for dinner, she thought. She lifted her hands to stroke the back of her neck, to put cool bathwater on the nape of her neck. She opened her eyes and looked down at her body, almost submerged, and was not pleased to notice a certain droopiness here and there. She poked her belly and watched the shudder of her plumpness, and felt regretful. But oh well, she thought; she was strong, and philosophical. Her body continued to serve her reasonably well. It remained healthy, and able. And she didn't think that a body, or even a body and a face, created seductiveness. It was something inside people, a hunger that looked out through their eyes.

I'm going up to Erna's, she'd say to Herman. We might take in a movie.

Last night she'd had a dream. She was in a room with
Bobby and a bunch of other people. She and Bobby had
happened to glance at each other. And this glance had created
such a sudden, driving need in them that Bobby got up from the
table around which they were all sitting, smoking cigarettes and
drinking beer (she thought this was odd, because she neither
smoked nor drank), and he pulled her into the bedroom and
onto a big square bed, warm and rumpled. He stripped off her
clothes, and his, and knelt over her, and she lifted her hips and
took him inside her—and then she noticed for the first time
that there were two other people in the bed, two men, one on
either side of them. The man on her right was Steven Grayson;
he was trying to read a magazine. The man on her left was
Lionel, her ex-husband; he was on his side, his head propped up
on his hand, and he watched, with a smile, as Annabelle and
Bobby had urgent, frantic sex. And when they had finished
Bobby collapsed at the end of the bed and Lionel said to
Annabelle, "Hey, wow, that was beautiful."

She shifted in the bathwater. It had made her uneasy,
Bobby and Lionel and Steven Grayson all together in one of her
dreams. Not while she was dreaming it, for dreams have a logic
of their own. But when she awakened; she was uneasy then.

Annabelle got out of the tub and dried herself while the
water gurgled down the drain. She put on clean underwear and
her yellow dress. She dried the tub with the bath towel and
draped the bathmat over the edge of the tub. She opened the
bathroom door and stepped out into the hall, carrying her
laundry, which she dumped into a hamper that stood in the
kitchen, next to the washing machine.

Annabelle looked outside and saw that Rose-Iris was taking
the washing from the line, dropping the clothespins into a
canvas bag that Herman had fitted to a coat hanger, putting the
clean clothes into a basket. I just did the ironing, thought
Annabelle, and here comes more of it.

She got out the ingredients and began making a salmon
loaf. She looked in the fridge for salad things and saw lettuce,

tomatoes, cucumber, green onions. There was fruit, too; maybe she'd make a fruit salad for dessert. She turned on the oven and got a loaf pan from the cupboard.

Rose-Iris came in lugging the laundry basket, which she put on top of the washing machine.

"Where's your sister?" said Annabelle, as Rose-Iris began folding clothes.

"Out playing with the dog."

It's better than climbing trees, thought Annabelle, as she began mixing up the salmon loaf. Or cliffs.

"Ma, I want to be a secretary when I grow up."

Annabelle could see it, too. She saw Rose-Iris teetering on high heels, wearing a skirt and a sweater and makeup on her face, her hair combed back. She saw her sitting, knees together, holding a notepad and a pen, scribbling quickly and confidently, taking down the words of her boss. Annabelle couldn't see the boss, she could only hear him, droning, and she watched proudly as Rose-Iris wrote shorthand.

"Good," said Annabelle, approving. Being a secretary was a real career. It had some substance to it. Unlike waitressing, which was the only job Annabelle had ever had.

"In junior high I can take typing," said Rose-Iris. "And shorthand."

Rose-Iris was going to be ambitious, Annabelle realized; that was good. She'd been ambitious herself—not to have a career, though. Annabelle's ambitions had been for motherhood.

"I took typing in school," she told her daughter. "And shorthand, too."

Rose-Iris looked dubious.

"I wasn't very good at shorthand," Annabelle confessed. "But I was pretty good at typing." She put down the spoon and typed in the air, very fast. "We could probably get you one, at a garage sale or something. A typewriter. So you could practice at home."

"And then I could get jobs in the summertime."

Annabelle nodded, looking at Rose-Iris proudly. She wondered, if she hadn't had that abortion, would she have had an ambition? To be a secretary? Or a teacher, maybe?

Just then Camellia erupted into the kitchen. She was carrying a plastic bucket that had once held ice cream. She held it out to Annabelle, clutching it by the handle so that it dangled in the air. "Look!" she said. "Blackberries!" Her legs were scratched and her hair had debris in it, bits of moss and tree bark and forest dust.

"Dessert!" Annabelle crowed, taking the bucket. She put it on the counter and hugged Camellia, who smelt hot and sweaty. "Someday," she crooned, smoothing Camellia's disheveled hair, "we'll have so many things."

"What?" said Camellia, smiling.

Annabelle leaned against the counter, her arm around Camellia, and looked across the room at Rose-Iris, who was folding the last towel in the basket. "We'll have a dryer. And a freezer, full of food. We'll have a bathtub with a shower."

"We'll have our own dog," said Camellia.

"We'll have a typewriter," said Rose-Iris, grinning.

"And a VCR," said Camellia.

"We'll have silverware," said Annabelle.

"And a CD player," said Rose-Iris.

"We'll go on a trip," said Annabelle.

"We'll have a house on the beach," said Camellia.

"And relatives," said Rose-Iris. "More than just Uncle Warren."

Annabelle frowned at her, and was going to speak, but then somebody knocked on the door. She moved across the room so that she could look through the screen, and saw the young woman from the newspaper standing there.

"Herman isn't here," said Annabelle.

"Well actually, it's you I'd like to talk to, if you have a couple of minutes."

Annabelle stared at her. What was it about this girl that was upsetting her?

The girl had seen her in the restaurant with Bobby, Annabelle remembered.

She thought about Herman finding out about Bobby. Warren was right. She had to be much much more careful.

She shivered, and watched her hand reach out and push the door open. She stepped outside. "I'm going to my garden," she said. "You can come, if you like."

In the garden Annabelle said, "What's your name?"

"Diana."

"Diana." Annabelle looked her over. "If I were your mother, I would have named you—well, maybe Dianthus. But probably Rose." She turned. "I have six rosebushes." Her hand, indicating the roses, rippled slowly through the hot languid breath of her garden.

"They're beautiful," said Diana.

"They're grouped together like this, as you see," said Annabelle, "in the middle, here, so that they can get full sun."

"It's a beautiful garden," said Diana. She turned, slowly, surveying it. "Those hollyhocks are wonderful."

But she wasn't really looking. Annabelle could tell. It was disappointing. Some little thing to share, some tiny thing in common—that's what people needed before they could talk to each other. But this silly girl was going to blunder on and talk anyhow; Annabelle could see it in her face, which was turned, distraught, to the hollyhocks. Annabelle drew herself up, pulling in her stomach, smoothing her hands over the roundness of her belly, noticing the flat front of Diana's khaki shorts.

"Wonderful," the girl repeated, looking into the curvaceous heart of a hollyhock blossom, her uplifted face gathering earnestness like dust.

"Truly, I do not understand what you're doing here," said Annabelle. The girl's presence no longer made her tense and uneasy. She felt safe in her sunny, fragrant garden...as though confident she could, if necessary, summon things to rid herself of intruders. Summon a slow-moving battalion of slugs, for instance. This girl with the taffy-colored hair, she'd run fast enough from a bunch of slugs. Except it was too hot for slugs. Summon quick-slithering garter snakes, then—she glanced at the edges of her garden, where the forest snuffled, curious, but saw no garter snakes; they'd be curled somewhere in the heat; swirled; arranged; concentric. The girl with the flat stomach and the strong legs, pale legs, creamy as Annabelle's own, she'd flee the garden in a panic should Annabelle summon a few garter snakes to speed her on her way.

"You're going to write an article about Herman's mini-zoo. But the mini-zoo's got nothing to do with me," she said, lifting the lolling head of a dahlia, letting its huge red flower rest for a moment on the palm of her hand. "Nothing at all to do with me." She moved along to a small bed of snapdragons. "These are called 'Rockets,'" she said. She reached to press a pink satiny jaw, and smiled when it opened, promptly, obediently. "See?" she said to Diana. "Did you see?" Diana leaned near, and Annabelle did it again.

"My grandmother showed me that once," said Diana.

Annabelle glanced across at a wire frame smothered in sweet peas. The vines were turning yellow in the heat. She wished the girl would go away, so that she could tend her garden.

"I don't think I'm going to do a story on it after all," said the girl, holding hands with herself in an intense manner.

"Well then," said Annabelle. "What on earth are you doing here?"

"I—you see," said Diana; she put her fists in the pockets of her shorts; "I don't approve of the mini-zoo."

Annabelle let her eyes grow wide.

Diana flushed. "I don't think animals ought to be in cages."

Annabelle slowly nodded. "I see. Well."

"I would like to try to persuade Mr. Ferguson to set them free."

Annabelle had a quick picture in her mind of the monkeys scampering along the streets of Sechelt, chased by Erna's dog. She must have smiled, because Diana took a step toward her and added, "Or at least set the raccoons free, and the foxes, and give the monkeys to the zoo."

"Bigger cages," said Annabelle absently.

Diana flushed redder. "People assume," she said, speaking quietly—which meant she was trying to control something, indignation or condemnation or something; into Annabelle's chest came a flash of anger—"people assume," Diana went on, "that because we seem to be smarter than animals, that makes us better than animals. More worthwhile."

"Oh for goodness' sake," said Annabelle.

The girl opened her mouth to speak again—and then suddenly her face got heavy, and young as it was, it sagged a little, revealing the strain that lay behind it. "I feel so stupid," she said, looking around the garden, dazed and unhappy. "I don't know what I expected to accomplish."

Annabelle, generous in relief, was about to offer the girl a bouquet of sweet peas when Diana said, abruptly, "Did you know that the president of the Law Reform Commission says the Criminal Code should be revised to give rights to animals?"

Annabelle, vexed, snapped her mouth shut and crossed her arms in front of her so that they were snuggled firmly under her breasts. She made her stare a steely one.

"He said they should have a status sort of like slaves," said Diana. "It's not much, is it? But it would give them rights to decent shelter, and enough food, and it would mean that people couldn't abuse them." She jerked her head toward the trees. "Those animals, they're being abused, Mrs. Ferguson. Those cages are far too small, for one thing. My God, they're going to go crazy with boredom in there."

Annabelle moved toward the rosebushes in the center of her garden. She could leave, of course; just walk right out of here, through the bushes, and stomp up the dirt path and into her house, where she could slam the door on this impertinent girl. But

Annabelle was curiously stimulated. She felt as if all the many flower-parts of her garden were leaning toward her and this girl, listening, straining to comprehend—as she was herself, surprisingly enough, even though it wasn't really worth the time or trouble.

"I don't agree with you," she said, and was pleased to hear that she sounded comfortable, reasonable, neither threatened nor threatening. "In the first place, Miss—" She turned and looked quizzically at the girl. "What's your last name?"

"Alberg."

Annabelle was for a moment frozen, suspended in that quizzical pose, looking back over her shoulder, her head tipped, waiting, courteously. "That's right. Your father's a policeman." She couldn't remember if adultery was actually against the law, or not. Laughter bubbled in her throat but all she did was smile. Then she turned and stepped again toward the roses. "There are rules about keeping animals, you know. Government regulations."

"I know."

"And there are people who go around making sure the rules are kept." She peered intently at the new growth on the rosebushes, looking for aphids.

"I know that," said Diana. "I talked to the wildlife guy. He said I wouldn't get anywhere with your husband." Diana gave her a tentative smile.

"And you won't get anywhere with me, either," said Annabelle sharply.

She had heard the truck pull up next to the house.

"If you talked to the wildlife people then you know that no rules are being broken here," she said quickly, moving toward the brush that separated her garden from the house. "Some snoopy person complained about the mini-zoo, and they looked into it, because that's their job." She pulled back the branches. "Come on, come on," she said impatiently, and the girl hurried up past her, and through the brush.

"You shoulda told me you were coming back," said Herman excitedly, slamming the truck door. "Did you bring a photographer this time?"

"I'm not here for that," said Diana stiffly. She started to walk out of the yard, but Herman put up an arm to stop her. "So—shit, you mean that article's gonna be in the paper without a picture?"

"I don't know," said Diana, with a swift glance at Annabelle.

"There might not be any article, Herman," said Annabelle.

"What the hell are you talking about? What's she talking about?" he said to Diana.

"I—we don't think there's much of a story, really," said Diana. "I'm sorry." Once more she began moving toward the road, and her car.

"Wait a minute, wait a minute," said Herman desperately, spittle flying. "Goddammit."

Annabelle put a hand on his arm. "Herman—"

He pulled away. "Listen," he said to Diana. "Goddammit just stop and listen!" He reached out to take hold of her shoulder.

"Herman!" said Annabelle, grabbing at him.

Herman turned to her and, with a swipe of his left arm, knocked her to the ground.

The screen door banged shut as Rose-Iris ran from the house to her mother.

Herman looked from Annabelle to Diana, who stood stock-still, staring at him in horror. "Goddammit!" he cried. He rushed to his truck, backed frenziedly to the road, and drove away.

Annabelle got to her feet, rebuffing Diana's attempt to assist her. She smoothed her hair and pulled at the waistline of her dress, which had become twisted.

"Go away now," she said calmly to Diana, brushing dust from her dress. She peered closely at the skirt. "Oh look, Rose-Iris. There's a tear in my dress."

Suddenly she whirled to face Diana. "Go! Go!" Annabelle shouted, tears flashing in her eyes, and Diana stumbled off to her car.

Chapter Twenty-Seven

Alberg met Natalie Walenchuk where she worked: at a dog grooming establishment on Denman Street, in Vancouver's West End.

It was very hot in Bertha's Doggy Salon. Natalie Walenchuk was wearing shorts and thongs and a white T-shirt. She was the only person in the place. It was almost closing time, she explained, and she was working on the last dog.

Alberg pulled out a handkerchief and wiped his forehead, looking curiously at the row of large kennels upon which sat several smaller ones. Two of the small ones were occupied by Yorkshire terriers, who had barked excitedly and with considerable purposefulness when Alberg first entered.

On the grooming table stood a large, blond dog. "It's a standard poodle," said Natalie, when Alberg inquired.

A harness was attached to the ceiling but Natalie wasn't using it for the poodle. She held his muzzle in her left hand and with her right operated a razor, shaving the dog's face, from the eyes down, and his throat. It was like she was shearing a sheep, Alberg thought, watching as the dog's muzzle appeared to lengthen, and his eyes to grow larger.

"Okay, fella," said Natalie, giving the dog a slap on the flank. "On to phase two." She pulled up a stool, picked up a pair of long-bladed scissors, and began trimming. Her back was to Alberg. The dog rested his chin on Natalie's shoulder and gazed at Alberg with a calm intelligence the staff sergeant found disconcerting.

"Come on through, if you like," said Natalie.

Alberg opened the gate next to the counter. He wandered around the table until he could see Natalie's face, which was set and grim.

"Brush off that chair and sit down."

Alberg looked at the chair. Like everything else in the place, it was covered with dog hair.

"Here," said Natalie, throwing him a towel.

The dog turned his head to look curiously at Alberg, then sighed, and rested it again on Natalie's shoulder, watching the pedestrians pass in front of the shop.

"Were you and Steven—good friends?" said Alberg, wiping the seat of the chair.

"Yes," said Natalie curtly, the scissors snapping as she quickly, expertly, cut the woolly hair close on the dog's back.

Alberg peered into the canvas bag that was attached to the end of the table, then dropped the towel into it. "Lovers?" he asked, sitting down.

Natalie glanced at him irritably. "Is that any of your business?"

"I don't know," said Alberg. "Maybe not."

"Gotta move now, fella," said Natalie to the dog, pushing her stool back from the table. She began brushing the long, curly hair on the dog's left front leg, using an instrument that looked to Alberg like a short-handled rake. "No. We weren't lovers. Steven was gay."

The dog yawned, slowly, hugely. Natalie looked up and caught Alberg's eye. Her brown hair was short and thick and wavy. Her face shone with sweat. She had dark blue eyes and her teeth looked almost artificially straight and white. She started working on the dog's right front leg.

"Was there anybody special in his life? A sexual relationship, I mean."

"No," said Natalie. "I don't think there ever had been. I used to worry about him—one-night stands, you know. I kept hoping he'd meet somebody." She stopped brushing and stared at the wall, where there were shelves full of merchandise—collars and leashes, food and water dishes, anti-flea shampoo. "He was my friend. I loved him." She blinked rapidly, and swept tears away with her fingertips. The dog looked down at her; Alberg figured he knew that his front leg was done, and was wondering why Natalie wasn't moving on. He moved his muzzle close to Natalie's left temple and began sniffing, delicately. Natalie stood up. She turned her back to Alberg and looked out the front window, her hands in the pockets of her shorts.

Alberg heard the fans—there were two of them—and the patient, rhythmic panting of the dog standing on the table. In their cages the Yorkies moved restlessly. They must be awfully hot, thought Alberg, waiting. But he saw that each cage contained a water dish.

Natalie returned to her stool and began brushing one of the poodle's back legs.

"Did you know he hadn't been back to Sechelt for ten years?" said Alberg.

"Yeah. He didn't think much of the place."

"How come he decided to go home this summer?"

Natalie put down the brush and picked up the scissors. She cut the air a few times while she studied the dog. Then she began clipping the right front leg. "Well, see, he'd done something." She lifted her head and rested her arm on the dog's back. "He told me about it—oh, a few months after we met. He did this awful thing, he said. And he was waiting for a chance to put it right." She shrugged and went back to the dog. "He never did tell me what he'd done. But it was something pretty serious. Or he thought it was, anyway. And then, last month he called me up, all excited, and said he was finally going to take care of it."

"How? What was he going to do?"

Natalie looked up from her clipping. "What does it matter, for God's sake—he's dead, right? I just hope he had the satisfaction of getting things squared away before it happened." She bent to the dog again.

Alberg watched her for a while. Then, "Natalie," he said. "It's possible that his death wasn't an accident."

Natalie looked at him uncomprehendingly.

"We don't know anything for sure. But it's possible."

She stared at him. "What are you saying? You think he— you think he jumped off that cliff? On purpose?"

"No, that isn't likely."

"You're damn right it isn't likely. So what, then?" She caught her breath. "You mean, somebody pushed him off?"

"We're investigating that possibility," said Alberg.

Looking dazed, Natalie put down the scissors and sat back. She folded her arms and hunched her shoulders slightly, hugging herself.

"Did you hear from him," said Alberg, "after he left for Sechelt?"

Natalie nodded.

"What did he tell you?"

She was watching his face intently, hungry for information Alberg hoped she already possessed. "He said—" She shook her head.

"Did he call you? Or write to you?"

"He called."

"Often?"

"Two or three times, maybe." She shivered. "My God, my heart's beating so fast I can't believe it." She stood, quickly, and embraced the dog, who looked somewhat surprised but gave the side of her face a dutiful lick.

"Natalie," said Alberg. "I really need you to help me on this."

"He was going to give somebody money," she said, her hand pressed against her chest. "He phoned me on Thursday. He was in Vancouver. He had to come back to get the money."

"Was he being blackmailed?"

She sat down on the stool. "No. I don't think so. This guy, he didn't know Steven was going to give him money. At first he wouldn't even agree to see him."

"Do you know his name?" said Alberg.

Natalie shook her head. The dog lifted a paw and nudged the air in her direction. "I told him to try again," she said. "This guy told him to fuck off. Steven called me. 'He won't see me,' he says, and he's so upset, he's nearly crying. 'What am I going to do?' he says. And I told him to call the guy again. 'Try again,' I said. 'Try again.'" Her voice rose to a cry. "That's who did it, isn't it? That must have been who killed him."

Alberg looked around for a clean towel, found one, and handed it to her. The big blond dog nuzzled her hair as she wiped her face.

"I have to ask you a couple more questions," said Alberg.

"Sure."

"I figure you must have tried to make him tell you what he was feeling so guilty about. Am I right?"

"Yeah, sure. Of course."

"So what did he say? I know he didn't tell you—but what did he say?"

She considered this for a while, remembering. "The most he ever said was this. See, I was bugging him about it again…I thought it would be a good thing for him to talk about it, you know? I mean, it wasn't just morbid curiosity on my part."

Alberg nodded.

"So anyway, this one time I said, 'Whatever it is, it can't be all that bad,' or something like that. And he got really upset, and he said, 'What's the worst thing you could imagine?' And I laughed and said, 'Well you didn't kill someone, did you?' And there was this awful pause and then he said, 'Not directly.'"

"What did you think he meant?"

"I guess somebody died, and he felt responsible, even though he probably wasn't." She picked up the scissors and opened and closed them, studying them closely, as if she'd forgotten their purpose.

"Did you talk about this again?"

Natalie shook her head. "I didn't really want to." She looked up at Alberg. "I wish I had, though. I really wish I had."

Steven Grayson had lived in a small apartment in Kitsilano, two blocks from the beach. There was an elementary school across the street and more apartment buildings on either side. From the living room, sliding doors led onto a balcony barely big enough for one chair.

Alberg stood in the middle of the living room and looked around. It was very quiet, and very hot. The sun poured into the room in streaks, between the slats in Levolor blinds that had been left partly open.

He felt a personal responsibility for Steven Grayson's death, because he'd almost witnessed it. Some son of a bitch had been stumbling down the backside of that goddamn cliff, fleeing a murder scene, while he, Alberg, sat on the sand babysitting the corpse.

Steven had been an orderly person, he thought, looking around. The coffee table held a dozen magazines, stacked neatly by category: news magazines, photography magazines, travel magazines. The paperback books filling the shelves against one wall were all fiction, arranged alphabetically, by author. Steven had had a high-quality sound system, and the compact discs, too, were organized—jazz in one box, rock in another, some classical music in a third. The sound-system components were the only things in the room that would have cost him serious money.

On the walls of Steven's apartment hung framed photographs which Alberg assumed Grayson had taken himself. Some of them Alberg liked a lot. Pewter driftwood, on a beach drenched by a silver tide. A full white moon in a navy sky, peeking over a snowy hillside. A sheet of still water bordered by leafless trees; Alberg craned his neck to look at it upside down; the reflection was only marginally less defined than the trees themselves.

He went into the kitchen and opened cupboards and drawers, but didn't find anything interesting. The fridge had been cleaned out but not turned off.

The apartment had two bedrooms, the smaller of which Steven Grayson had used as an office. Here Alberg found cameras and equipment in a closet, and a filing cabinet next to a small desk. A glass-fronted bookcase held hardcover photography books. On the desk were containers of pens, pencils, paper clips; an in-and-out tray; a telephone with a Rolodex beside it; and drawers containing supplies.

Alberg put on his reading glasses, opened the top drawer of Steven Grayson's filing cabinet, and began to examine the contents.

The sunlight gradually withdrew, and Alberg, squinting, turned on the overhead light, and the desk lamp.

He went through everything in the filing cabinet, and everything in the desk. He became aware of hunger, but ignored it.

He heard himself humming, slowly, under his breath. He did this a lot; he assumed it helped him concentrate. But he wished it weren't the theme from *The Mickey Mouse Club* that he hummed.

Eventually, he was finished. He sat back in Steven's desk chair, took off his reading glasses and rubbed his eyes. He was tired, but he was also engrossed. Intent upon the puzzle that was Steven Grayson; because in the understanding of his life lay the solution of his death.

Chapter Twenty-Eight

Alberg was at his desk early the next morning. He made several calls, then went down the hall to see Sid Sokolowski, who was talking on the phone at his desk in the main office, behind Isabella's counter.

Sokolowski hung up as Alberg poured himself some coffee. "I was talking to the guy about getting your list," said the sergeant. "Of the property owners on the Thormanbys."

"And?"

"He says we'll have it by noon, but I wouldn't count on it."

"Why not?" said Alberg, stirring sugar and cream into his coffee; Isabella hadn't yet arrived, so he was free to do this openly.

"His name's O'Hara," Sokolowski said meaningfully.

"So?"

"Irish," Sokolowski pronounced.

Alberg shook his head. Sokolowski believed that certain character traits, both positive and negative, were part of a nation's DNA. He would not have agreed that this made him a bigot.

"If you go down there at noon and scowl at him, Sid, I bet you'll get some action."

"Maybe," said the sergeant grudgingly. "What did you learn in Vancouver?"

Alberg sat on the edge of Sokolowski's table, which was positioned right up against his desk. The sergeant used his table as a place to sort things; there were many piles of paper on it. "His friend Natalie says he was going to give the money to somebody. It was supposed to be—a reparation, I guess."

The sergeant looked skeptical. "What did he do?"

Alberg shrugged. "I don't know. But I'd like to find out. Meanwhile, check this out, will you, Sid?" He gave Sokolowski a warranty registration form. "It was in his office. But the camera itself is gone. I think he had it with him when he was killed. When we get the description we can contact pawnshops, secondhand stores—"

"Et cetera, et cetera. Will do."

Alberg stood up and put his mug down next to the coffeepot. "I've got a couple of people to talk to. I'll check with you when I get back."

"Wow," he said fifteen minutes later, looking out through the glass doors in the high school principal's living room.

"Sit down," said the principal, whose name was Hugh McMurtry. "How about a cup of coffee? Or would you like something cold?"

"Coffee's fine," said Alberg.

The doors were open to a small brick patio, in the center of which was a plot of earth, home to two red rosebushes. A few steps led down from the patio to a walk that stretched along the beach. Beyond that, Trail Bay lay still and gleaming in the sun. Alberg heard sea gulls, and some children, laughing and shrieking. He stepped out onto the patio and saw them splashing in the shallow water near the shore,

FALL FROM GRACE 175

watched by two women in shorts and T-shirts who were sitting on beach towels nearby.

"It'll just be a second," McMurtry called from his kitchen, which was separated from the large living room by a counter.

"This is quite a view," said Alberg, as McMurtry joined him on the patio.

"It is, isn't it," the principal agreed.

He was older than Alberg, probably almost retirement age. He wore light pants and a polo shirt. His hair was gray and thinning, and he was about fifteen pounds overweight. But he was tanned, which Alberg envied. People who tanned, he thought, always looked slimmer and healthier than people who didn't.

McMurtry gazed out at the ocean. "I look at that bay and I think of Hong Kong," he said. "Look how empty it is. We've got so much space, in this country. Sometimes it doesn't seem fair."

Alberg in his mind's eye saw Trail Bay thick with houseboats, and decided he'd like to put that off as long as possible.

They moved inside, and McMurtry slid the door closed. "Do you want cream? Sugar?" he said, going to the kitchen.

Alberg hesitated . "No, thanks. Black is fine."

The principal set the mugs on the coffee table. "I went to the office," he said, "after you called, and looked up Steven's file." He looked unhappily at Alberg. "I still can't believe you think he was murdered."

"We don't think anything yet, Mr. McMurtry." Alberg took out his notebook. "Do you remember him pretty well?"

"I remember them all pretty well," said McMurtry with a smile.

"Was he a good student?"

"Average, I'd say. Except for photography, of course."

"He was good with a camera, was he?"

"Oh yes. He took all the pictures for the school newspaper, and for the yearbook, from grade ten on."

"What can you tell me about his friends?"

"Well, everybody knew Steven, because of the photography. But I don't remember him having any close friends. He always seemed to me to be pretty much on his own."

"Did he have a girlfriend?"

"Not that I know of."

"Do you think he was homosexual?"

The principal looked surprised. He shook his head. "No. Sometimes you have a hunch. But it's seldom that kids that age are open about it. Most of the time they're fighting it, if it's there. It scares the hell out of them. They don't want to be different. Not in a town this size."

"Probably not in any town," said Alberg.

"In some of the bigger schools there's a constituency. So they can acknowledge each other. And that makes it easier."

"In Steven's case, you didn't even have a hunch?"

"No."

"Did he do drugs?"

"I never had any reason to think so."

Alberg closed his notebook. "Any of his photographs still lying around?"

"As it happens," said the principal, "we had a reunion in the spring. A ten-year reunion. So we pulled the yearbook, of course, and some of the newspapers from that year. And that was Steven's year."

"Did he show up for the reunion?"

McMurtry shook his head.

"Can I have a look?"

"Sure you can." McMurtry stood up. "We can go over to the school now, if you like."

"Great."

McMurtry went down the hall into what Alberg assumed was a bedroom. Alberg heard murmurings; McMurtry's wife, he'd been told, was an invalid.

"Okay, let's go," said the principal, returning to the living room. Alberg thought he looked guilty; Alberg would have liked to meet his wife.

Annabelle wandered, restless, through her house, aware of its emptiness and quiet. In the room with the window wall the heat was
overpowering; she'd had to move some of the tenderer plants out of
there, and now her family complained about the four-foot hibiscus
taking up space in the living room, and the seven-foot weeping fig that
was crammed into the girls' bedroom, and the five azaleas in the
kitchen. And Herman hated the miniature rose in their bedroom; he
said it stuck him with its thorns whenever he had to get up in the night.

Herman got up a lot in the night. He had taken to prowling
around the yard every hour or so, checking on the animals in
their cages. Protecting his investment, he said. Since the cops
wouldn't do their job.

The phone rang.

"Where the hell were you last night?"

"Oh Bobby, I'm sorry." Annabelle twisted the telephone
cord around her hand. "I couldn't come. I had an accident."

"Did you get hurt?"

"No no. Oh no. Only my dress. I'm fine."

She almost smiled, to hear him thinking so busily.

"What kind of an accident was it?"

"Oh heavens." Annabelle's laugh sounded artificial, even to
her. "I told you, it was nothing." She pretended that she saw her
children running toward the house. "Oh Bobby, I have to go.
I'll see you—oh, tomorrow, okay? Okay? Bye." Annabelle hung
up, trembling, before he could protest.

She went outside, and the screen door banged behind her,
bouncing in its frame. She walked quickly past the animal
cages, averting her eyes, and kept on going until she got to the
edge of the gravel road, where a big fir tree grew. She sat on the
carpet of needles and leaned against the trunk.

There flashed into her mind a picture of Steven Grayson
falling from the cliff. Had it felt like flying, for a moment? Or
had he known, all the way down, that flying was impossible?

Annabelle rested, in the dry heat of the day.

Percy Grayson put a sign in the window announcing that his shop was closed. "What's this all about, then?"

"We're investigating the circumstances of your nephew's death," said Alberg, "because it wasn't a natural death."

Percy rubbed vigorously at the top of his head, which was bald. "It surely wasn't. What a god-awful thing."

Alberg figured Steven's uncle was pretty close to sixty. He was a big man, six feet tall, tanned and fit. He was wearing dark brown slacks and a short-sleeved tan shirt with thin dark brown stripes.

"Just a hell of a thing."

"Thanks for taking the time to see me," said Alberg, opening his notebook. Percy adjusted a discreet SALE sign that hung on the wall above a rack of summer clothing. "I used to be a fisherman," he said. "Did you know that?"

Alberg shook his head.

"Well I did. Then six years ago this summer we had the best sockeye run in seventy-five years. I made myself a packet. So the wife says, let's do this or let's do that, and so on and so forth. But I knew exactly what I was gonna do." He gestured proudly. "Get myself a store. Sell men's clothes. And that's what I did."

"It's a very nice store," said Alberg.

"Come on, sit down, we might as well be comfortable."

They were in an area at the rear of the shop, near the four changing rooms. There was a grouping of chairs and a sofa, and a big wooden coffee table bearing a selection of magazines. Most were news magazines, but Alberg saw a copy of Vogue, too, and realized that most of the people who sat there waiting were probably women.

"I'm not gonna be much help to you," said Percy. "See, in the last ten years we hardly saw Stevie at all."

"We think the reason he died has to do with his life here," said Alberg, "before he went away. That's what I want you to talk about."

Percy looked doubtful.

"Tell me about his parents. Was he close to them?"

"My brother Harry," said Percy, after a pause, "he was gone a lot. Out in the woods. He could be in a logging camp for weeks, even months at a time. That job's even worse than fishing, if you ask me. And then when he did get home he'd lay down the law." He shook his head in disgust. "Stevie got along good with his mom, though."

"What can you tell me about his friends?"

"Nothing. All I remember is, he was always taking pictures."

"He was a good photographer, right?"

"Yeah, I guess so. Damned annoying, though. Never asked your permission, always snapping away. Sometimes it was just because he was nervous, I think." Percy shook his head. "Mustn't speak ill of the dead," he said tiredly. "He was a good boy, Stevie was."

"Did you see him when he came home this summer?"

"We did, yes. The wife and me, we had the two of them to supper right after he arrived."

"Did he tell you why he'd come back?"

"Just said he'd come for a visit. That's all."

Alberg sat back. "What kind of a man was your nephew turning out to be, Mr. Grayson?"

Percy pondered the question, staring at his shoes, which were brown, highly polished loafers. Finally, "I don't have any idea, really. You couldn't get real close to Stevie," he said heavily. "At least, I couldn't."

Annabelle, who had fallen asleep under the tree, awoke gradually, feeling a sweet burgeoning inside her. For a moment she thought that when she opened her eyes Bobby would be there, smiling down at her. But it wasn't Bobby, it was Camellia. She was sitting cross-legged, looking intently at Annabelle. And Annabelle turned her head slowly to the left and saw that Erna Remple's mangy dog was there, too, and that he had fallen asleep in the heat with his muzzle in her hand, in Annabelle's hand; she felt his warm anxious breath on her palm.

The sweetness inside her began to ache.

"Don't be mad, Ma," said Camellia—softly, so as not to waken the dog.

Annabelle, gazing at Camellia, thought: Bobby Ransome was my childhood sweetheart. She liked the words: "childhood sweetheart."

She heard a whirring sound, and looked up and saw a flock of medium-sized brown birds swoop down to occupy the branches of a tree across the road; their flight had been so single-minded that she thought the tree might be magnetized in some way, and the birds powerless to bypass it once they were within its range.

She looked down at the dog, who was twitching in his sleep. "I'm not mad," she said to Camellia.

Camellia stood up, and the dog awakened, and lifted his head. He looked at Annabelle, whose hand still rested, palm up, on the ground beside her. Then he moved close to Camellia and swiped at her grimy knee with his tongue, and trotted off up the gravel road, toward home.

"Can I help you make supper?" said Camellia.

"When it's time, you surely may." Annabelle got to her feet and wiped her hands on her dress. She began to follow Camellia across the yard. Then she stopped, and walked to the edge of the road, where Herman had hammered a sign into a hole in the dirt.

"Mini-Zoo," it read. "Adults $2, Kids $1."

"Camellia," said Annabelle. She held out her hand, and Camellia took hold of it with both of hers.

"Swing me around, Ma," said Camellia.

"Tomorrow," said Annabelle, "we're going to start doing something. You and I and Rose-Iris."

"What? What're we going to do?"

"See this sign here?"

"I see it."

"Starting tomorrow, we're going to take this sign down every morning. And put it up again every afternoon. And we're not going to tell your dad."

Camellia frowned at the sign. "Why're we going to do that?"

"Because the mini-zoo is, in my opinion, a silly idea." Annabelle swooped down and picked up Camellia and headed for the house. Camellia's legs circled Annabelle's waist, and her arms were around Annabelle's neck. Camellia threw back her head and laughed at the bright summer sky.

Back at the detachment, Alberg sat in his office with the door closed and the window open wide. On his desk lay a large brown envelope stuffed with yearbooks and copies of the school newspaper from 1978 to the graduation ceremonies in 1980; he'd found nothing useful there. He was flipping through his notebook, jotting down on a pad of lined yellow paper what he'd found out about Steven Grayson's last weeks:

Up to June 17, the kid had lived his life as usual.

June 17: he calls his mother and tells her he wants to come home for a while.

June 18–28: he finishes several assignments, and gets extensions on several others.

June 29: he takes the ferry to the Sunshine Coast; according to Velma Grayson he intends to spend two or three weeks.

July 3: he calls Natalie; the guy he wants to see won't see him. She tells him to persevere.

July 19: he goes to the Bank of Montreal in Sechelt, where he runs into Keith Nugent and arranges to borrow his boat on

Saturday, the 21st. Then he tries to withdraw most of the contents of his savings account. But the bank won't let him, because it isn't his branch. He takes the ferry to Vancouver and gets it from his own bank. He phones Natalie and tells her everything's going to be okay.

July 20: he tells his mother he's going to meet somebody the next day, Saturday, but that it won't take long and he'll be back in time for dinner with his aunt and uncle.

July 21: he falls from the cliff top at Buccaneer Bay wearing a belt containing twenty-three thousand dollars.

Sometime between July 3 and July 19, he must have persuaded this guy, whoever he was, to see him.

Alberg made another list: what was it that he wanted to "put right"? why did he decide to do it now? what happened to the missing camera?

Then he got a call from Natalie Walenchuk.

"I have something here," she said. "It's some pictures. Some photographs. And negatives. I forgot all about them."

"What photographs?"

"They're Steven's. He left them with me. He said he'd phone me from Sechelt when he'd finished whatever he was doing, and then I was supposed to burn them in my fireplace."

"Have you looked at them?"

She hesitated. "Yeah, I did. They're very ordinary. Mostly just pictures of people. I don't know who they are. You'll want to see them, right?"

"Right," said Alberg.

"Well I'm coming over there in the morning," said Natalie. "I want to meet his mother. Pay my respects. I could bring them."

Chapter Twenty-Nine

"**I** thought you must have left town," said Warren.

He'd gone into the drugstore for some throat lozenges—Bobby was the furthest thing from his mind, for once—and there he was. Buying himself a hair dryer, for Pete's sake. He looked jumpy, Bobby did; as if he'd been trying to steal the thing. But he was standing in the lineup so obviously he planned to pay for it.

"Why'd you say that?" said Bobby, turning swiftly to Warren.

"Haven't seen you around," said Warren. "That's all I meant."

"Yeah, well, I'm not gonna *be* around much longer," said Bobby, getting out his wallet. He had a way of moving, Bobby did, that made a person cautious. Made you watch him very carefully. So you could get out of the way in a hurry.

Warren was shifting from foot to foot, feeling awkward, wanting to break away and go find the throat lozenges. But being too nervous to do that, for some reason.

"Oh yeah?" said Warren.

"Yeah. Gotta move on, you know?"

"So is your stepdad better, then?"

"Yeah," said Bobby. "Better enough."

Warren said, "Well I'm on my break, and it's already used up." Bobby was paying for the hair dryer now. Warren said, "Well, seeya," and he backed off toward where he thought the throat lozenges might be.

He didn't like it at all that Bobby followed him over there, carrying the drugstore bag containing his new hair dryer.

"Is he taking good care of her, Warren?" said Bobby softly.

Warren didn't have to ask who "her" was. "Her" was Annabelle. Warren was exceedingly alarmed, as he scanned the selection of lozenges. There was everything from cherry to eucalyptus looking him in the face. Bobby was waiting for him to answer, so he said, "Yeah, I'm pretty sure of it, Bobby." He picked up a package of mentholated cough drops, then put them down again.

"She happy with him, is she?"

"Yeah, I think so, Bob," said Warren. Maybe cherry would be better, he thought.

"I'm gonna replace my car," Bobby said abruptly.

"Oh yeah?" It's damn hot in here, thought Warren, reaching for a package of black lozenges. I've gotta get out of here, he thought, before I drown in my own sweat.

"Yeah," said Bobby, picking up a box of Vicks. "Gonna be on the road. Gotta get a reliable set of wheels."

"You got the money for that?"

"Why? Aren't ex-cons supposed to have money, Warren?"

"Oh, hey, sure, Bob, I'm sorry, I just thought—"

"I don't have it yet, as it happens," said Bobby. "But I'm gettin' it."

"Good, good," said Warren.

"So I thought maybe you could advise me," said Bobby. He put the cough drops back. "You know. The make, the model, the year."

"Yeah, I could do that, Bob," said Warren, easing past him in the narrow aisle.

"Good," said Bobby, following him to the cashier.

Warren looked blindly into his wallet. He felt himself flushing, and fumbled in his pants pocket for change.

"I forgot to go to the bank," he said to the cashier, who shrugged.

She was chewing gum and wore a lot of makeup.

Bobby reached in front of him and slapped a Loonie down on the counter. "My treat," he said, and Warren watched as he left the drugstore.

"I need another quarter," said the cashier, snapping her gum.

Warren dug again into his pocket and came up with a quarter. He picked up his cough drops and started for the door, walking slow, but when he went through it onto the sidewalk Bobby was still there, leaning against a blue '79 Datsun.

"I'll stop by, then," said Bobby. "About the car."

Chapter Thirty

Velma Grayson opened her front door. When she saw Alberg, she said, "Did you arrest somebody?"

He shook his head.

"It's the only thing I can think of that might make me feel better."

"May I talk to you for a few minutes?"

"Of course," said Velma, and held the door open.

Alberg hesitated. He couldn't hear the furnace. But he didn't want to take any chances. "Do you think we could talk out here?"

They sat on the veranda, in a pair of green-and-white-striped lawn chairs.

"I should offer you some tea," she said.

"No, really. I don't need anything." He opened his note-book. "I've spoken to his friend Natalie," he said, and told her what he'd learned.

"But what did he have to feel guilty about?" said Steven's mother, bewildered.

"He wouldn't tell her."

Velma looked perplexed. "But he's been gone for ten years."

"I know. Maybe it happened before he left."

She got up and went to the edge of the veranda, and leaned on the railing. "I don't have any idea what it could be," she said dully, staring at the willow tree that grew between the house and the street.

"You might have the key to it, though," said Alberg.

She turned to face him, her back to the railing. "What do you mean?"

"It looks like he made up his mind to come home during his phone conversation with you on June seventeenth. Because he didn't start shuffling around his work load until the next day. I'd like you to think back very hard to that conversation. What he said to you—but especially what you said to him."

"It was just like all our conversations. He called home regularly. To make sure I was well. To keep in touch. And to hear what was going on in Sechelt."

Alberg waited. Her front lawn was brown. So was the one across the street. Everybody's lawn was brown.

"Bank tellers," said Velma, "we hear just about all the news there is. And Steven wanted me to pass it all on to him. And I did so, with pleasure." She sat down again, her hands resting on her thighs. "I liked it that he still had an interest in the town."

"What news did you have for him that day?" said Alberg.

She'd told him that Mr. McMurtry, the high school principal, was retiring after this year. And about Wendell Simpkins getting fined for dumping his restaurant trash into the ocean. And Gloria Jang, who had gone to school with Steven, was pregnant again for the fifth time. And Joe Borovsky got drunk at the Legion Hall and drove through a stop sign near the Old Age Pensioners' Hall and nearly hit a child on a bike. And Bobby Ransome who'd gone to jail years ago was back in town, because his father was sick. And Peter Jenkins had left his wife, Maude. And the Glasscos' house had been robbed.

"That's it?" said Alberg, and Velma said it was.

"Okay," said Alberg. "That's very good. I appreciate it."

"I don't see how it can help you, though."

"Well that's because we're not quite finished yet. We're going to go over it again, now. And I want you to tell me everything you know about these people. Will you do that?"

"Of course," said Steven's mother.

Chapter Thirty-One

It was late afternoon and Hetty was preparing to go out on her bicycle, to patrol the northwest quadrant of the village, when her nephew arrived, unexpected but welcome.

She offered him tea or coffee but he didn't want any.

They sat down at her kitchen table, and silence moved into place between them. He rested his elbows on the table and picked up the salt shaker and poured some salt into the palm of his left hand; then he didn't seem to know what to do with it. He got up and brushed it into the sink. And sat down again. Trouble was written all over his face.

"Aunt Hetty?"

She looked at him inquiringly and nodded, showing him reassurance instead of the alarm she felt.

"Ah, I gotta move on, I think."

Hetty couldn't hide her dismay. She reached over to put a protesting hand on his arm...and from among her memories came an image of Bobby squatting next to a parked car, fumbling with a valve cap.

"I know," he said, patting her hand. "But I gotta."

He'd collected a whole jar of them, from cars all over Sechelt. "Henry's better. My mom's stopped worryin' about him so much, anyway."

And his dad had made him put them all back.

"So—uh, I'm gonna be on my way."

Nobody saw him, when he was collecting them. But a lot of people saw him the second time around. And not many were prepared to believe that he was putting their valve caps back.

"The thing is…" He got up and pulled something from his jeans pocket, and handed it to her.

It was the note she'd given him, folded twice: it said, "You're in my will. The house. And money." She looked up at him, puzzled.

"I was wondering—" He was shifting around uneasily. "See, Aunt Hetty, I kinda need something right now. New wheels. A car. Because I gotta do some traveling."

Hetty began nodding her head. "Isee. Isee."

"Could you? Is it possible?"

She was thinking rapidly. She'd have to summon her lawyer. Arrange to sell something. Or cash in a bond. "When?"

"When do I need it? Fast. Real fast, Aunt Hetty."

She could deliver a letter to her lawyer in the morning. "Dontknow. Try. Come—" She gave up the struggle and reached for a notepad. "I'll find out," she wrote. "How much?"

"A couple of thousand?" He hesitated. "Five, maybe?"

"I'll try," Hetty scrawled.

Chapter Thirty-Two

"**S**omebody told me today that he was murdered, Karl, that young man on the beach; is that true?" She had come to his house in Gibsons straight from work; the library stayed open until nine o'clock in the summertime, and although it was usually staffed by volunteers in the evenings, someone had called in sick and Cassandra had filled in for him.

"Come inside," said Alberg. He closed the screen door behind her but left the other door open. It was still very hot in the house, but beginning to get cooler outdoors. "We don't know yet. Maybe."

She sat down in the wingback chair by the window and put her big denim handbag on the floor. "My God. I can't believe it."

"Hey, I'm about to have a beer and a sandwich. How about you?"

"No, thanks. I just—it's terribly upsetting. What've you found out?"

"Not much," said Alberg vaguely, hands in the pockets of his faded jeans.

"Oh you're so damned annoying." Cassandra felt rattled. Spooked. And not at all calmed by Alberg's large, solid, noncommittal presence. She sank back in the chair and stared moodily out the window.

"Well," said Alberg after a minute, "I'm going to get you a beer and a sandwich anyway."

"Not tuna," said Cassandra. "I hate tuna."

"Okay," said Alberg, and disappeared into the kitchen.

The younger of his two cats came slinking around the corner of the long chesterfield that divided the room into living room and dining area. She was a spayed female, black, with a white smudge on her nose, white front paws, and a white chest. Cassandra looked around for one of the scrunched-up balls of foil that usually lay about for the cats to play with, but she couldn't spot any. "Sorry, cat," she said.

Through the open door and windows she heard a car pull up in front of Alberg's house. It'll be Diana, she thought. She tried to make her gaze casual and disinterested as she peered through the twilight. But it wasn't Diana.

Cassandra watched with growing alarm as she approached the door, a young woman in walking shorts and a T-shirt, wearing sandals, a leather bag slung over her shoulder. She was dark-haired and really very young.

"Karl," Cassandra called out, getting to her feet, "someone's coming to your house." Maybe it's one of Diana's friends, she thought. Of course it is. Who else could it be? On the other hand, she thought, moving reluctantly toward the door, he was about to be fifty and due for a midlife crisis, and maybe she, this young person out there on his porch, maybe she was it.

He emerged from the kitchen just as Cassandra opened the door.

"Mrs. Alberg?" said the young woman.

Cassandra, disoriented, muttered something unintelligible, and thought of Hetty Willis.

"Natalie," said Karl, coming up behind Cassandra, who noticed that he didn't sound surprised to see her.

The girl held up a large manila envelope. "I decided not to wait till morning."

Alberg reached around Cassandra and pushed open the screen door.

They sat down in the living room, and Alberg made introductions.

Natalie, on the chesterfield, clutched the envelope. "I went to your office first," she said, "and they told me how to find you."

"I know. They called me."

Cassandra picked up her denim bag. "I should go, Karl."

"No, don't go," he said quickly. "Really. Stay. I'll get us some coffee."

But when Cassandra offered to do that for him, he didn't object.

"How are you doing?" said Alberg to Natalie. "Are you all right?"

She shook her head. "Not really." She placed the envelope flat on her lap and stroked it, smoothing it.

Alberg heard sounds from the kitchen. He wondered if Natalie liked cats. Did she have a boyfriend? A lover? Where did her parents live? Had she told them about Steven?

"He told me once," she said suddenly, "—he said his earliest memory was his father's arms. He said they were brown, and very strong." She looked over at Alberg, sitting in the wingback chair. "His father was a logger."

Alberg nodded.

"He was standing and his father was crouched behind him, with his arms around him. Steven said he remembered seeing his dad's arms, and the sleeves of his flannel shirt rolled up past his elbows, and his hands. The hair on his arms and hands was bleached by the sun, he said. It looked like gold flecks. Sparkles. He said it was a good memory." She dug in her leather bag for a package of tissues. "Shit."

Cassandra came in with a tray, and Alberg helped unload mugs, cream, sugar, spoons, and the coffeepot. By the time the coffee had been poured and served, Natalie had collected herself.

"You graduated this year?" said Alberg, and Natalie nodded. "What's your degree?"

"Education."

"Education," he repeated approvingly. "Have you got a job in September?"

"Yeah," she said. "I'm one of the lucky ones."

"Where?"

"Prince George."

Alberg thought about Janey, wherever the hell she was, and Diana; Bachelors of Arts, the both of them. He often felt glum and fearful, contemplating his daughters' futures. You could do a lot worse, he thought, than teach school in Prince George.

"Okay," he said. "Let's have a look." Natalie handed him the envelope and he pulled out the photographs.

A younger Hugh McMurtry in a school hallway, looking patiently at the camera, obviously wanting to be on his way.

Two women in a parking lot, at night. One was laughing, with her head thrown back.

A chunk of rain forest. It could have been anywhere on the B.C. coast. Huge trees, ferns, logs, brush—all surrounding a clearing through which a small stream flowed.

Alex Gillingham, perched on the end of his examining table, hands folded on his thighs, wearing his stethoscope, a white coat, and an indulgent smile.

A young man lounging on a bench in the corner of a locker room. Wearing sweats and running shoes; his feet drawn up. He gazed at the camera impassively; a chunk of blond hair hung over his forehead.

The same young man with his arms around a dark-haired girl; he was kissing her neck.

Hetty Willis. Younger. Another outside shot; night. It looked like the same parking lot. She was peering around a tall man whose back was to the camera.

Finally, an old man wearing overalls, a cap, and round glasses with wire frames. He was sitting on a bench against a brick wall. His breast pockets were full of ballpoint pens. He looked very happy.

As Alberg looked at each one, he passed it on to Cassandra.

"Who do you know, here?" he said when they'd both seen all of the photographs.

"Hetty Willis," said Cassandra. "Alex Gillingham. And that piece of forest."

"Are any of them familiar to you?" said Alberg to Natalie.

"No," she said, shaking her head.

"What did Steven say about them?"

"Nothing," she said firmly. "He gave me the envelope, like I told you. He said he was going to phone me from Sechelt when he'd finished things here, and tell me to burn it."

"And you asked him what was in it."

"Sure I did. He said, 'Pictures.'"

"And then you probably asked him why he wanted them burned."

"Sure. He said, because they were a part of his life that would soon be over."

"But why wouldn't he burn them himself?"

"Because he didn't want anything lying around, when he got back, that he didn't want to see."

Alberg turned to Cassandra. "Do you know who this is?" he said, pointing to the kid kissing his girlfriend.

"No," said Cassandra. "But isn't this the same guy, in the picture with Hetty Willis?"

Alberg looked at it more closely. "Yeah. It looks like the same jacket." He shuffled through the photos again. "McMurtry. Gillingham. And by God"—he moved one of them directly under the light from the standing lamp next to the sofa—"I think this is the Ferguson woman. The one laughing."

"And the old man in the overalls used to manage the Petro-Canada station," said Cassandra. "He died a few years ago."

"What can you tell me about the piece of forest?"

Cassandra laughed. "It's a clearing behind the high school. It's a make-out place," she said, and instantly blushed. "Has been for years," she added lamely.

"What do you think?" said Natalie to Alberg. "Will they be any help?"

"Probably," he said. He stood up and headed for the kitchen, in search of sandwiches and beer. He just didn't have the faintest idea how.

Chapter Thirty-Three

"I can't do it, Bobby," said Annabelle on Wednesday. "Not today."

"That's what you said yesterday."

"Yes and I might say it again tomorrow, too. I can't just up and do whatever I like, you know. I'm a married woman." Annabelle was standing in the kitchen, keeping her voice low even though she knew there was nobody else in the house, keeping her eye on the door.

"A married woman," he snorted. "Some kind of a married woman you are."

"I'm the only kind I know how to be."

"You'd be a different kind if it was me you were married to."

She didn't bother to respond to that. "I have to go, Bobby." The azaleas lined up on the buffet looked positively parched, she noticed.

"Some kind of a friend you are, too."

"Oh, Bobby," she said, exasperated. "It is so much trouble, having you in my life."

"I need to talk to you, Annabelle. I told you. I really do." He hesitated. "I'm going away. And I gotta tell you why."

Annabelle's gaze fixed on the screen door. "What do you mean? You just barely got here, for heaven's sake."

"My aunt's giving me the money."

"Well talk to me on the phone, Bobby."

"I can't talk about it on the phone," he said flatly. "I'm not gonna beg you, for Christ's sake."

Annabelle could see Camellia through the screen, watering the animals. "I could meet you tomorrow afternoon."

"For sure, this time, Annabelle?"

"For sure."

"You promise?"

"I promise."

Annabelle went to the buffet and rubbed at the soil in the azalea pots. It was dry as a bone. She watered them, then she watered the rest of her plants. This took her almost an hour.

Then she found herself in the bedroom, going through her side of the closet, tossing clothes out over her shoulder. Most of them were landing on the floor, although some got as far as the bed. She flipped impatiently through the hangers, assessing each garment against some need or credo that she hadn't identified but to which she was responding with urgency. If Rose-Iris were to have come into the room and said, "Ma, what are you doing?" Annabelle would have replied, "I'm cleaning out this closet, there isn't room in it for a single more thing."

She whipped a red dress off its hanger, and then a green one: maybe I'm getting rid of all my dresses, she said to herself. Is that what I'm doing? But no, her hand had moved past the yellow dress, and the pink one, so that couldn't be it.

She didn't understand why he'd decided to leave. She was quite certain he'd be better off here. There were all sorts of jobs he could do. Logging. Or working on the tugboats. All sorts of things.

She shook her head, as if to dislodge things caught in the fringes of her brain. If she could shake them into her blood they might come out with the next menstrual flow and she'd be done with them, rid of them. Oh dear oh dear, thought Annabelle.

She was suddenly tired—her body was throbbing with exhaustion—but she squatted down, her hands pressing on her kneecaps, and peered into the darkness of the bottom of the closet. She smelled the smell of foot sweat down there, and saw huge dust balls.

Yesterday she'd planted another rosebush. She didn't want any more. Seven was enough. Maybe six had been enough.

Annabelle hauled out sneakers and pumps and sandals, sending them flying one by one with the back of her hand.

She thought, whenever I go out of the house, I hear the animals. They make sounds that are listless and desolate. They have exotic voices, and speak something that isn't words.

It was the heat, maybe.

"Ma! Ma!"

Annabelle's heart stopped beating; then it rushed to start again, tripping over itself. She scrambled to her feet and raced out of the bedroom; would there be blood? would she be calm? would she know what to do?

She found them outside, dancing from foot to foot in the dust of the yard, and behind them the animal cages lay in a sullen sprawl.

"What is it?" said Annabelle, breathless. "My heaven, you scared my heart clear out of my chest, I thought one of you was dead."

Their eyes were large, and Camellia was blinking rapidly. "There's stuff on the window wall," she said.

"Paint," said Rose-Iris, walking backward, her hand stretched out toward Annabelle. "Come and see."

Annabelle followed them around the corner.

Huge letters, spray-painted in black. They made tears come to her eyes. They hurt her in the chest. "Whore of Babylon," they spelled. Annabelle glanced around quickly but there was nobody else in the yard, no cars on the gravel road.

"Somebody must have done it in the night," said Rose-Iris.

"Yuck," said Camellia, with a shiver. "Will it come off, Ma?"

"Of course it'll come off," said Annabelle. "We'll roll up our sleeves and get ourselves a couple of stepladders and some turpentine and a pile of rags and we'll get that off there right now, that's what we'll do." She pushed her hair away from her face with trembling fingers. "Come along," she said, "and be smart about it." She marched around the corner and toward the shed, her daughters tumbling along in her wake, and they collected what they needed.

Much later, they stood back and looked.

"That glass, it's never been so clean," said Annabelle, panting. She dropped to the ground. "I'm spent," she said. "Thank you for your help, Rose-Iris."

"That's okay, Ma," said Rose-Iris, sitting beside her.

"And me, me," said Camellia. "For the iced tea."

"And thank you, too, Camellia," said Annabelle, "for the iced tea."

"Ma," said Rose-Iris, craning her neck to see behind her. "Look. You forgot to take down the sign."

"Ah yes," said Annabelle calmly. "I must have done. For there it is, sitting in its hole, pointing right at us."

The girls began to giggle.

The three of them put away the ladder, and the turpentine, and Annabelle threw the rags in a plastic bag and sealed it with a twist tie. She told the girls to wash up, and asked Rose-Iris to start dinner. Camellia groaned when she was asked to set the table, and stomped around the kitchen for a while, but Annabelle ignored her fussing and went on into the bedroom. Soon things were quiet out there; she heard them talking, and china and cutlery clinking, and heard something sizzling and then she smelled it, too, it was hamburger, Rose-Iris was probably making Hamburger Helper.

Annabelle hung up all of her clothes, smoothing them on their hangers with her hands, which had smudges of black paint on them, and smelled of turpentine. She needed a bath, but she wouldn't have time before Herman got home. And it would be more practical to have it afterward, anyway.

He made a lot of noise driving up, as she'd known he would.

She looked quickly around the room, as if another exit might reveal itself; she thought about the window; but how undignified that would be; and she'd made her bed, after all.

He yelled something at Arnold, in the yard, and stomped through the kitchen without speaking to the girls. He came into the bedroom and slammed the door behind him.

She looked at him as if she were tranquil, reached for tranquillity somewhere inside her, tried not to flinch when he came near, and didn't flinch, didn't feel it, really, not the first blow, and then she found herself on the floor looking at dust, smelling dust, tasting slivers of blood.

I will not make a noise, she thought.

I cannot do this anymore, she thought.

Chapter Thirty-Four

"**I** don't get it," said Sokolowski, staring at the photographs. "I remember this guy," he said. "He died. I know Gillingham, too. And Hetty Willis." He looked up at Alberg. "The cat lady. She can't have anything to do with this. What could she have to do with it?"

"I don't know," said Alberg.

"I also know her," said Sokolowski, pointing. "The girl getting her neck kissed, there. She works at my bank. Her name's Wanda." He peered closely at the picture. "She's a lot younger here. Maybe this guy's her husband, who works at the Petro-Can station. Nah. Warren's got dark hair. Who the hell is this guy, anyway?"

"His name's Bobby Ransome," said Alberg.

The sergeant handed back the photographs. "So what're you going to do?"

"I'm going to see these people. All except the dead guy."

"Yeah, right," said the sergeant, smiling despite himself. "We got the description of the camera, by the way. It's a very,

very expensive camera. So I'm putting it out to the pawnshops, et cetera, toot sweet."

"Good," said Alberg. "How about phone calls from the Grayson number?"

"Too soon for that. But we got the property owners. Not by noon, though. The guy sent it over, must have been four, five o'clock."

"Anything interesting?"

"Well I don't know, do I?" said the sergeant plaintively. "What am I looking for, anyway?"

Alberg was moving paper clips around on his desktop. "Sid. What do you know about this Ransome guy? He got sent up for drugs about ten years ago."

"Before my time," said Sokolowski. "Why?"

"He went to school with Grayson. Got out of the slammer about eighteen months ago. He's been living in Vancouver, but he showed up back here in early June. And Velma Grayson reports this to Steven when he phones her, and Steven immediately decides to come home for a while."

"Coincidence," said Sokolowski significantly, "happens more often than people think."

Alberg got up to open his office door. "Jesus it's hot," he muttered. "But she tells me all this, Sid, and I look up Ransome's sheet, and lo and behold, it turns out it's Ransome in all those photos."

"But you said the kid felt responsible for somebody dying," said the sergeant. "This Ransome thing, it was just a drug bust, wasn't it?"

"That's what I want to find out," said Alberg. "Get somebody to drag the files out of dead storage. Court records, exhibits entered—everything there is."

"Anything else?" said the sergeant, watching Alberg as he absentmindedly picked up the pile of evaluation forms, tapped the edges against the desktop to even up the stack, and put it down again.

"Yeah. Get a list of Ransome's friends and relatives, and check it against the property owners. Also, let's find out exactly where this guy is, and then let's keep a quiet eye on him."

Hetty Willis sat on one of the love seats in her sitting room with the scrapbook open on her lap, waiting for her lawyer. But when somebody knocked on her door, it turned out to be the policeman.

"Miss Willis," he said, with another of his smiles. "I wonder if I could ask you to take a look at a photograph?"

She nodded, curious, and he opened a large envelope and pulled out a picture.

It was a photograph of her and Bobby, and it made her smile to see it, and then her smile faded and she grew puzzled, for wherever had it come from?

"Have you seen it before?" said the policeman; Alberg, his name was.

And Hetty's heart was pounding as she shook her head. How on earth had this policeman come upon a photograph of her and her nephew?

"Do you remember when it was taken?"

She stared at it, thinking. "Younger." She thought some more. She nodded, and pointed to Bobby. "Gradation." She shook her head impatiently, tapping the photo. "Grrradation." Finally she hurried into the sitting room for her notebook. "Nephew's graduation," she wrote, and tore off the paper, and gave it to Alberg.

"Is this your nephew? Bobby Ransome?"

Hetty nodded vigorously.

"Do you know who took the picture?"

She kept her head ducked down, looking hard at the photograph. "Donknow. Dinsee." She glanced away; her heart was beating very fast. "Where? Wasit?"

"You mean, where did I find it?"

She nodded.

"Well, I think it was taken by a young man named Steven Grayson," said Alberg. "He died, last Saturday. This was with some other pictures that a friend was keeping for him."

Hetty's mouth dried up. She tried several times to speak. The policeman waited politely. Hetty didn't want to speak, didn't want to know. But she asked it anyway. "How?"

"I'm afraid somebody killed him," said Alberg.

Tears filled Hetty's eyes with the suddenness of pain. She waved off Alberg's hand, raised instinctively to protect or comfort her. She felt centuries old as she stood and walked uncertainly to the front door. She opened the door and waited with her head bowed until he had passed through onto the porch. She thought he was saying something but she wasn't sure. She closed the door gently in his face, and hoped he would overlook her discourtesy.

Chapter Thirty-Five

Herman went away right afterward.

Then Annabelle called out from the bedroom, lightly, "Go ahead with dinner, girls, call Arnold and go ahead, I want to have a bath before I eat."

They didn't argue or protest because there were things they understood, young as they were, and that was awful, but good.

Annabelle slipped quietly into the bathroom and soaked for a long time, holding a cold washcloth against the side of her face. She lay in warm water and pressed coldness against her face; it was an interesting sensation, and seemed likely to completely dispel the pain. She felt a blitheness of spirit growing inside her and it brought tears to her eyes; this was what was called a paradox, but she understood it very well. She lay in the bath in pain, and yet felt happiness grow, or relief; they were the same thing after all, weren't they? Because Herman would stay away all night, and all the next day. And when he came home for dinner tomorrow he would arrive in the yard quietly, and sit quietly at the table, and speak kindly to the children, and in the night, in the warm moistness of their bed, he would quietly apologize, and he would not insist on having sex. So Annabelle had at least thirty-six hours of happiness to look forward to, and she was grateful for that.

She was also relieved to have learned that Herman hadn't meant anything specific by the writing on the window wall. If he'd known anything for sure he would have given her a lot worse beating than she'd gotten, and he would have said something, too. So it was as usual. Time had passed since the last time he'd gotten jealous, enough time so that he'd gotten jealous again. He had some weird clock in him, Herman did, and it kept better time than he knew.

Annabelle sat up, wincing, and wet the washcloth again under the cold-water tap. She wrung it out and settled back in the tub, pressing the cloth cautiously against the right side of her face.

After her bath she brushed her hair and put on clean clothes and went out to the kitchen, where Camellia was doing the dishes. And maybe it was that, the sight of her smallest child doing the dishes, or maybe it was Arnold out in the yard feeding and watering the animals, or maybe it was Rose-Iris sitting in a lawn chair in the room with the window wall, staring out through the window at nothing…whatever it was, Annabelle was suddenly bursting with energy.

She started cleaning the house. She cleaned vigorously, without stopping, for three hours. By the time she'd finished, the sun had lowered itself so far in the western sky that the day was teetering on the brink of night.

The children had trailed along after her for a while, whining with dismay, but Annabelle, singing "Onward, Christian Soldiers" as she worked, ignored them except to tell them cheerfully to get out of her way or stop bothering her.

She cleaned the bathroom and the kitchen. She cleaned the big bedroom and the girls' bedroom. She would have cleaned Arnold's bedroom, too, except that he flung himself past her and stood in front of his door with arms and legs outstretched, barring her passage, and there was a look of frantic pleading on his face, so Annabelle laughed and turned away.

She washed floors and polished windows. She wiped out the fridge and the cupboards, and cleaned the top of the stove, though not the oven, and went around the house with a spray bottle of Mr. Clean rubbing at dirt on walls and window ledges.

She was doing the inside of the window wall, a task that took almost half an hour all by itself, when she said to Rose-Iris, "Heat me up some of that hamburger stuff, will you? And maybe make a pot of tea."

When she finally finished she was tired and sweaty and filled with satisfaction. I'll have to have me another bath before I go to bed, she thought, and that reminded her of another chore. She hurried into the bedroom, stripped the bed and remade it with clean sheets.

"Come on, Ma," said Rose-Iris. "It's ready."

Annabelle sat at the kitchen table and ate hungrily. She had a plateful of Hamburger Helper, a mug of sweetened tea and two pieces of white bread. She always bought whole-wheat bread for the rest of the family, because it was good for them, but she got white bread for herself because she preferred it. Annabelle loved real butter, too, but seldom bought it because margarine was cheaper. She had been very happy when for her birthday last March Rose-Iris and Camellia had given her a pound of real butter. It was a joke present, but it was a very good present.

Arnold had gone off into the living room to watch TV and Rose-Iris was in her room, getting ready for bed. Camellia sat at the table, her chin in her hand, watching Annabelle eat. "The house sure is clean," she said.

Annabelle nodded. "It's so clean I won't have a thing to do tomorrow. I can spend hours in my garden."

And hours with Bobby, she thought.

Camellia pushed some bread crumbs around on the surface of the kitchen table. "What did those words mean, Ma? The ones we took off the window wall."

Annabelle swallowed what was in her mouth and took a long drink of tea. She stood, and picked up her dishes. "They're words from the Bible," she said calmly, putting her plate and mug in the sink. "Somebody's mind dredged them up from the Bible, and smeared them all over the glass. It's a good thing they were put on glass, I can tell you," she said, squirting dish detergent into the sink. "It would have been a darn sight harder to get them off wood, for instance." She turned on the hot-water tap. "It's time you were in bed, Camellia. It's getting late."

"Tell me a story about when you were a little girl," said Camellia. "Please?"

Annabelle sighed, and flicked water at her.

Camellia ducked. "Please?"

"Get yourself into bed," said Annabelle. "Then maybe I'll tell you a story."

She was washing her dishes when Arnold wandered into the kitchen.

"Is Dad coming back tonight?" he said.

Annabelle kept her back to him. It was in the presence of her son that she felt most troubled, as though this was where her greatest failure lay. Which was very odd, under the circumstances.

She put her plate in the drainer and began washing the saucepan in which Rose-Iris had heated her dinner.

"Because if he isn't," said Arnold, "I could get up in the night, and check on the animals."

"I don't think you need to worry about the animals," said Annabelle.

"But Dad worries about them," said Arnold.

She heard chair legs scrape across the floor, heard him sit down. He was probably straddling the chair, like his father liked to do.

Annabelle rinsed out the saucepan and set it in the drainer. She let the water out of the sink, wrung out the dishcloth and wiped the counters, sluiced clean water around in the sink. She folded the dishcloth and then she turned around.

She saw a tiny flinch occur in Arnold's face when he got a good look at the bruise on her cheek. His eyes slid away from her. She'd have to put makeup on that bruise, tomorrow.

"If I happen to wake up," he said, "I'll go out and have a look around."

Annabelle nodded. She wanted to reach out and touch his face, and pull him close to her for a big hug. But she was afraid that he would draw away from her, out of contempt, the worst kind of contempt, the kind that grew reluctantly out of love.

"You're a good person, Arnold," she said.

He shuffled awkwardly to his feet. "I'm gonna go watch TV."

Camellia called out from the girls' bedroom.

Annabelle found them both in bed. Rose-Iris was reading a book and Camellia was lying down, the sheet up to her chin, the rest of the covers folded neatly at the bottom of her bed. Annabelle, standing in the doorway, gazing upon her daughters, realized that she was smiling.

"Tell me a story," said Camellia.

"A story about what?"

"Tell me about Sunday dinners," said Camellia. She patted the edge of her bed, and Annabelle sat down.

"Sunday dinners. The ones you mean, that was when I was just about Arnold's age, and we lived not far from my grandparents."

"Your mother's mother and your mother's father," said Camellia.

"Yes," said Annabelle. "That's right."

"And Uncle Warren was just a bitty baby," said Camellia.

"Yes," said Annabelle.

"And your grandma and grandpa were very old," said Camellia.

"Not so very old," said Annabelle. "They were about sixty, I guess."

"Your grandpa was tall and skinny," said Camellia.

"Let Ma tell it," said Rose-Iris irritably. She'd put her book down, with a bookmark in it, and had linked her hands behind her head.

"Yes, my grandfather was tall and skinny," said Annabelle. "He wore round eyeglasses, and his hair, which was white, was combed straight back from his forehead. He always seemed to be wearing a suit, although he must have worn other things some of the time."

"At night," said Camellia, giggling. "He must have worn pajamas at night."

"And the suit was always gray," said Annabelle, smoothing her skirt. She leaned back on her hands and crossed her ankles. "I remember that his pants had belt loops but he never wore a belt, he used suspenders instead. And he'd have on a white shirt, and a tie that was mostly gray."

"What about his shoes?" said Camellia.

"Black," said Annabelle promptly.

"And tell me about your grandma," said Camellia.

"She was a little person," said Annabelle, and Camellia giggled again. "She sat very straight and some of the chairs, like the dining room chairs, were a little bit high, I guess, because when she sat on them her feet didn't quite touch the floor. She wore dresses all the time, all the time, and a round brooch at the neck, and black shoes with sensible heels, that laced up. She had white hair, too, and it had lots of little waves in it. She grew African violets," said Annabelle. "My grandfather built a little greenhouse for her, in their back yard, and it was jam-packed with African violets."

"And they'd come for dinner on Sundays," said Rose-Iris, being helpful.

"That's right. And it seems to me—" Annabelle leaned forward, her hands loose in her lap. "Memories are very funny things. You can be absolutely sure of something and then find out that you were wrong about it. It's very disconcerting."

"What's 'disconcerting'?" said Camellia.

"Annoying," said Rose-Iris. "Confusing. Like that. Go on, Ma."

"Well," said Annabelle, "in my memory we had roast beef and Yorkshire pudding every single time my grandparents came for dinner. But we probably didn't. But that's the way I remember it."

"And you'd have to set the table," said Camellia.

"Yes. But I didn't mind. I liked setting the table."

"First you put on the tablecloth," said Camellia.

"First she put on the silence cloth," said Arnold.

They all three turned and saw him lounging against the door frame.

"Well," he said defensively, "I can be here if I like."

"Of course you can," said Annabelle. "Yes, that's right, first the silence cloth. And then the tablecloth. And then the silverware and the china."

"And the napkins," said Rose-Iris. "In the napkin holders."

"That's right," said Annabelle.

"Then you'd have to peel the potatoes," said Camellia.

"And put the pickles in the pickle dish," said Rose-Iris.

"And you'd have roast beef," said Arnold, "and Yorkshire pudding."

"And maybe carrots," said Camellia.

"And a lemon pie for dessert," said Rose-Iris.

"Because that was your dad's favorite," said Arnold.

The children looked at one another.

Arnold ambled off down the hallway toward his room. Rose-Iris sighed, and picked up her book.

"Thanks, Ma," said Camellia, turning over so that the light from Rose-Iris's bedside lamp wouldn't shine upon her face.

"Goodnight," said Annabelle. She went into the room with the window wall, where she sat in a lawn chair and looked through glass at the black, starlit sky.

Eventually, she went to bed.

That night nobody in the house awakened.

In the morning when Arnold went out to tend to the animals he found the lock on the shed door broken, and the bags of feed inside slashed and emptied, and he saw that another cage had been opened, and the raccoons were gone.

Chapter Thirty-Six

On Thursday morning Alberg caught up with Alex Gillingham while the doctor was doing his hospital rounds. Alberg pulled out the photograph and put it down on the counter at the nursing station. Gillingham looked at it uncomprehendingly and said, "What is it?"

"It's a picture of you, Alex. Steven Grayson took it."

"He did?"

"You don't remember?"

Gillingham shook his head. "But he always had a camera with him. It got so you never even noticed it."

"There's another thing," said Alberg.

"Go ahead."

"He apparently felt responsible for somebody's death."

"Who, Steven?"

"Yeah. You got any ideas?"

Gillingham thought for a moment. "The only person in his life who died that I knew about was his father."

"Yeah. But I think this thing happened before that."

"I can't help you, Karl. Sorry."

Alberg put the photograph back in the envelope. "Thanks anyway."

He went to the detachment and called in Sokolowski and Carrington.

"I got zilch," said Sokolowski heavily. "Went back to the islands, rechecked everybody, nobody saw a thing."

"What about the marinas?"

Sokolowski shook his head.

"When am I going to get the files on Ransome?"

"Tomorrow," said the sergeant. "If we're lucky. What I can't figure is why he's still hanging around, if he's the perp."

"I don't know, Sid," said Alberg. "But I want to make damn sure we know it if he changes his mind."

"Don't worry. If he hits the ferries or the airport, we'll know about it."

"So you're pretty sure it's this Ransome, Staff?" said Carrington.

"No. Not sure. But maybe it's him," said Alberg.

"The guy could have been killed for that camera of his," said Sokolowski. "By a berserk tourist he met on top of the cliff."

"A berserk tourist," said Carrington. "Ha. I like that."

"A thief who missed all that cash?" said Alberg.

"Maybe he fell off the cliff before the guy could grab it," said Sokolowski. "It could be he was just in the wrong place at the wrong time. Him and his belt full of money. And his two-thousand-dollar Hasselblad. People have died for less than that before now."

"He was for sure in the wrong place at the wrong time," said Alberg. "As it turned out."

"A berserk tourist," said Carrington. "Ha."

"Carrington," said Alberg. "I want you to get me a list of everybody Grayson knew in the last three years he lived here. That means faculty and students at the high school, plus anybody else his mother or his uncle can think of."

"Right," said Carrington.

"Cross off anybody who doesn't live on the peninsula anymore," said Alberg. "Get phone numbers for the rest. Once we hear from the phone company—the numbers that were called from his mother's house—we can look for a match."

When Sokolowski and Carrington had left his office, Alberg pulled in front of him the pile of evaluation forms, which even if he did the whole works today would still be two weeks late getting to Vancouver. He put on his reading glasses.

"Sokolowski," said the top form. His eye skimmed the blanks to be filled in. "Number of years on the Force. Number of years at the detachment. Current duties and responsibilities. Recommendation for promotion? Recommendation for a merit increase?"

Christ, Alberg said silently to himself. I cannot deal with this. Not now. He shoved the stack of forms away from him.

He thought of Sid. And Sid's wife, Elsie.

He reached for the forms again.

And then he heard a tap on his door. "Come in," he called out, and his heart lifted to see Diana standing there. "Come in, sweetie," he said, taking off his glasses.

"Have you got a minute?" she said, sitting down in the black chair.

"Of course I have. Are you here in an official capacity?" said Alberg with a smile, pointing to her notebook. He wondered what reporters wrote in their notebooks. Most of them had tape recorders now, too. It didn't seem to do them any good. They still got most things wrong. Not Diana, of course. Her newspaper stories were extremely well written, thoughtful and intelligent...but of course, he thought, looking at her in sudden dismay, he was in no position to judge their accuracy.

"Well, yes," said Diana. "If you've got time," she said, pushing her hair back from her forehead, "I'd like to talk to you." She laughed. "Interview you. Is that okay?"

"Interview me about what?"

"I went to see that mini-zoo guy," said Diana, opening her notebook, "and what a jerk *he* is. And I talked to the guy with Wildlife Management, which is part of the Ministry of the Environment." She dug in her large straw handbag and pulled out a pen. "And now I need to find out what the police position is." She looked at him expectantly, pen poised.

"What the police position is on what?" said Alberg carefully.

"On the mini-zoo, Dad," said Diana.

Alberg looked out the window at the heat. "The police don't have a position on the mini-zoo," he said.

"Why not?" said Diana.

"Well, Diana. Because it's not necessary. That's why."

"Have you had any complaints about it?"

"Not as far as I know."

"You mean to say, Dad, that not a single soul has protested to you about that awful place?"

"Yeah, one single soul has. You."

She looked at him thoughtfully. "You're not being honest with me."

Alberg shifted in his chair. "I don't know what you mean," he said, with dignity.

"You are not telling me everything."

He squinted at her. "What the hell are you talking about?"

"How come you're not telling me about the broken cages?"

"Why should I tell you about them?"

"Or the bags of feed cut open?"

He looked at her sullenly.

"Or the death threat that awful man got, not that he doesn't deserve it." Diana shook her head reproachfully. "How can journalists do their job, Dad, when we don't get cooperation from the police?"

Alberg was silent.

Diana glanced at her notebook. "How's your investigation proceeding?"

"We've been distracted from our investigation," he said dryly, "by a homicide. Maybe you heard about it."

She looked chagrined, which gave him some pleasure. "I'm sorry, Dad."

"I can't discuss these things with you, Diana. You know that."

"You're happy enough to talk to us when you need us," said Diana, flushing. "When you need people to do a search, or whatever, you're sure willing to talk to us then."

"Diana, I can't discuss ongoing investigations with you. Not as a reporter, and not as my daughter. When there's something to say to the press you can be sure I'll say it. But there isn't. Not yet."

"Are you investigating that Willis woman?" Diana blurted.

"What, the cat lady? For murder? What do you know that I don't?"

His daughter closed her notebook and stood up. "You don't seem to be doing a great deal that's useful," she said coldly. "You don't care about the animals in that man's zoo. You probably don't care about his wife, either. He hits her, you know. I saw him."

"Diana," said Alberg. "You stay away from that place. Do you hear me?"

"Are you speaking as a father?" she said. "Or a cop? Because if you're being a father, I'm past the age of majority. And if you're being a cop, you have no right to order me around."

"Diana," said Alberg, but she was already out the door.

Chapter Thirty-Seven

Annabelle was deep in sleep when she felt her shoulder being shaken. She opened her eyes and drew back in a quick flinch when she saw Herman standing by the side of the bed. He ignored this, although she knew he'd seen it, and handed her a mug of coffee.

"It's three o'clock," he said. "It's your turn, Annabelle."

"Oh my goodness Herman I can't believe you meant it."

"I been out there since eleven. You only gotta stay till it gets light. That's only a couple hours."

Annabelle took the coffee and sat up in bed. She reached for the switch on the lamp, but Herman stopped her.

"We don't want no light showin'," he said, keeping his voice low. "She'd know we were up."

Annabelle leaned against the headboard and took a sip of coffee. "Well I might as well get going," she said, and sighed. Herman put his hand on her shoulder. She waited, in case he wanted to say something. But he didn't. So she got up, and got dressed, while Herman got undressed, and climbed into bed.

The dark night was pierced and flooded with light from a fixture attached to the gable of the shed. Annabelle sat in a lawn chair next to the house. She wondered how the animals could sleep. Maybe they were huddled in their cages with their paws over their eyes.

Herman hadn't gone away for a night and a day after all. He'd slept all night in the truck, parked a little way down the road, and then he'd driven off to work in the early morning before anybody was up. As soon as he'd gotten home from work and seen that the raccoons were gone, he'd driven back into town to get what he needed to install the yard light.

It was so bright that nobody would come near the place now, Annabelle had told him. Surely it was unnecessary to stand guard. But Herman said he had an investment to protect; he would stand watch half the night and either Rose-Iris or Annabelle had to do the other half; Arnold and Camellia were too young.

Now that she was out here, sitting in the lawn chair with her coffee, she was almost content.

After an hour or so she went inside for more coffee.

When she sat down again she caught a whiff of the fragrance of her rose garden as it drifted through the brush.

She smelled the animals in their pens, and the roses. There wasn't even a breath of a breeze. She moved her arms, trying to create a ripple in the air, but all that did was set the uncommon warmth of the night to stirring.

Annabelle, sitting in the hot, dark night, began to feel like someone enchanted.

She wasn't surprised when she saw a movement across the yard, on the light-pool's opposite shore. She wondered if it was a raccoon. Maybe raccoons had set their brethren free, she thought, and leaned forward slightly to see.

Into the light crept a figure, and Annabelle saw that it was human. She watched, fascinated. The figure stopped, and stood still; it stood there, motionless, for such a long time that Annabelle began to think she'd been mistaken; it wasn't a person at all but a shrub, some kind of vegetation that had been there all the time, just inside the boundaries of the artificial day in which the animals were submerged. Then it moved, and Annabelle saw that it had something in its hand. Annabelle put her hand up to her mouth. She didn't know what she ought to do. She hadn't discussed with Herman what would happen if either of them actually caught the vandal in the act. She got to her feet and moved backward a few steps, until she had reached the side of the house, and got down on her haunches; the smaller she could make herself, the better, she thought.

She peered across darkness into the light-flooded mini-zoo and watched as the figure made its way past the first cage, which Annabelle knew was empty, and past the second one, also empty, to the third. Annabelle tried to remember what was in that cage. Then she heard chirping sounds—squirrels, that was what was in there.

The figure at the cage was crooning, now, and working away at the wire. Annabelle moved a little closer, slowly, cautiously, not making a sound. But even if I do make a sound, she told herself, he won't hear it with the squirrels chirping like that.

The figure became still, and turned suddenly, and looked directly at Annabelle.

But she can't see me, thought Annabelle, for she's in light, and I'm in shadow. She stood up, slowly. The cat lady—Bobby Ransome's Aunt Hetty—straightened from her crouching position in front of the cage. She shaded her eyes with one hand. Annabelle moved to the lawn chair, and sat down. The cat lady looked at her intently, and Annabelle looked back. Yes, thought Annabelle calmly, I guess she can see me after all. She picked up her mug from the ground and took a sip of coffee.

The old woman held what Annabelle took to be a pair of wire cutters. She had gray hair that she'd wound up and pinned on top of her head. She wore heavy shoes, and a skirt that almost reached her ankles, and a cardigan buttoned up to the neck, and of course her black shawl. She stared at Annabelle for a long time, until Annabelle finally realized that something more was needed. So she lifted her hand and slowly touched it to her forehead, in salutation.

The old woman hesitated, then turned back to the cage, and, with several looks back across her shoulder at Annabelle, resumed her work with the wire cutters. Annabelle watched, and listened for sounds from the house, but heard none; she was getting worried, though, because of all the excited noises coming from the cages.

In a few more minutes the old woman was finished. She pushed herself to her feet, reached toward the cage, and pulled. A chunk of the wire cage came away. The old woman looked steadily at Annabelle for a minute. And then she walked away.

Annabelle sat quiet in her chair, sipping coffee, watching the broken cage, and eventually the squirrels crept to the opening, and scurried out. They sat on their haunches for a moment, looking around. And then they raced toward the woods.

Annabelle closed her eyes and let her head drop to her chest, as if she had fallen asleep.

Chapter Thirty-Eight

"**O**h boy," said Hugh McMurtry, studying the photograph Alberg had handed him. "That was a while ago." He laughed. "It's one of Steven's, I guess. He must have taken, oh, dozens of pictures of me, and the rest of the staff, too."

"Any particular reason for this one?"

"I can't even recall the occasion, whatever it was."

"How about this picture?" said Alberg.

"Why, that's Bobby Ransome. Looks like it was taken in the boys' locker room. Where did you get these, anyway?"

"What can you tell me about him?"

"Bobby?" McMurtry sat back and spread his arms along the top of the sofa. The glass doors were open and every so often a cool breeze from the sea drifted into the room. "Basically, he was a good kid. But he got into trouble—joyriding, drinking; you know the kind of thing. And he dropped out of school in grade ten. Usually that's it. A kid drops out, and you lose him for good. But four years later, Bobby came back."

"Why?" said Alberg.

McMurtry grinned shyly. "Well, I think I had something to do with it. I'd see him in town, working as a laborer, and I'd put the bug in his ear. He started coming up to the school, hanging around after classes. Finally he came in to see me, asked how it would work, if he came back. It took another year, but eventually, he did."

"How'd he make out?"

"Fine. Just fine. Everybody admired him for having the guts to sit in a grade ten classroom with kids four or five years younger than he was. But then—he was a powerful presence, Bobby was."

"How do you mean?"

McMurtry shrugged. "He was the kind of person people are aware of. Charismatic, I guess you'd call him."

"So what happened?"

"Well, he graduated. And he married his girlfriend. And then I think he planned to take a heavy-duty mechanics' course."

"Uh-huh."

"I went away that summer, I remember," said McMurtry absently, looking out at the roses growing on his patio. "And when I got back, Bobby had been arrested for selling drugs, and sent to jail." He glanced at Alberg. "He's back in town now, so I've heard."

"Was this arrest a big surprise to everybody?"

McMurtry looked uncomfortable. "Yes. No. I don't know. I mean, he was kind of a wild kid, from time to time. Maybe," he said wearily, "maybe we should have kept a closer eye on him."

Alberg studied the photograph. "How well did he know Steven Grayson?"

McMurtry shook his head. "I have no idea. Probably not well at all."

Alberg had to wait a long time before Hetty Willis opened her front door.

"I'm sorry to bother you again."

She clung to the edge of the door. Several cats swirled languorously around her feet.

"I'd like to talk to you about your nephew. Bobby."

Her expression remained unreadable, and for a long time she didn't move. Some of the cats slithered out onto the veranda. Alberg willed himself to relax. He tried smiling inside his head. And maybe that worked; finally she pulled the door open and allowed him to enter.

They stood in the entrance hall, Hetty looking up at him, blinking behind her glasses.

"You were upset, I think, when I showed you that photograph."

He had the feeling that she was waiting patiently for him to finish, and leave.

"Can you tell me why?"

She made no response. Alberg remembered an old man he'd known saying that once you get to a certain age "the whole shitteree is fast wearing out—any minute, something essential could go on you." Maybe Hetty's hearing has suddenly gone on her, he thought.

Hetty was flipping rapidly through a mental list of her relatives and friends. She began with Rachel, her sister-in-law, because Rachel was Bobby's mother, after all. But Rachel's attention was still riveted upon the failing health of her second husband. And there was nobody else Hetty knew who cared about Bobby.

She looked despairingly at the policeman. Her responsibility for her nephew lay heavily upon her.

If she was wrong, she thought, confiding in the policeman would do no harm. And if she was right—well she had more responsibilities than one.

She took Alberg into her sitting room, and handed him the scrapbook.

Chapter Thirty-Nine

Herman had been beside himself when he awoke Friday morning and found Annabelle ostensibly asleep in the lawn chair and the squirrels gone. "First the skunks, then the raccoons, now this," he'd hollered. "Well there for sure goes my damn zoo," he'd said, almost in tears about it, and he raged off in the truck, forgetting all about Arnold.

Annabelle had kept to her plan, though. She'd walked into town, when it was time, and gone to Bobby's house, just as they had arranged it.

He'd been waiting for her in the living room, his face striped with light that sifted in through the blinds. "Jesus, I thought I wasn't ever gonna see you again," he said, taking her hands, pulling her upstairs.

"You said you wanted to talk to me, Bobby," she said, trying to sound stern. He slipped her bag from her shoulder and reached behind her to unzip her dress and there was such hunger in her that she was trembling.

"Oh Jesus, Annabelle," he said, and took her breast in his mouth, and they tumbled onto his bed.

Oh she loved his eyes, double-lashed, outlined by nature as if with a dark smudgy pencil. They were as green as the green water in a lake Annabelle had been to once; as green as seawater sometimes is. Even Erna had remarked enviously upon his eyes.

And oh she loved the mole next to his hipbone. She liked to touch it with the tip of her tongue. It was not merely a dark spot of skin but a protuberance; an entity that had come to rest there alongside his hipbone: maybe it even moved around, exploring the surface of his body with the same tactile curiosity that possessed Annabelle—although she had never seen it anywhere but there, alongside his hipbone.

She liked the way he touched her; not soft, tentative brushings like feathers or a summer breeze but strong, bold strokes that made her muscles ripple, setting up inside her the beginnings of tumult.

She liked the way his lips grazed her body as though it were a pasture of sweet grass.

And after they'd made love she pressed her face into the warm dampness of his hard belly and felt between her breasts his erection begin to return; she liked that, too.

She reached out to stroke Bobby's brown back, which was shiny with sweat; he was sitting, naked, on the edge of the bed. He turned to give her a smile. He had more than one smile, and some of them were scary, but this particular smile was so open and winning that it made her heart ache.

Annabelle sat up and looked on the floor for her clothes.

"I'll get them," said Bobby. He scooped up her panties and sundress and put them on the bed. Then, as Annabelle watched disapprovingly, he reached for his jeans and pulled them on. A man who wore no underwear, Annabelle believed, was not a man to be completely trusted. It might have been the only thing about Bobby that she didn't like.

She watched as he thrust bare feet into his sneakers.

"I'll be back in a minute," he said, and went down the hall to the bathroom.

She got dressed and found her purse, which he had tossed upon the room's only chair, and was brushing her hair when he came back. She smiled at him in the mirror as she pulled back her hair and fastened it with an elastic band.

"Annabelle," he said, putting his hands on her waist. "I've got something to tell you. I don't wanna tell you this. But I need to, Annabelle."

Annabelle glanced at the window. The blind was down but the window behind it was open; the shade fluttered every time a breeze blew in, and then bounced softly against the windowsill. Annabelle would have liked to know what time it was. She'd forgotten to wear her watch again.

"I wish you'd change your mind," she said, looking kindly at him, "and stay in Sechelt." She pulled strands of hair from her brush and looked around halfheartedly for a wastebasket, then scrunched up the hairs in her hand and placed them neatly on top of Bobby's dresser. She moved to the chair and put the hairbrush away. "I can't be late getting home," she said, slinging her purse over her shoulder. He was a pretty sight as he stood there, tall and tanned, with wide shoulders and a smooth strong hairless chest; there was a thicket of hair under his jeans, though, a splurge of coarse, reddish hair; it made Annabelle sigh to think about it.

"I can't stay in Sechelt," said Bobby, grim-faced, "because of what happened last weekend."

Annabelle crossed her arms, frowning. "What?"

"You know about my temper," he began. And all of Annabelle's alarm bells went off at the same time.

"I can't stand around here any longer, Bobby," she said quickly. "I have to be getting home." With a glance back at the disheveled bed, she headed for the hall.

Bobby stepped between her and the doorway. "Don't run away from me, Annabelle."

"I'm sure I don't know what you're talking about." She looked into his green eyes. "I have to go now. I really do."

But Bobby blocked the doorway. "Annabelle please, just listen."

"Bobby stop this, stop it immediately." She recognized the tone of her voice as the one she used on her children when she was correcting their table manners. She didn't do that often enough, she thought, looking blankly at Bobby. She couldn't, when Herman was around. Annabelle wiped her forehead with the back of her hand. She didn't want either of them. I don't want anybody at all, she thought, turning toward the window, where the blind tapped gently at the sill, I only want me, she thought, and the notion of being alone speared her chest with sudden, unexpected longing.

Bobby pushed himself away from the doorjamb and put his hands in the pockets of his jeans. "Yeah," he said bitterly. "Okay. Fine. Go."

She pushed past him, into the hall, and ran down the steps. Then she came to a halt, staring at the dirty glass panes in the front door.

"Bobby," she said.

"I'm here." He was right behind her.

With profound reluctance, she turned, slowly, and took his hands, which were square and brown and clean.

"Tell me, then," she said.

Chapter Forty

"We got no evidence, you know, Karl," said Sokolowski.

"I know it."

"Even if he did it, we can't prove anything."

"We can get his picture out to Thormanby," said Alberg. "Put him on the island at the time Grayson died, at least. It's a start. Then we can bring him in, talk to him, and take it from there. Maybe the camera will turn up."

Hetty Willis's scrapbook lay on the desk in front of him. It contained mimeographed programs from school concerts. An invitation to Bobby's high school graduation. Photographs of Bobby in Halloween costumes. Photographs of Bobby with his parents, and with Hetty. Notes that he'd written her, thanking her for Christmas and birthday presents. Newspaper clippings about his arrest, trial and sentencing. And letters he'd sent her from prison.

Photographs had been entered as evidence of a drug transaction between Ransome and two fourteen-year-olds who had later testified for the prosecution.

Bobby had received a sentence of seven years, because the drugs he was convicted of having sold had been imported over the U.S. border.

But he actually served eight and a half years, Hetty had told Alberg; eighteen months had been added to his sentence after he escaped and was recaptured.

The photographs that sent him to jail had been mailed to the RCMP anonymously. But Bobby knew who'd provided them. "Steven?" Alberg had said, and Hetty Willis had nodded.

"What I don't understand," said Alberg to Sokolowski, "is who the hell died? That Steven felt responsible for?"

The sergeant shrugged. "I guess that part of it's wrong."

Chapter Forty-One

"**I** thought you could give me a sandwich," said Bobby, "and then we could go to the bank together." He was very restless in his body, and kept looking out the window.

It was astonishing, thought Hetty, what fixes a person can get into in a lifetime.

She shook her head.

"No, what?" said her nephew. "No sandwich?"

"Money," said Hetty quickly, before she lost her nerve. "No money."

She saw his consternation, and felt a great echoey emptiness.

He stood quite still, towering over her; she had the sense of his blotting out the sun.

She thought about the cats, about how she needed them. She had always cared about animals, but since her brother's bizarre death on the horns of a deer she had, illogically, focused her life upon them. A person has to have something, thought

Hetty, looking up at Bobby, craning her neck because she was so short.

And frail, she thought. For the first time in my life, I feel frail.

Most of the murders in the world happen among family members. She watched the news. She knew.

But she also knew that he would never hurt her.

"How come you changed your mind?"

"Notgood."

"Not good. Not good. Shit. Fuck." He threw himself onto the love seat. "Do you know what you're doin' to me, Aunt Hetty?"

"No," said Hetty.

"You're killin' me." He gripped his head with both hands. "Killin' me."

"Notme," said Hetty. She was crying again. She hadn't wept for years, and now it seemed like she was doing it all the time. "You," said Hetty, through her tears. "You."

Chapter Forty-Two

"**M**y goodness, why are you two hanging around the house?" said Annabelle. She was flying from room to room, wielding a duster. "Where's that mangy dog, anyway, Camellia? Why aren't you outside playing with that mangy dog?"

"He's not mangy," said Camellia, following her from the kitchen to the living room, which was a long, narrow room with only one window in its end wall. "I don't feel like it."

"Why don't you sit down, Ma?" said Rose-Iris uneasily. "Have a cup of coffee or something."

"I don't want to sit down," said Annabelle.

"Well I don't want to go out and play, either," said Camellia.

Annabelle stopped dusting and put her hands on her hips. "I don't like that whine in your voice," she scolded Camellia.

"It's not a whine," said Rose-Iris. "She's just worried, that's all."

"I'm worried, that's all," said Camellia.

"Oh for goodness' sake," said Annabelle, dusting the television set, "what've you got to be worried about?"

"You, Ma," said Rose-Iris. "We're worried about you. Why're you acting so funny?"

"It's you two who're acting funny, if you ask me," said Annabelle, bustling past them on her way back to the kitchen. "Here it is beautiful weather again and you have no chores to do, because I've given you the whole day off. Arnold at least has a brain in his head. He knows what to do when he's given a day off, he's gone off to play like a normal child." She had begun to shiver. "But you two, you just hang around, mope around, getting in my way."

Annabelle remembered, suddenly, a day last autumn when she'd been walking up the gravel road to Erna's house. The sky at the top of the hill was brilliantly blue. The trees stretched up and over the road, and the wind was blowing strong, lifting leaves from the trees and hurling them down; the air was filled with them—a golden rain of autumn leaves. And Annabelle, walking up the road, lifting her face to the sky and the golden falling leaves, had thought she heard laughter.

"Maybe when your dad gets back with the truck," she said now, trying to control her shaking, "maybe we'll go somewhere. To the beach, maybe. I'll cook a roast and we'll slice it up and pack us a picnic and go to the beach. That's what we'll do." But she couldn't stop shaking, and Camellia began to sniffle.

Then they heard a car.

The children looked at one another and then back at Annabelle, and they were all thinking, well it isn't the truck, and it isn't Uncle Warren's van, and then they heard a car door bang and up to the screen came the girl from the newspaper.

"Will you please go away," said Annabelle, suddenly enraged.

She struck the screen door with the heel of her hand. It slammed open, nearly hitting Diana. Annabelle strode through it, across the yard and around the corner to where Diana's car was parked, next to the broken-down gas pumps. She opened the driver's door and stood there.

"Get into your car and drive away," she said. Diana gaped at her, looking very silly, Annabelle thought. The girl came near: thank God, thought Annabelle, she's going without a word.

But instead of getting into her car, Diana said, in a very soft voice, "Can I help you?"

Annabelle looked at her incredulously.

"Please let me help you," said the girl.

There was such tenderness in her voice that Annabelle was embarrassed for her. And then Annabelle realized that her face—Annabelle's own face—was wet with tears; dripping with tears. And that Camellia and Rose-Iris, staring at her, were transfixed with fear.

She looked intently into Diana's face.

"Let me take you into your house," said Diana, "and maybe your daughters and I can make you a cup of tea." She put an arm around Annabelle's shoulders and led her inside.

A few minutes later they were sitting around the table, the four of them.

"I have a friend," Annabelle said. "Who's in trouble." Her daughters were listening intently. "Now it's trouble of his own making, mind." Camellia glanced at Rose-Iris. "There isn't a thing I can do. To help him," said Annabelle, rubbing the palms of her hands against her skirt. She had put on the blue and white sundress again, she noticed.

She saw Rose-Iris look quickly at the door.

"Here's Dad," said Rose-Iris, and Annabelle held her breath to listen.

She nodded. "Yes," she said. "It is indeed. Herman is home," she said to Diana over the pounding of her heart, which had moved up into her throat; if it stays there, she thought, it is going to be extremely difficult to talk, and to breathe, too.

Herman flung the door open and stood in the kitchen, staring down at her. He didn't seem to be aware that there was anyone else in the room.

He knows, she thought, looking up at him.

Everything went into slow motion then.

They all stood up from the table, Diana, and Rose-Iris, and Camellia, and Annabelle. Diana took a step toward

Herman, and then a step back. Camellia moved toward the wall. Rose-Iris placed herself between Herman and Annabelle.

Nobody said anything. Through the screen Annabelle heard the truck motor making ticking sounds in the heat; Herman had driven it right up to the back door. She was glad he hadn't driven it through the window wall.

This was the last thought she remembered having.

"You whore," said Herman, breathing hard and fast.

Annabelle turned herself into a sponge.

"You been doin' it again," he said.

Nobody moved, because everybody knew that if they moved, so would he, and everybody thought that maybe if they didn't move, neither would he.

"You filthy whore," said Herman, his voice rising. "After what I done for you." He raised his hand, which he'd made into a fist, and pulled it back, and came for Annabelle.

"No! No!" cried Rose-Iris, and grabbed him around the waist.

He flung her off and struck Annabelle across the side of the head. Annabelle fell to the floor, but scrambled clumsily back up again.

"Don't!" shouted Diana, and Annabelle saw her looking frantically around the room.

Annabelle lifted her arm to shield herself but Herman struck her again, in the neck, this time.

"No Daddy, no!" said Rose-Iris above the wailing of Camellia, who was crouched in the corner with her hands over her ears. Rose-Iris tried to cling to Herman's arm. Herman threw her aside.

Herman, sobbing, clubbed Annabelle again with his fist, and again she fell, and struck her forehead against the edge of the buffet.

"Daddy please," said Rose-Iris, crying, clawing at him, "please don't do it."

"I ain't your fuckin' daddy," Herman roared. He turned on Rose-Iris and picked her up by the shoulders and shook her. "I ain't your daddy, you hear that?" He threw her to the floor.

"Herman!" cried Annabelle, staggering to her feet.

But Herman reached down and cuffed Rose-Iris, who was lying on the floor, trying to curl up into a ball.

"Herman, no!" screamed Annabelle. Herman kept on hitting Rose-Iris, and from the corner of her eye Annabelle saw Diana reach down and pick up a chair.

Annabelle turned, opened a drawer, and fumbled for a knife.

Chapter Forty-Three

Warren picked up Wanda at the ferry terminal in Langdale that afternoon; she'd been in Vancouver, at a bank tellers' seminar. He was in his work overalls and she was in her city clothes. He felt proud of her, driving along the highway, taking sidelong glances at her whenever he could. She was a real pretty woman, Wanda.

He didn't have to go back to work, so when they got home Wanda changed and they went out into the backyard for a couple of hours before supper.

"Maybe I should get a bunch of these," said Warren, indicating the two railroad ties in the middle of the yard, "and make a raised bed back here." He was taking a break from the siding to build boxes to surround the bases of the cherry trees. He planned to fill them with bark mulch.

"What do we need a raised bed for?" said Wanda. She was sitting on her sloped-back red workout chair, lifting weights.

"It's easier on your back," Warren told her. "You don't have to stoop down to do the weeding. You sit on the edge of it, see, and you reach in."

"I don't stoop down," said Wanda, breathless. "I get down on my hands and knees."

There was a small garden beside the garage, which stood at the back of the yard. Wanda had planted some herbs there, and a zucchini, and a couple of tomatoes.

"Yeah, well, you wouldn't have to get down on your hands and knees," said Warren, measuring, marking the tie with a thick pencil, "if you had a raised bed." He reached for the power saw.

"That thing's hideously noisy," said Wanda when he'd finished. She was wearing shorts and a T-shirt, and sneakers, and she had a headband on, and wristbands, too, to soak up the sweat.

He started to say something, then stopped. "Did you hear something?"

"Only that saw," said Wanda, all concentrated on her weights. Warren used to think about doing weights. No way he'd do them now, though.

He fitted the two pieces of tie together, marked the second tie, and did his sawing.

"I hope that's the end of that," Wanda grumbled.

"That's it," said Warren. "Now I've just gotta nail them together, and I'm through."

Wanda was naturally skinny; Warren couldn't figure why she'd gotten so keen on getting fit, anyway. She said it was for strength and flexibility.

Again, Warren thought he heard something.

He had a very bad feeling. He wished for a moment that his backyard wasn't enclosed by a six-foot cedar fence. He wanted to be able to see through it.

He went to the gate, opened it, and looked along the side of his house. Nobody was there, and he heard nothing but the sprinkler on the lawn across the street, and he saw the back end of the van, parked in front of the house, and no other vehicles. He closed the gate and stood there listening, but heard nothing.

He went back to the lawn and sat down. "Wanda, something weird's going on."

Wanda, laboring with her weights, said, "I didn't hear a thing, Warren, you imagined it."

Warren heard it again, whatever it was. He got up and went back to the gate and opened it. A cement walk ran along the side of the house and then around in front. There was nobody there.

Suddenly a woman appeared around the corner of the house. She looked terrified. Warren had never seen her in his life before.

"Are you Warren?"

He nodded, speechless.

She went back around the corner. Warren couldn't figure out what the hell was going on. But his heart was thumping, and there was a metallic taste in his mouth, and he absolutely knew something terrible was going to happen.

He watched the corner intently. And suddenly Annabelle appeared.

"Wanda," said Warren, quietly.

It seemed to him that she was beside him in an instant. She looked at Annabelle and sucked in her breath. Warren didn't know what to do. He felt Wanda slip past him, ducking beneath his arm. She walked toward Annabelle and as she got closer she walked faster, and her arms lifted, and when she reached Annabelle she put her arms around her and drew her close, and all Warren could think of was that Wanda was getting blood all over her.

Chapter Forty-Four

Annabelle waited in a room that had no windows. It was painted green. There was a rectangular table in it, and two wooden chairs. It wasn't a particularly threatening room, but Annabelle wished there were some things on the walls. It wasn't threatening; but it wasn't clean, either. Annabelle didn't sit down on a chair, at the table, because neither the chairs nor the table were clean.

She wiped the palms of her hands again and again down the sides of her blue-and-white-striped sundress. The dress was stained, of course. Annabelle was pretending that the stains were gravy.

At least her skin was clean now. Her hands were clean. She looked at them again, making sure. She held them out in front of her, inspecting closely around the nails. She thought she could see flecks there, around the edges of her fingernails; flecks of gravy.

That'd teach her, she thought, rubbing the palms of her hands against her dress, that'd teach her to cook a roast in the middle of the hottest summer in the world. If you cook a roast and then you cut it with a dull knife, why that's what's going to happen, the blade's going to slip and oh God you've cut yourself you've cut yourself now, there's gravy all over your dress no too red too bright it's juice from the roast you've cooked it rare Herman's going to be mad...

She knows she felt it go in, she knows she has to think about that but she can not think about that now—now she only hears the sounds, the grunting, and cursing, and shuffling, and hard breathing, and then some shouts, children crying, oh dear God no please and yelling it out, no no no, and Herman sobbing and then a thwacking sound and then oh God his shriek—

Annabelle had never before in her life heard such a sound. But when she heard it, she recognized it. It was the sound you make when it's the last sound you'll ever make. It was the shriek of dying.

Chapter Forty-Five

"Why didn't you call me?" said Alberg to his daughter.

"She wanted her brother. She said her brother would call you. He did, didn't he?"

"Yes, he did."

"So that was okay, wasn't it?"

"Are *you* okay?"

"It was self-defense," said Diana, ashen-faced. "And her daughter, he was beating on her daughter, too."

"Sit down, Diana." He stepped out into the hall. "Keep her in the interview room," he said to Sokolowski. "Tell the rest of them I'll see them in a minute." He went back into his office and closed the door. "We'll need to get a statement from you."

"It was self-defense." Her voice was shaking. So were her hands.

"It's okay, sweetie. You'll be okay. You just tell it exactly as you witnessed it."

"We were sitting at the kitchen table—"

"Not now," said Alberg quickly. "Not to me. I want you to tell it to Sid Sokolowski." He took her hands, which felt very small and cold. He looked at her helplessly. "I love you, Diana."

"I love you, too, Pop."

"It's a damn circus around here," muttered Sokolowski from behind his desk. "What with all these damn kids."

And Bobby Ransome had disappeared.

"Any word from Thormanby?" said Alberg.

Sokolowski shook his head.

Alberg leaned on the desk. "Listen, you know Diana was there when the Ferguson thing happened; would you take her statement?"

"Sure," said the sergeant. He looked down, pondering something, and Alberg knew what it was. He was wondering what the hell Diana had been doing out there. He wanted to know that himself.

"Do you have to talk to the kids?" said Warren. He put his arms more tightly around the girls; eight-year-old Arnold was sitting on Wanda's knee. He hoped she knew how good she looked, with a kid on her lap.

The big blond cop looked at the kids and smiled. "I'd like to talk to them, yes." He got down on his haunches in front of Warren and the girls. "Would that be okay with you?" he said to Camellia and Rose-Iris. They both nodded. Well they were a lot calmer now, thought Warren, and the cops were probably used to talking to kids, so it'd probably be okay. He felt uncertain, though, because he was the only relative around—the only functioning relative, anyway.

"I'll tell you, sir," he said to Alberg, "I'd feel a lot better if I could call my folks. Would that be okay?"

"Sure," said Alberg.

"They live in Fort Langley. It's long distance."

"That's okay," said Alberg. He stood up and said to the woman behind the reception counter, "Would you make a call for Mr. Kettleman here, Isabella?"

So Warren gave her the number.

And then he and the kids went with the big cop behind the counter, and Warren talked to his dad, who said they'd get over to Sechelt right away, and that's sure what Warren had wanted to hear.

"The police want to talk to the kids, Dad," he said, trying to keep his voice low, even though he knew this Isabella woman could hear every word.

"Well sure they'll want to talk to the kids, Warren," said his dad.

"Is it okay then?"

"Sure it's okay," said his dad.

But Warren was very glad somebody else had been there, too, so the cop had more than Annabelle's word, and her kids' word, to go on.

He stayed there with them when the cop asked them questions. And then he got asked some questions, too. And so did Wanda. He looked around for the girl who'd brought Annabelle to the house but he didn't see her.

"She's talking to another officer," said Alberg, when Warren inquired, "down the hall there."

"So what's going to happen to Annabelle?" said Warren finally, since nobody was volunteering any information about this.

"I'm going to talk to her now," said Alberg. "Meanwhile, you and your wife can take the kids home with you."

"Yeah, but before I go," said Warren. He stood up then, for some reason, and with his right hand on Rose-Iris's shoulder, and his left hand on the top of Camellia's head, he said, "I want to know what's going to happen to my sister."

"I can't tell you that just yet," said Alberg. "But I'll know a lot more after I've spoken to her. Give me half an hour or so. Okay?"

"Okay," said Warren reluctantly. Wanda stood up, holding Arnold's hand, and the five of them went outside to Warren's truck. He was very surprised to realize that it was still Friday, and only four-thirty in the afternoon.

Chapter Forty-Six

"May I please change my clothes?" said Annabelle.

Her upper lip was badly swollen, she had a black eye, and there was a bandage on her forehead, just at the hairline.

"In a few minutes," said Alberg. "Your sister-in-law has brought something for you to put on."

"It won't fit me," said Annabelle, clasping her hands.

"They're your own clothes," said Alberg. "She went to your house to get them. First of all, Mrs. Ferguson, I must inform you that you have the right to retain and instruct counsel without delay."

She was shaking her head.

"And that if you can't afford a lawyer, one will be provided for you."

"I don't want a lawyer."

"You're sure?"

"I'm sure."

"Okay. I'm going to turn this tape recorder on. Now, tell me what happened."

Annabelle shook her head back and forth, back and forth.
"Oh no, oh dear, such a mess, such a mess." She began to weep.
"God forgive me. It was me. I killed him."

"No," said Alberg. "You didn't kill him."

Annabelle froze. "He's—I—he's not dead?"

"He's going to be okay."

Every trace of color washed from Annabelle's face. "Thank
God," she whispered. She ran her fingertips over her face,
repeating "Thank God, thank God," touching her injuries,
stroking them tenderly. "But I hurt him," she said.

"He's hurt, yes."

"Will I go to jail?"

"That's not up to me."

"Am I under arrest?"

Alberg sat down in the other chair. "No, Mrs. Ferguson.
You're not under arrest. But you have to tell me what happened."

She turned away from him, touching her face again.

"Mrs. Ferguson."

"How are my children?"

"They're fine. They're with your brother and his wife."

"Arnold, too?"

"All of them. All three of them."

Annabelle wiped her cheeks with her hands. "Where's—
where's Herman?"

"In the hospital. Tell me what happened," said Alberg
gently.

She stood up, and went around to the other side of the
table.

"I don't know if I can," she said, looking at the door.

Alberg waited.

"He hardly ever hit me in front of the kids." She leaned
against the wall. "I don't know how he found out," she said
wearily. "Maybe he didn't." She pushed her hair away from her
face, and winced when her hand brushed against her swollen
lip. "He guesses. And of course I feel guilty. Because either I am
guilty, or I was guilty, or I will be guilty. And so part of me

thinks I deserve it—*part* of me," she said, and for the first time Alberg saw that there was anger in her. "Only part of me."

She slumped against the wall again. "He came into the kitchen, we were sitting down having a cup of tea—" She looked at Alberg. "Your daughter was there," she said, as if she'd just remembered. "She was there. And in the middle of it all, I saw her looking around, and I knew she was looking for something to hit him with." She turned away, weeping, her cheek against the wall. "She's a stranger. And she was going to hit him." She closed her eyes and took a big breath. "She was going to hit him, and Rose-Iris was hanging on to him, and I was just standing there. Waiting for him to beat me some more.

"I could see on his face that he didn't want this to be happening. I felt so terrible for him, just for a minute."

She turned away and moved hesitantly to the end of the room, her left hand never leaving the wall, as if she were blind.

"He's never known what to do about me. So he hits me. But he never hit the kids before. Never."

She stopped, huddled in the corner. Alberg got up to hand her his handkerchief. She took it, and wiped her face. He sat down again.

"Rose-Iris was yelling at him to stop, and calling him 'Daddy.' And he said, 'You're not my kid, you little bitch.' Something like that." She moved out of the corner. "When I met Herman, he said he didn't care that I was pregnant with somebody else's child. He said he didn't want to know who it was. He said we'd have our own kids, too, and he'd treat them all the same. And he did. Right up until today."

She sat down, and for a long time she didn't say anything. When she did begin again she spoke abruptly, impatient to get it over with.

"He kept hitting her, and I got up, and I took a knife out of the drawer and I stuck it into him, and he fell down on the floor. We ran out of the house and got in your daughter's car and she drove us to Warren's house. And that's all. When can I see my children?"

"Right now. I'm going to release you on what's called a promise to appear. You'll have to appear in front of a judge. I'll let you know when." He stood up. "Make sure you stay away from Herman. Okay?"

Annabelle nodded. "I never told anybody," she said, staring at the floor.

"You never told anybody what?"

"Who her father is. Not until today. Today I told Rose-Iris, because she asked, and I had to." Tears were spilling from her eyes.

"It'll be okay."

"And Warren heard. Because he was there."

"I'll get your clothes for you," said Alberg, going to the door.

"Nobody knew," said Annabelle, through her tears. "Until today. Not even Bobby knows."

Alberg stopped, with his hand on the doorknob. "Bobby who?" He turned around. "Bobby Ransome?" Annabelle nodded. Slowly, Alberg sat down again.

Chapter Forty-Seven

Warren was sitting in the living room with his folks, who had arrived about an hour earlier, and Annabelle's three kids. His head was awhirl every time he looked at Rose-Iris, because Rose-Iris was nine going on ten which meant that Bobby Ransome had been getting the both of them pregnant at the same time, Wanda and Annabelle.

And Warren didn't like the thought of that one little bit.

If Wanda hadn't had an abortion, her kid with Bobby would've been the same age as Annabelle's kid with Bobby. They would have been related.

Wanda, of course, was furious to learn this.

What a mess, thought Warren, feeling bleak and lonely.

His dad was sitting there looking at the kids in wonder, as if he'd never seen kids before: pictures come to life, that's what they were to him.

His mom was sitting on the very edge of the sofa. Her knees were pressed together and so were her ankles. She was wearing white slacks and a pink top that didn't tuck in, because her waist was kind of thick. Her face had a surprised look on it.

Nobody was saying much. They were all waiting for the phone to ring, for the police to tell them Annabelle could go home.

Camellia was lying back in Warren's arms sort of like she'd collapsed there, her head resting against his left shoulder and her legs flung out, one of them hanging down and the other lying over his right knee. She had her right hand on top of his hand, which was on the arm of the chair, and her left hand kept going up to her face: Warren thought maybe she felt like sucking her thumb and wasn't doing it because it would have been babyish.

Rose-Iris was sitting on the floor between Warren's chair and his dad's, and she'd made Arnold sit next to her. She'd told him she needed him there—Warren had heard her whispering to him. So Arnold was sitting there with his knees drawn up, looking out for Rose-Iris. Who had some cuts and bruises on her, but nothing serious. At least that's what they'd said at the hospital. Warren thought it was pretty serious, all right.

"Warren," said his dad, "why don't your mom and I take the kids off for a hamburger." He reached down to smooth a piece of Rose-Iris's hair away from her face; Warren was astonished at how gently he did this. "Give us a chance to get to know them a little."

Warren and Wanda exchanged glances.

"How about it, kids?" said Warren's dad.

The kids seemed to think it was all right, so they went off with Warren's folks, and Warren and Wanda sat alone in their living room, staring at one another.

They'd been sitting there for not more than fifteen minutes when there was a knock on their front door, and Warren went to see who it was.

"Hiya," said Bobby. "You got a minute?"

Warren, looking at him, wanted very badly to say no. But he brought him into the living room, and Wanda said she'd go and make coffee.

"So you need a set of wheels," Warren said heartily, having figured out why Bobby had come.

"Yeah," said Bobby. "Something cheap." He was sitting forward on the sofa with his feet apart, forearms on his thighs, hands hanging loose.

"What do you want to spend?" said Warren.

"I dunno," said Bobby. "Two, three grand, maybe."

"Old man Ivory has an '85 Aries he wants to sell," said Warren. He sat down on a leather chair that used to belong to his dad.

Bobby didn't respond to the Aries.

"It needs rubber," said Warren. "And it blows a little smoke. But the body's good."

Bobby looked at him with amusement.

Wanda came in from the kitchen. "Coffee'll just be a minute," she said.

"Okay," said Bobby, and his gaze followed Wanda as she left the room.

"So what are your plans?" said Warren, leaning back into the leather chair, trying to get his body to relax.

"Plans," said Bobby thoughtfully, as if he'd never heard the word before. He looked away, toward the open window, and the hot summer evening that lay beyond it. "How do you figure he knew I was here, Warren?"

"What?" said Warren. He glanced toward the doorway. "What's that, Bob?" He wondered if the coffee was already made, and Wanda only had to pour it into cups, or if they were going to have to wait for it. Even with one of those automatic drip things it seemed to take a long time to make a couple of cups of coffee. She'd probably make a full pot, too, which would take even longer. Warren took a quick glance at Bobby, who was looking down at his hands, shaking his head.

"The stupid prick," said Bobby.

He didn't say it very loudly. Warren decided to pretend he hadn't heard.

"Yeah, that'd be a good car for you, Bob," he said. "I'll give old man Ivory a jingle in the morning, then I'll get right back to you. Wanda," he said fervently, springing to his feet. He took the coffeepot from her. "Hey, I'll get the cups and stuff, let me get them," he said, handing back the pot.

"Oh dear Jesus," he whispered in the kitchen. He put his hands flat against the wall and leaned in so that his forehead was pressed there too. "Sweet Jesus," he whispered.

He went over to the counter and threaded his fingers through the handles of three coffee mugs. He shoved three spoons into the breast pocket of his overalls, clutched the cream and sugar in a clumsy embrace and went back to the living room.

"Why on earth didn't you use a tray?" said Wanda, exasperated, and Warren wondered if she was deaf or dumb or blind or what, she looked perfectly calm, and she was sitting there on the sofa right next to Bobby just like he was a normal person. Warren put the things down, spilling a little cream in the process.

"Good grief," said Wanda, and she hopped up and went perkily out of the living room.

Warren stood in the middle of the room feeling blank, like a piece of paper nobody had thought to write on. He just stood there, watching the doorway, listening to Bobby's steady breathing coming soft and slow from the sofa, until Wanda reappeared with a dishcloth. And then he just stood there watching her wipe up the spilled cream. And then he just watched the doorway again, blank and patient, until finally she came back and plopped herself down on the sofa and started stirring sugar into her coffee. Warren took a deep breath and sat on the very edge of the leather chair.

"I don't know how he knew you were back, Bobby."

Wanda, frowning, looked up at him. "Who?"

"Somebody musta told him," said Bobby.

"Who?" said Wanda.

"But why would he want to know?" said Warren.

Bobby poured cream into his coffee and Warren watched the two things swirling around in there, white and black, mixing together, turning coffee-colored. He smiled at the thought.

"What on earth are you guys talking about?" said Wanda.

She was feeling poutish, Warren noticed. He was damn sure that wouldn't last long.

Bobby was looking at him now, and his eyes were still cold, but the expression on his face wasn't cold.

"I'm fucked, buddy," said Bobby. "I am well and truly fucked. You know that, don't you?"

"If you say so, Bobby," said Warren carefully.

Wanda pulled away from Bobby, just a little. She picked up her mug and held it in both hands, blowing delicately on the hot coffee. Warren saw that Wanda had decided not to talk for a while. When she was quiet, Wanda listened very hard, and her mind got very sharp. So this was good, thought Warren.

"He felt guilty," said Bobby. "The fucker felt guilty."

He got up from the sofa, moving in that swift, smooth way he had. Bobby was a big man, and you didn't know how rapidly he could move until he was suddenly right there next to you instead of only on the way.

"Do you know why I'm here, Warren?" he said, leaning down, close to Warren's face. "And it's not about buyin' a fuckin' car." Warren stared at him, unwilling to speak, unwilling even to think. Bobby turned away. "Ah," he said. "What's the use. I don't think I give a fuck."

Wanda was darting little looks up at him from underneath her eyelashes. Her face looked hard and edgy. Warren thought, if you hit her even with a pillow little chunks of her face would fall off. He thought about Annabelle. Oh please no, not now, he said to himself, and wrestled Annabelle out of his brain.

"So he calls me up," said Bobby dully.

"I don't know if we oughta hear this, Bob," said Warren, standing up, but Bobby ignored him.

"Three times he calls me up. Twice I tell him, go fuck yourself. The third time, he—" Bobby looked at Warren, disgusted. "Shit, the guy was pissing himself. So I say yeah, okay, sure, what the hell." He walked restlessly to the fireplace and picked up a framed photograph that stood on the mantelpiece. "You're a good-looking woman, Wanda," said Bobby, staring at the photo, which was of Wanda and Warren the day they got married. "No kids yet, though. How come you got no kids?" He turned to look at Warren. Warren thought he saw the shadow of a smile on Bobby's face. He felt the sting of anger.

He didn't answer Bobby. Neither did Wanda; she just drank some of her coffee. But Bobby hadn't expected an answer anyway. He was putting the photo back on the mantel, making sure it was in exactly the same place, at exactly the same angle.

"I was in prison for eight years," said Bobby, touching the photo with his fingertip. "Hell, you know what happened. After three years and eight months I blew the joint. And four days later they picked me up. So I got eighteen months added on." He turned to Wanda. "That's when I told you to get the divorce."

Wanda nodded.

"And so you did."

Wanda nodded again. She looked very small sitting there. Warren wanted to go over to her and sit next to her and put his arm around her but he couldn't move. It was like they were the three points of a triangle, he and Bobby and Wanda, and if he moved the whole triangle would crumble into nothing, and so would they. So he stood still again, waiting again. And although he felt acutely attentive, unusually alert, his heart was beating at a normal pace, and he was not afraid. He was very grateful for that.

After a minute Bobby sighed, and moved, and then Warren could move, too.

"So I tell him where to meet me. And he meets me." Bobby groaned, and slapped his temple, hard, with the heel of his hand.

"Bobby," said Warren. "Don't do this, man."

Bobby whirled around and stared at him, then at Wanda, then back at Warren. "You owe me. Right? Nobody else in the world owes me nothin'. But you two, you fuckin' owe me."

"Yeah. Okay, Bob," said Warren. "You're right."

Bobby nodded, satisfied. "So okay then. Listen." He looked at Wanda. "Listen."

"I'm listening," said Wanda. Warren's glance flickered over to her; she'd sounded cold, which he didn't think was a good idea.

But Bobby didn't seem to have noticed. He moved restlessly back and forth across the living room. "My mom phones me. She says my stepdad's pretty sick. So I decide to come home, spend a couple weeks, if there's decent work I might even stay. I'm fuckin' fed up with the shiteating odds and ends I get in Vancouver. So I get over here and all of a sudden Grayson's on my case. I can't believe it. I put him off, put him off again.

"Then, I'm gonna borrow my stepdad's boat, gonna go off to an island, camp out for a few days. And he calls again. And this is when I say sure. Okay. I'll see you."

He reached into the adjoining dining room and grabbed a chair. So swiftly and suddenly did this happen that it caused Warren's heart to leap.

Bobby straddled the chair. "So I go over to Thormanby and I put up my tent next to a place my cousin's got there. I don't want the son of a bitch anywhere near my campsite, so I tell him to climb up the back of the cliff and meet me at the top.

"By now a little bit of me's startin' to look forward to this. I'm gonna make the sucker crawl. I'm gonna make him grovel. I'm imagining this and it's fuckin' near makin' me happy. So I go up there, and I wait for him."

He stood, shoving the chair away with his foot. "See, my life is pure shit. I got nothin'."

Warren ducked his head in embarrassment. He put his hands behind his back and studied the big square rag rug that covered the middle of the living room floor.

"I'm tired," Bobby went on, relentless. "I'm bitter. And I got nightmares I figure won't ever go away."

Outside, in the twilight, somebody turned off a lawn mower. Warren hadn't even been aware of it until it was silenced. Now the stillness was profound.

"When I got up there," said Bobby quietly, "the guy offered me money."

Warren looked up.

Bobby was nodding. "Yeah. Twenty-three thousand dollars, he said. Said he'd been savin' it up to give me."

Warren glanced at Wanda, who was staring, fascinated, at her ex-husband. "So what'd you do?"

Bobby put his head back and laughed. "I said I'd take it. Sure. But then—" His face twisted, as if he'd felt a pain somewhere. He shook his head. "That stupid fucker. He's got this belt thing, right? Stuffed with dough. And he's got this fuckin' camera, hangin' around his neck. I say 'Yeah, okay, I'll take your money,' and he grins all over his face and Jesus fuckin' Christ the next thing I know he's got this camera up to his eye and he's snappin' fuckin' pictures of me—pictures of *me*, I cannot believe this stupid fucker, this asshole, and I just lost it, I lost it, I grabbed his fuckin' camera and I grabbed him—" Bobby stopped. "I don't know what happened." He was staring out the window. "I guess I shoved him." He turned slowly to Warren. "Anyway. He went over the edge."

Warren was pretty sure he'd stopped breathing. He thought probably everything in his body had stopped working. He hoped it would all start up again, in a second or two.

"I musta lived it over a thousand times," said Bobby tonelessly. "You know—if I'd done this, or if he'd done that." He sat down on the sofa.

"What about the money?" said Wanda.

Bobby looked at her with reluctant admiration. "This is a woman with her eye on the main chance," he said to Warren. "The money went over the cliff, sweetheart," he said to Wanda. "Which is where you guys come in." He smiled at her. "My aunt finked out on me. And I gotta get outta here. So I need your car."

"Van," said Warren.

"What?"

"We haven't got a car. We've got a van."

And then Warren's folks were at the door, back from the restaurant with Annabelle's kids.

"You can have it," Warren said hastily to Bobby. "Hey," he said heartily, turning to his dad. "Guess who's here?"

There was some chitchat, but all the time Warren was moving Bobby toward the door, trying to keep Bobby behind him; he didn't want Rose-Iris getting curious about him. He got Bobby outside and walked him to the van.

Back in the house, Warren pulled Wanda into their bedroom and shut the door. "He said don't call the cops."

"Well of course he did. What would you expect, for heaven's sake," said Wanda, reaching for the phone.

"No," said Warren, grabbing her hand. "Don't. I—"

"Don't be a jerk, Warren. What can he do?"

"I told him about Rose-Iris."

"Why, for heaven's sake, did you do a thing like that?"

"I don't know. Don't call them."

"Warren. They'll catch him, and he'll go back to jail forever, and you'll be done with him, he'll never get out."

"Oh yes he will," said Warren miserably. "He'll come back. You just watch and see if he doesn't."

But Wanda ignored him, and called the cops.

"It's just a matter of time," said Alberg, more to himself than to Sokolowski. They'd checked Bobby Ransome's parents' house and had found no sign of him.

"So how come you're not going home?" said Sokolowski.

"How come you aren't, either?"

Then Carrington knocked, and opened the door. "I've got good news," he said, "and bad news."

"Just give it to us," said Alberg irritably.

"A woman called, now we know what Ransome's driving. That's the good news. The bad news comes from the hospital."

Chapter Forty-Eight

It was evening when Annabelle got home. There were a few clouds stretched thinly across the horizon and the sun, burning through them, turned the clouds and all the world to gold.

Annabelle stood next to the old gas pumps and looked at the house with the window wall and wondered what the judge would say. Would she have to go to jail? It wouldn't be good for Rose-Iris to have two parents who were jailbirds. Annabelle giggled a little at this, but she felt tears trembling in her eyes because what on earth would become of them, her children, if she were to go to jail? She took a few deep breaths, to steady herself.

She couldn't see into her house because of the sun shining on it. From a distance, she thought, these windows will look as if they're made of gold.

She walked toward the house and around the corner and approached the animal cages, to look in upon the foxes and the monkeys. She would have released the foxes, except she was a little afraid that they might bite her. She would call the SPCA first thing in the morning. She noticed that the animals had plenty of water, and wondered who had given it to them. She thought of Herman and turned quickly around—but no, he wasn't there, he was in the hospital…they'd told her he wouldn't die, but he'd lost a lot of blood—lost a lot of blood, thought Annabelle; but he won't die; won't die.

Maybe the judge would want her to appear quickly. Maybe tomorrow, she thought. Maybe I won't have to go to jail.

Pull yourself together, Annabelle, she told herself sternly.

She drew herself up and walked purposefully toward the house. She opened the screen door, crossed the hall—and then she was in the kitchen.

She had been steeling herself for this. She had to confront the kitchen before seeing her children again. She had to look at the scene of her crime, and wash Herman's blood from the floor, and weep, and fashion a penance for herself.

And so she entered the kitchen. And looked bravely around her.

And saw that there was nothing to confront.

The kitchen was spotless and serene. No blood to clean up. Nothing was out of order, out of place. It's Wanda, she thought, amazed. Wanda, who had come to collect the clothes Annabelle was now wearing, must have cleaned up the kitchen. And watered the animals, too. Annabelle, frowning, put her hands on her hips and surveyed the kitchen critically. She felt she had been robbed of something.

Finally she went into the room with the window wall and sat down in the lawn chair. She was very restless. Something, somewhere, was quickening.

Or maybe it was just not being able to clean up the blood.

There is not much of Herman in this house, she thought— and out of the blue she was struck by a desolation so intense that she doubled over, whimpering, her eyes squeezed shut, breathing with as little of her lungs as possible: a terrifying blackness had engulfed her. Lightly, she rubbed the center of her chest, saying to her pain, please please let go please let go; she willed it to dissolve, to sink into her bones and tissues, to become part of her; it's all right she said, silently, soothingly to her pain; it's all right, and she thought of pains she might have had that would have been worse.

The evening was deepening, thickening, as Annabelle went from her house and along the hard-packed trail and through the brush into her garden, which was awash in a dusky glow and the fragrance of roses. Her rose garden had begun and ended with Bobby. It was a private joke. Notches on her belt—a coded record of her sexual explorations. There was no rosebush for Herman.

Annabelle's roses were pale perfumed smudges in the twilight. She couldn't decide—did she want to leave this place, this droll house with its wraparound window wall, this garden with seven rosebushes as its centerpiece? How many times had she moved in the last ten years? She couldn't remember. And each time, she'd moved the roses too and each time, they had survived. But Annabelle thought they might die if she tried to take them from this garden.

And maybe she, Annabelle, oughtn't to be uprooted again, either.

She left her garden and returned to the house. She flipped on the floodlight, and the kitchen light. She must phone Warren, who would be worried. And she must bring the children home.

Then she heard Warren's van: he'd brought them to her, then. Quickly she looked into the kitchen mirror: would they flinch from seeing her?

Bobby knocked on the screen door. She regarded him for several seconds, she in the kitchen, he outside, and she was reminded of seeing him before in just that way, through the screen; only it was day, then, and the sun was pressing against the side of his face, glittering in his hair.

He opened the door and came inside without being invited.

"Jesus," he said, looking grimly at her injuries. "I heard about it from Warren. You okay?"

Annabelle nodded.

"He's not okay, though, huh?" said Bobby.

"He's not going to die," said Annabelle.

"That's good," said Bobby. "I guess."

"Do you think they'll send me to jail?"

Bobby laughed. "Nah." He looked at her more closely. "Seriously?"

Annabelle nodded.

"The way I got it from Warren, you were protecting the kid. That right?"

Annabelle hesitated. "Yes."

"No way you'll go to the slammer. You press charges, you could get Herman sent there."

His hands were in his pockets, and he was jangling something, car keys, probably, Annabelle thought.

"Annabelle, I'm on my way outta town."

"I thought you probably were. Sit down for a minute."

"Yeah, okay," said Bobby. He sat down at the table. He sat like Herman did, straddling the chair. "But before I go, I wanted to see you. And tell you that I saw the kid."

Annabelle nodded.

"She's a real pretty little thing. I dunno if you knew," said Bobby, his arms resting on the back of the chair, "when I got sent up, Wanda, she was, uh, expecting. And she had an abortion. Because of me going to prison. I mean, she didn't know how she'd look after it, on her own. Well you know, for Godsake."

"Yes," said Annabelle.

"Well anyway," said Bobby, "I just wanted you to know, I'm glad you didn't get rid of yours."

"Of course I didn't get rid of her. Why did you think I got you to sleep with me again, after all that time, and you married to somebody else, except to get pregnant?"

Bobby stared at her. "You're puttin' me on."

Annabelle shook her head. "I knew we could do it, you and me. Because we had before."

He gazed at her. "You really wanted a kid bad, didn't you?"

"I wanted four of them. The three I have. And the one I *did* get rid of."

"So," said Bobby uncomfortably, after a minute. "Is she smart, or what?"

"Smarter than you are," said Annabelle, and she laughed out loud.

"Yeah, you got that right," said Bobby, grinning.

They were looking at each other and smiling and their eyes seemed to catch in midair. Annabelle felt like crying.

"Annabelle, you know, I was broken up about it when you went and married what's-his-name, the guy who couldn't have kids."

"Lionel."

"Yeah. Because there I was, I'd gone back to high school and everything, just for you, to prove myself—"

"You do things for yourself, Bobby Ransome. Like we all do."

"Yeah, well. Probably you're right." He looked at her for a long time. "You gonna be okay?"

"Sure." She ducked her head and was looking down at the tabletop, blinking hard against tears, when horrendous noises erupted with terrifying suddenness out in the yard.

"Fuck," muttered Bobby, springing to his feet. "What the hell's that?"

Annabelle heard bellows of rage, and smashing sounds. Uncomprehending, she stood up and stared at the door.

"What the fuck's goin' on?" said Bobby, frozen in a half crouch.

Annabelle moved to the door and looked through the screen. "Oh my God," she cried, and ran outside. "Herman!" she screamed. "Stop it! Stop it!"

In the floodlit yard he was flailing at the remaining two animal cages with a tire iron. His shirt was torn and blood-stained. He was shouting things that were unintelligible.

"Herman! Stop it!" said Annabelle, but he ignored her. She turned swiftly, to run to the telephone.

"What the hell's going on?" said Bobby, coming through the screen door.

At the sound of Bobby's voice Herman stopped banging at the foxes' cage. He turned and stared at Bobby, thunderstruck. He looked from Bobby to Warren's van and back again. "You fucker," he said, and he staggered toward Bobby, raising the tire iron.

Bobby started backing up. "Forget it, man," he said, and Annabelle could see that he wasn't afraid, just wary. He was a lot bigger than Herman, and he wasn't injured, and those things seemed to make up for the fact that Herman had a weapon.

"Bastard," gasped Herman, reeling toward Bobby. "I'm gonna kill you, you bastard."

"Herman, no," said Annabelle, and she thought to herself I cannot do it again even if I had the knife in my hand this very minute I could not do it again.

Herman stopped, and turned to Annabelle. "Bitch. Whore." He changed direction, and moved toward her with unexpected swiftness.

"Hey, Herman, hey!" called Bobby. "You son of a bitch come on over here, come on, come and get me, you're chicken shit, man, come on—leave her alone, don't touch her you bastard!" He was racing across the hard-packed earth. "Put that down!" Herman lifted the tire iron. Bobby swept down upon him, grabbed it, and brought it down hard on Herman's head.

"Oh Jesus," said Bobby, panting. He dropped the tire iron and took hold of Annabelle.

Annabelle heard sirens, and they became louder and louder as she watched blood trickle in a thin stream over the hard-packed earth, which was too dry to soak it up.

"Oh Bobby. Ahhhh...Bobby..."

"Shh," said Bobby, weeping, wiping tears from her cheeks. "Shh, Annabelle, shhh. It's okay. It's okay."

Chapter Forty-Nine

"**N**o hard feelings."

That's what Bobby had said when the cops dragged him and Annabelle into the police station, and he'd seen Warren and Wanda waiting there.

"No hard feelings."

Warren hoped fervently that he'd meant it. Because in today's world even killing somebody wasn't necessarily enough to lock a guy up for the rest of his life.

Now they were back in Warren's house, which was very crowded; he thought it looked like an emergency shelter, with people sleeping all over the place. And that's pretty much what it was, when he thought about it.

They'd given their bedroom to his folks, who'd hung around waiting for Annabelle until they'd missed the last ferry, and of course there wasn't a room to be had in town, what with all the tourists. So Warren and Wanda were camped out in the rec room in the basement. There was a second bedroom which

Wanda used as a sewing room; it just had a cot in it. So Annabelle would go on the cot, and the three kids could sleep on the floor.

Things were pretty strained, which wasn't surprising. Annabelle in particular was white in the face and shaking all over. After she'd been to the cops for the second time that day, she'd come here to the house and gathered the kids around her, hugging all three of them at the same time, and it'd been quite a while—a minute or two, at least—before she'd seen that her folks were there too.

Now all the adults were in the living room, having a cup of tea. Though Warren would have preferred a beer.

"Is Herman dead this time?" said Warren's dad.

Everybody looked at him in horror. Everybody but Annabelle, who laughed. It sounded a tad hysterical, though, to Warren.

"No, Dad," she said. "He's pretty tough, I guess."

"Bobby'll be going back to jail I guess," said Warren's mom.

"It's highly likely," said Wanda dryly.

Warren looked around at his brittle, wary family. Maybe they could do it, he thought. Leave the past in the past.

But it wasn't going to be easy.

He didn't think he, for one, was going to manage it.

"I always said he'd come to no good," said Warren's mom, and he winced.

"There were—extenuating circumstances," said Annabelle carefully. Warren knew she didn't want to say too much in front of the kids.

"You can come live with us, you know, Annabelle," said their dad. "We've got lots of room." That was certainly true enough, thought Warren. But Annabelle said no thanks.

"I'll be getting me a job," she said firmly.

"That would be good," said Arnold. "Just until Dad's better."

Nobody knew what to say to that.

Annabelle folded him into her arms. His head was hot and damp. She kissed his hair, humming.

Chapter Fifty

"He was goin' after her, man; what was I s'posed to do, let him whack her?" He was sprawled on a chair tilted back against the wall, his thumbs hooked over the edges of the seat. His legs were stretched out in front of him. He wore a denim shirt with the sleeves rolled up, jeans and sneakers. No watch, no rings, no belt. "Ask her. She'll tell you."

"I already asked her."

"So?"

"You're right. She told me."

"Okay then." Ransome let the chair fall forward onto its front legs. "I'm outta here."

"There's something else," said Alberg. "There's Steven Grayson."

Ransome continued to look at him, expressionless. "I hear he fell off a cliff."

"Yeah." Alberg sat on the edge of the table. "I thought you might have seen it happen."

Ransome lifted his right hand, pointing to himself, looking amazed. "Who, me?"

"Yeah," says Alberg. "You were over there, right?"

Ransome didn't respond.

"On Thormanby. Camping."

Bobby looked around the interview room.

"There's some people over there who've identified your picture," said Alberg.

"So why ask?"

"You left in kind of a hurry, too, I guess. There's a tent, some camping gear, apparently abandoned."

"Yeah, well, I'm an impulsive guy." He moved restlessly in the chair. "Look, I'd like to get going, if it's all the same to you."

"That's right, you're on your way out of town, aren't you? You going back to Vancouver?"

"I dunno, man. Haven't thought it out yet, where I'll go."

"Did you have a job there?"

"Yeah I had a job there."

"What kind of a job?"

"A bunch of jobs, man, a bunch of piss-ant jobs, what's it to you?"

"He went to Thormanby to meet somebody."

"Yeah? Who says?"

"His mother says."

Bobby looked skeptical, but uneasy.

"See, this is what I know, Bobby." Alberg stood, and leaned against the wall next to Bobby's chair. "He kept phoning you. And you kept hanging up on him. And then one day you gave in, and said you'd see him. So he got all this money out of the bank and hiked up to the top of the cliff at Buccaneer Bay to meet you. But I guess you decided you didn't want his money. I guess you figured it'd be more satisfying to kill him."

"Don't be a fuckin' idiot," said Bobby. "I grabbed him, like this—"

He stood, suddenly, reaching for Alberg's shoulders. Alberg's hands shot up and out, knocking Ransome's arms down. They stood face to face, very close to each other. Charisma, shit, thought Alberg, staring him down.

Bobby grinned. "You're pretty fast," he said. "For an older guy."

"Sit down," said Alberg.

Bobby hesitated, then slumped back into the chair.

"So you grabbed him," said Alberg. "Then what?"

"I grabbed him by the shoulders," said Bobby dully. "I took his goddamn camera and heaved it into the fuckin' forest and then I grabbed him and I was gonna beat the shit out of him. I shoved him—fuck, man, I *shoved* the guy, right? I *shoved* him, is all. If it hadn't been for the fuckin' cliff—"

"So what do you think?" said Sokolowski.

"I think he's telling the truth." Alberg rubbed his temples wearily with the heels of his hands. "We better have a look for the camera. Where he says he threw it, it's pretty dense brush in there. It's possible nobody's found it."

"So—what're you saying?"

"If there's anything in the camera to show provocation, maybe Bobby's luck is changing. With a good lawyer, he ought to be able to get away with manslaughter." Alberg stood up and looked around for his reading glasses. "It's time to go home."

"Staff," said Sokolowski. "I gotta ask you."

"I'm coming in to do them on Sunday. Really. Honestly. Cross my heart."

"Good," said the sergeant, relieved.

Chapter Fifty-One

"This clearing is where the drug deal happened," said Alberg the next morning, pointing at a photograph.

"Uh-huh," said Diana, chin on her hand.

Alberg hesitated. How the hell had Cassandra known it was a teenage makeout place? She was thirty years old when she moved to Sechelt.

"This is Hetty Willis, Bobby Ransome's aunt," he went on, pointing to another picture. "And here's Bobby with Wanda."

Diana wasn't giving this her complete attention, he thought, irritated. Everybody always complained about how he never talked about his work. Now here he was talking about it, and his daughter wasn't even listening.

"I'm buggering off out of here," he said, "in a little while."

"Who's this?" asked Diana.

"That's Bobby Ransome's father. He used to manage the Petro-Canada place."

The phone rang. It was Cassandra, wishing him a happy birthday. "Oh, thanks," said Alberg, trying to sound like he'd forgotten it was his birthday. Which Diana certainly had. And Janey. And he hadn't heard from Maura, either.

"Have you been outside yet?"

"Nope." He'd gotten cards from Isabella, and from Sid and Elsie, and Sanducci had given him one, too. And so had his parents. But not a word from his children, or his ex-wife who was supposed to still be so fond of him.

"When you've been outside, call me," said Cassandra, and hung up.

"What the hell was that all about?" Alberg muttered. "Now Gillingham," he said, picking up the doctor's picture, "he swears he didn't have anything to do with anything. He did, of course," he said confidently to Diana. "He just doesn't see it yet. Someday he'll remember. And this one," he said, tossing Gillingham away and picking up Annabelle, "she had a child with Bobby." He scrutinized the photograph.

"Bobby Bobby Bobby," said Diana. "I guess this photographer guy was in love with him, was he?"

Alberg looked at her, amazed.

"Pop," said Diana. She got up and went to the living room window.

"Yeah? What?"

"Come over here," she said.

"What for?" said Alberg. "What is it?" He joined her and peered outside. "Jesus Christ. What are those?"

"There's fifty of them," said Diana.

"They're pink, for God's sake."

"They're a present," said Diana. "From Cassandra and me."

"They're flamingos. They're plastic flamingos," said Alberg, aghast.

"We're making you dinner, too," said Diana. "But this is your main present." She kissed his cheek. "Happy birthday, Pop."

Get to know the entire Alberg & Cassandra series!

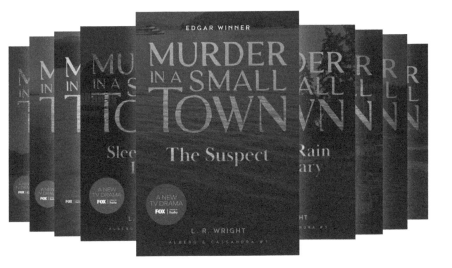

"Excellent writing, inventive plots and realistic characters distinguish Wright's mysteries....The suspense becomes tormenting as the author leads readers through blind alleys and, finally, to an astounding revelation adroitly concealed until the story's close." —*Publishers Weekly*

FIND OUT MORE ON FELONYANDMAYHEM.COM: